WICKEDLY YOURS

The Wickeds Book 4

KATHLEEN AYERS

❧ I ❧

Wales would never be her favorite place. Gloomy with a gray cast that never seemed to leave, Wales was full of ill-tempered dark, mysterious folk who glared at her with suspicion and at times open dislike. One of the those being the ancient, deaf cousin that dwelled within the walls of the gray stone edifice of Twinings, the Duke of Dunbar's far-flung Welsh estate.

All the isolation and lack of sunshine did however give one plenty of time to mull over one's actions. Assisting in the ill-fated abduction of your sister-in-law, for instance.

Lady Arabella Tremaine, sister of the Duke of Dunbar wandered about the overgrown gardens of Twinings, a letter clutched in one hand as the damp mist of Wales wet her hair and cheeks. The letter was from Arabella's dearest friend, Lady Miranda Reynolds. Well, no longer Reynolds, for Miranda had married the Earl of Kilmaire in a small wedding nearly a month ago.

A wedding Arabella should have been part of, were she not banished to this pile of ancient stone in the middle of nowhere.

Acid congealed to form a pit of bitterness in Arabella's stomach. Her hand curled into a fist, half crumpling the letter, as she pressed both against the unwelcome ache. This was what came of protecting her brother from himself. Indignation filled her as well as a spike of jealousy at her friend's news.

Opening the fine vellum once more, she struggled to read her friend's words. Miranda's handwriting was deplorable, nearly impossible to read, but one thing stood out.

'Your brother gives you leave to return to London for the ball Grandmother is hosting to celebrate my wedding.'

"How lovely of Nick." She hissed her brother's name in contempt at a spray of morning glory vine. The vine was clearly struggling to survive in the dank, overgrown garden of Twinings. As was Arabella.

Icy cold rage encased the length of her body at the thought of her brother, His Grace the Duke of Dunbar. Sending her to this prison, to be watched over by a small army of Welshmen, most of whom she couldn't understand when they spoke. No one lived at Twinings save Cousin Millicent, who was not only deaf but half-mad. Some days Arabella felt as if she were Anne Boylen or some other tragic figure of history who had been imprisoned unjustly. Well, she had to admit, her imprisonment was not *completely* without cause.

"All because of Jemma." A bird flew out from the morning glory vine, terrified at the venom in her voice.

"Arabella? Darling are you out there?" Footsteps sounded on the cobblestone path as her aunt, Lady Cupps-Foster approached. "I've received a letter from your brother. It appears your banishment will be short-lived. Thank goodness. While I am a great admirer of the country, I do not care for Wales in the *least*."

Poor Aunt Maisy. Stuck here with Arabella for the last few months at Nick's request to keep her niece out of trouble. As if her aunt didn't have her own life. Aunt Maisy was the closest thing Arabella had to a mother, since the death of Charlotte Tremaine years ago. Not that Charlotte had been much of a parent. A sour taste settled on her tongue as it often did when she thought of her little-mourned mother. "Has Nick written to me as well?"

The smile on her aunt's pretty face faltered as she approached. Eyes the color of sapphires were shadowed with apology. "I'm sure Nick thought a letter to me would suffice." Her aunt tried to smooth over Nick's rudeness. "He *is* allowing you to return for Miranda's wedding celebration. The Dowager Marchioness is hosting herself and the event is planned a fortnight hence to give you and I plenty of time to arrive in London. We must hurry and pack." Her aunt's excitement at returning to London was evident as she took Arabella's arm. "Dearest, do not frown so. You don't wish to wrinkle. Time enough for such things when you are my age." Aunt Maisy tugged Arabella in the direction of the house. "Oh, I do so love a wedding celebration, especially one held in honor for our dear Miranda."

Arabella was put off by her aunt's easy acceptance of Nick's reasoning. "He allows me back only for Miranda and no other reason."

"What difference does it make why he allows you to return to London?" She pulled Miranda close. "Things between you and your brother cannot be mended while you are in Wales. After Miranda's celebration you will have ample opportunity to apologize for your actions."

"Nick will never understand that I only sought to protect him from...*her*. Why could he not have married Miranda as I'd hoped all these years? Grandfather must be spinning in his grave. The very idea that he married a member of the family responsible for my father's denouncement from society and ultimately his death befuddles the mind. Is it too much to

3

hope that my brother would consider such a thing as he rattles about London?"

Aunt Maisy pursed her lips as if deciding whether to say more. "Your brother has *not* been in London, Arabella. He's been at The Egg since his marriage."

The Egg was the nickname of the Dunbar family seat close to the Scottish border. The estate was nicknamed such because the house was constructed of blinding white limestone, nestled amongst the dark, rocky cliffs that bordered the sea. The impression, as one approached, was of a giant egg in a nest. The Egg was an oddly whimsical name given it was the ancestral home of the most infamous duchy in England. The journey to The Egg was lengthy and the estate isolated. Nick rarely traveled there. He must have wanted privacy for he and his bride.

"It's a pity Jemma hasn't tripped and fallen into the sea." Arabella wasn't feeling charitable towards the woman her brother married.

Her aunt bit her lip. "Your sister-in-law is with child, several months gone."

"Several months?" Arabella chose to ignore the fact that in addition to her other sins, her actions towards Jemma inadvertently endangered an unborn child.

"You will be an aunt."

Guilt stung Arabella. She pushed it aside, clinging to the hope that her feelings towards Jemma were justified in some way. "Are we sure the child is Nick's? After all-"

Aunt Maisy came to a stop, her fingers digging into Arabella's forearm as she turned to face her. "How *dare* you."

Arabella turned away from the vehemence in her aunt's tone.

"That child is the *heir* to Dunbar. Should you *ever* voice such *concern* in your brother's presence, Nick may send you away to an even more remote location. Regardless of what you think of Jemma, such a thing in not in her character. I have been assured of the child's paternity."

"I do not," Arabella sputtered, "understand your *acceptance* of Nick's marriage to her. I find it rather appalling.

"Do not make me a liar, Arabella. I have spent my time in Twinings writing your brother letters begging him to forgive your misguided attempt to protect him. I've made it clear you did not *mean* to actually have your brother's bride abducted by her former suitor and his mother. Jemma was in shock over her father's treachery. Which, I may add, she is not to blame. Corbett and his mother preyed upon you and manipulated you. At least that is what I've relayed to Nick."

Swayed. Manipulated. Cajoled. While she detested the fact that her anger allowed Corbett to use her in such a way, Arabella still thought her actions *somewhat* justified. Protecting her brother and the Dunbar honor had motivated her. She still could not understand why Jemma was the woman her brother chose.

"Should you continue down this path, Arabella, you will never have your brother's forgiveness, nor Jemma's."

"I don't care—"

"You *should*. The bitterness that has festered for years in your heart finally seeped out and nearly *killed* an innocent woman. Do you wish to end your days alone with nothing but your anger to warm you? The honor of the Duke of Dunbar is *not* at stake." Two spots of color appeared on her aunt's cheeks. "Your parent's death was a terrible thing, but *your* father pulled the trigger ending his life and that of your mother, not Jemma's nor any other member of the Lord of Marsh's family. Nick has promised Lord Marsh that not a whisper of what transpired between Marsh's younger brother and your father shall ever be heard."

"Why wouldn't Nick wish to clear Father's name? I don't

understand why he wishes to protect the Marsh family from the shame that has haunted ours."

"Our family's reputation was infamous long before Jemma's father arrived to frame yours for treason. More importantly, Nick *loves* Jemma. He will do anything to protect her, even if it means sending his beloved sister to the other side of the world. It's best you remember that." Aunt Maisy tugged her forward. "Come. Nick has instructed Peabody to send the family coach to fetch us. We will have to inform Millicent. Poor dear, she had just gotten used to us being at Twinings and now we are to leave. Perhaps I can convince her to visit us in London."

"Cousin Millicent hasn't left Wales in forty years. You are bound to be disappointed." Reluctantly Arabella allowed herself to be dragged forward. She did so desperately wish to go home.

✣ 2 ✥

Rain dripped down the coach windows as the day turned more gray than usual. The Dunbar coach had arrived exactly on schedule bearing two especially large footmen, a groom and the driver. The footmen Arabella recognized from their original journey to Wales. The young groom was little more than a stable boy named Teddy Mac, an unfortunate lad Nick found picking pockets on the London docks. John, the driver, had driven the duke's coach for many years. The men, with the exception of Teddy Mac, all bore rather stoic expressions. She couldn't imagine how dull it was to traipse back and forth to Wales at the whim of the Duke of Dunbar.

Arabella sighed and tucked her feet more firmly against the heated brick beneath her sturdy boots. Warmth wafted pleasurably up her skirts but still she shivered. The journey would take a few days as the coach was in no mad rush to get to London and the weather poor. There would be time to stop and rest the horses, much to Arabella's relief. Between the damp weather and the condition of the roads, any respite from the coach would be welcome.

Camden, a small town just across the Welsh border was the first stop in their travels. She and Aunt Maisy would spend the night at the Duck and Crow, Camden's finest inn. Arabella wished desperately for tea and a hot bath.

"I am certain I shall never be warm again." Her aunt tucked the blanket around her form, shivering as she swaddled herself inside the thick wool.

"Or dry. I don't know how much longer I can tolerate the feel of my damp skirts. Toadstools could fall out at any moment." She gave her aunt a weak smile.

"Your mood has improved, niece." She reached across and patted Arabella's hands. "I am pleased. Nick has put the past aside and you must as well. I know of the difficulties you've faced. The Devils of Dunbar have faced our infamy head on. Really, who believes in witches and such in this day and age? The old tales only give the *ton* something more to gossip about." Aunt Maisy sighed. "But, I was young once too. All the notoriety is much worse for we women and I know the stink of treason has made things challenging. Everyone's path is fraught with difficulty of some sort. I've had my own share."

Sometimes Arabella forgot Aunty Maisy had endured *more* than most women her age. Widowed three times, her aunt's first two husbands perished at young ages, leaving her a young mother with two sons to raise. Spencer Hammond, Baron Kelso was Arabella's eldest cousin. Spence was currently in India doing...*something*. Arabella was never clear on exactly what Spence involved himself in other than she had a vague notion he worked for the government in some capacity. Brendan, the Earl of Morwick was Aunt Maisy's other son, as wild and mysterious as the moors from which he hailed in the Dark Peak district of England. Unfortunately, Brendan's father disappeared while hunting shortly after his son's birth. It was assumed that the previous Earl of Morwick had fallen into one of the numerous caves that dotted the moors and perished. Aunt Maisy waited seven long years before he was declared dead. Brendan rarely traveled to London. Lord Cupps-Foster, Aunt Maisy's last husband produced no issue. He died a week after the wedding. Though she was still beautiful and enormously wealthy, no man in his right mind would court Aunt Maisy. *Cursed*, the *ton* claimed.

"I forget sometimes, aunt, that you have survived much and yet still smile."

"Your heart loves where it wishes, even if that love is not perfect. Proper. Expected." Aunt Maisy's eyes grew shadowed. "Your brother has found that which he cannot live without. You will understand one day."

The coach bounced, springs creaking as they rounded a bend in the road and slowed, finally coming to a halt.

Arabella peeked out the window. Another coach blocked the road to Camden. Smaller and shabbier than the Dunbar coach, it nonetheless was large enough so that they could not go around. "The road is blocked with another vehicle. I see no passengers outside and the coach bears no crest. Perhaps it is a mail coach bound for London."

Aunt Maisy's brow wrinkled. "I do hope you're correct, although I'm thankful we've these two strapping footmen at our disposal. I did wonder what Peabody was thinking when I first spied them since both men are a bit rough looking to be in service."

Arabella didn't answer. She found neither footman to be someone Peabody would hire unless her brother Nick instructed the butler to do so for both were large and muscular with the build of pugilists. And neither wore the Dunbar livery well, something Peabody was a stickler for.

Seagraves, the larger of the two was exceedingly polite, though his manners were a bit rough. He had taken especially good care of Aunt Maisy since leaving Twinings, asking several times if she was comfortable or if he could fetch her another blanket. The attitude of the other footman, Barker, left much to be desired. Barely civil, his insolent gaze had followed Arabella's every move as she settled herself for the journey. As soon as she and Aunt Maisy arrived in London, Arabella planned to tell Peabody to fire the man.

The coach door opened revealing the red-cheeked face of John, their driver.

"John," Aunt Maisy greeted him. "Is there no way around?"

"No, my lady. The coach appears abandoned for I see no driver or any passengers. Perhaps they've walked to Camden for help, though the horses appear to be fine." A look of worry entered his eyes. "I'm sure it's nothing, my lady, but I'll have Seagraves and Barker move the coach off the road while I inspect the vehicle for damage. Teddy Mac will stay here with you and the horses." He bowed. "Camden is only another hour and we'll be there well before nightfall."

"Very good." Her aunt sat back with a plop. "I long to be out of this coach and before a fire."

John closed the coach door and Arabella could hear him speaking to Seagraves and Barker.

"I agree." The chill and dampness had sunk into Arabella's bones and she longed to be before a warm hearth where she could discreetly lift her skirts.

A violent lurch rocked the coach. One of the horses shrieked in fright. John called for Teddy Mac just before a large thud sounded as if a body hit the muddy road.

Arabella met Aunt Maisy's horrified eyes.

"Surely," her aunt whispered, "no one would *dare* rob the coach of the Duke of Dunbar. It's unheard of." Boots crunched outside and moved closer to the coach.

"Someone *does* dare." Arabella threw off her blanket and reached underneath the seat where a compartment held a brace of pistols. Arabella knew how to shoot a pistol, though she doubted she'd have time to load either weapon. Hopefully the thieves who'd stopped the coach wouldn't realize that.

The door to the coach was flung open to reveal Seagraves, unharmed. "I'm sorry, my lady."

"Oh, Seagraves". Aunt Maisy placed a hand on her throat in relief. "What is the matter? It sounded like something happened to the horses. What—" Aunt Maisy's words dissolved into a gasp of outrage as the footman shoved his massive form into the coach. He settled next to her, pinning her smaller body against the squabs, the breath of his shoulders straining the Dunbar livery as he blocked her aunt's movements.

"Don't fuss so, my lady. I don't wish you to hurt yourself." His mouth drew down mournfully. "Nor do *I* wish to hurt you."

Aunt Maisy began to pummel Seagraves back with her fists, like a small child trying to move a boulder. The scene would have been ridiculous were the situation not so serious.

We're being robbed. Seagraves and Barker are part of it.

Arabella's fingers clawed at the compartment, desperate to pull out the pistols, but Seagraves stuck a booted foot against the opening. He shook his head. "Don't." He grunted. "I've no wish to hurt you either, my lady."

"Shut her up." Barker opened the door and jerked his chin in Aunt Maisy's direction. "Or I'll gag her."

Seagraves immediately placed one meaty paw across Aunt Maisy's mouth silencing her. Her aunt's eyes peered over his hand, eyes wide with affront.

Barker turned to Arabella. "Let's go, my lady." He sneered the words. Wrapping his blunt fingers around both her wrists, he pulled her towards him with little effort.

Her ankle caught on the brick, tearing her skirt. Arabella instantly regretted not grabbing the brick instead of trying for the pistols. She could have lobbed the hot piece of stone at Barker's head. Twisting and kicking, she screamed. "Your life isn't worth a farthing. My brother will see you dead for daring to touch us."

Barker's lips twisted, in what she thought was an imitation of a smile. She noticed he was missing two teeth, and another was broken.

"He's got to find me first."

"Ow." Seagraves muttered as her aunt bit his fingers. He removed his hand from her mouth long enough for Aunt Maisy to order him to release her. "Let me out. Let me out this instant." She slapped at the back of his neck, as she attempted to escape.

"My lady," Seagraves growled. "Please be still. If you bite me again, I'll have to tie you up. He held up a dirty length of rope in one hand.

Aunt Maisy's eyes bugged at the sight of Barker dragging Arabella out the door. "No! Leave her alone, you filthy mongrel." Her aunt struggled to grab hold of Arabella's cloak.

Barker shot Seagraves a pointed look and tossed him a scrap of cloth. "Gag her. Now. We're far enough from Camden but we can't afford to let anyone chance upon us. You're too bloody soft," Barker hissed. "Give her a good slap and she'll shut up all right." Barker tugged again and Arabella landed outside the coach.

Seagraves didn't answer, but his mouth grew taut. "You do your job and I'll do mine." He reached over and slammed the door.

Aunt Maisy's muffled cries continued to sound from the coach.

Arabella's shock and anger rapidly turned to fear as Barker began to drag her towards the other coach. She kicked furiously at his shins.

Her captor grunted in pain as one of her boot heels hit

their mark. He raised a hand and she shied back, certain he would hit her, but Barker lowered his hand with a snarl. Instead he shook Arabella until her teeth clattered together. Stubbornly she dug her heels into the mud and refused to budge, forcing him to drag her.

"What have you done to him?" Arabella choked out as she spied John face down in the road, a trickle of blood oozing from his skull. Teddy Mac sat next to him, a gag in his mouth, his hands and feet tied.

The young groom glared at Barker with anger.

"He's not dead." Barker caught her glance at the driver. "I just hit him. But he will be if you don't stop." He shook her again and grabbed her more firmly by the arm.

Arabella stopped struggling. She couldn't risk any harm coming to John or Teddy Mac. "What about my aunt?"

"She'll be fine with Seagraves." He led her to the other coach and swung open the dented and scratched door. "Here she is." Barker flung her inside.

A dank musty smell filled her nose and she fell against the floor of the coach. The blinds were closed, leaving the interior dark. Even though she could see little, Arabella sensed she wasn't alone.

Firm hands gripped her shoulders and lifted her onto the seat.

"What do you want?" She struggled to keep her voice from trembling though she was terrified for the safety of her aunt. "I demand you let us go. How dare you accost the family of the Duke of Dunbar. Surely you know who we are." Arabella moved herself to the far corner of the seat. "You will be found out before you can collect any ransom for me if that is your aim."

A shadowed hand moved the curtains allowing a fraction of light to filter through the dirty windows.

"You." A dizzying sensation made her ears buzz as she

regarded the man before her. He looked only slightly different from their last meeting. Still boyishly handsome, the smug grin he perpetually wore gracing his lips.

"Lady Arabella," he said softly. "How lovely to see you again."

3

ugustus Corbett, lately of Bermuda and the cause of Arabella's exile, sat back, his handsome features full of amusement as he enjoyed her shock at the sight of him. He adjusted the sleeves of his once fine coat, now tattered and frayed around the cuffs and edges. Several buttons were missing from the front or dangling by a mere thread.

"I have a proposition for you."

Arabella sat back against the ragged seat cushions, trying to ignore the distasteful stain in the corner of the floor hovering near the edge of her skirts. The coach was filthy and looked as if it had been used to cart about a herd of orphans. She gave Corbett a brittle smile. He didn't frighten her, not in the least. Corbett always reminded her of a child about to throw a tantrum.

"Is there a reason you stopped my coach? Accosted me and my aunt? Surely you could have sent me a note or visited me in Wales for tea." She gave him a pointed look. "Well, possibly not as my brother is determined to rid the world of your presence."

"Arabella." He shook his head and a shock of brown hair fell over his brow. "Accost is such an *ugly* word. I merely wished an opportunity to speak to you. And as for tea, well there were too many fierce Welshmen surrounding Twinings to make that a possibility."

"I have nothing to say to you. You manipulated me."

"My dear Arabella, *manipulate* is rather strong. I prefer, *influenced*. Mother may have bent the truth a bit about some things, but not about the deceit of Jemma's father, William. He *did* commit treason and allow the blame to fall on your father, that much is true. As to the shooting which made you an orphan..." Corbett lifted his hands carelessly. "Who is to say?"

"Your father protected him." Arabella needed no reminder of the death of her parents and the horror she witnessed as a child.

"True. My father was the Lord Governor of Bermuda and gave William a safe place to hide from your family for many years. What can I say? They were friends." His gaze traveled up the front of her serviceable brown wool traveling dress, seeming to strip it from her with a glance. "You wear such staid garments, Lady Arabella. Covered from neck to toe. One wonders what you are hiding?"

The question unnerved her, as did his attention. Arabella had spent a lifetime taking great care to be unattractive to the opposite sex. She did not elicit flattery nor flirtation. Gray and brown were preferred for her wardrobe, though she did not stint on the quality of the fabric. No embellishment. A severe cut, suitable for a matron or a vicar's wife. Not so much as a hint of her generous bosom could be seen.

"Instead of being concerned over my clothing, you would do better to be concerned for your welfare. It is doubtful you will survive another meeting with my brother."

He had the grace to flinch at her words. "I purchased

passage to America. I imagine your brother assumes me to be in Boston else he would have sent a small army to escort you back to London instead of a young boy and two questionable footmen. Besides, he never found me to be particularly daring. Or devious." Corbett's tone was smug. "Won't he be surprised? Besides the Devil of Dunbar could care less about *you,* Arabella."

"Do not call him that." Arabella hated the reminder that London society considered Nick to be cursed. As angry as she was at him, he was still her brother.

Corbett gave a choked laugh. "Ever the protective sister." He folded his hands into a peak and peered at her over his fingers. "How did you enjoy your banishment to Wales?"

Heat flew up her cheeks as his words hit home.

"Aren't you the least curious why I went to all this trouble? Placing two men in your brother's employ? Stopping your coach?"

Arabella opened her mouth to spit out a biting comment but stopped. She *was* curious. Of course, any intelligent young lady, perhaps one who wasn't still smarting over being sent far away from home as punishment, *would* have started screaming.

Glancing out the window to her left, she peered through the grime to see the Dunbar coach rock slightly. John and Teddy Mac were still outside in the muddy road. "What could you possibly offer me? You've nothing I want."

"You are such a delightfully sour creature, Arabella." His voice lowered into a silky whisper, "your reputation in the *ton* is well deserved."

"You know nothing of my reputation," she snapped. Her reputation was *unimpeachable*. Her entire life had been spent struggling to keep free of the gossip that swirled around the Duke of Dunbar and her family, like moths circling a lantern. Mindful of her father's reputation as a drunkard, not a drop of alcohol ever touched her lips. Charlotte, her mother, was a known wanton. God forbid anyone should ever hear a flirtatious comment from Arabella. She'd never even been to France least her loyalty to the Crown be questioned as her father's had been. "I am above reproach."

"Yes, my dear. You most certainly are. Every action is proper and orchestrated. You are a paragon of morality, a bastion of discipline, a woman who demands the respect of society. A woman whose dour manner and constant frowning have warned away all but the most determined. No matter how many orphans and widows you support, or ladies luncheons you host, you will always shoulder your family's reputation. But I suppose fear is preferable to frivolity."

Arabella's fingers twitched against her skirts as she absorbed every word, knowing how close to the truth he came.

"Despite your best efforts to garner a place for yourself you are not well-liked in the *ton*. No one regards you as a friend save Miranda. At best you are an acquaintance, invited so as not to insult your powerful and wealthy family."

Arabella sucked in her breath.

"But I feel certain you could have tolerated such treatment and convinced yourself you were happy, until your brother had the audacity to wed the daughter of *the traitor*. You've devoted your life to being, as you say, *above reproach* and your sacrifices mean nothing to him." He slapped his thighs and sat back. "How that must *rankle* you. If I were in your shoes, I'm not sure I wouldn't have committed murder by now. I wonder the news of your brother's affection for Jemma didn't hasten your grandfather's demise."

Arabella bit the inside of her mouth so hard she tasted blood, for she had often thought the same thing. "Do not speak of my grandfather." The previous Duke of Dunbar had gone to his grave cursing Nick for not inflicting the revenge the Dunbar honor demanded.

"Thankfully, Lady Miranda begged for your return to London. Your dearest friend. How she must long to rub her marriage, a great love-match, in your face."

"Miranda would never do such a thing," she sputtered.

Corbett gave a careless shrug. "You are regretfully, now all alone."

The sharp intake of air burned her lungs. Corbett was speaking out loud all the horrible things that plagued Arabella's thoughts since she had received Miranda's letter. And as for her brother and Jemma? Twinings had not softened her rage towards Nick and his bride in the least.

"Don't you long to have revenge upon them all?"

Her eyes snapped to his. "You know nothing of what I want."

Corbett raised his brow. He did know.

"I propose we marry." The light blue of his eyes darkened with determination. "It is the perfect solution and we will both have what we want most."

"You're joking." The very idea was absurd. Her hand began to twitch in earnest.

"Not at all. When you look at the whole of it logically, our marriage makes perfect sense." Corbett's eyes held a fanatical gleam, but his voice remained smooth. "Think of Jemma's horror. Your brother will be *incensed*."

"Nick will have you murdered in your sleep." Corbett was right. No one called on her unless she held a tea to discuss one of her charities. She was never asked to dance at the few balls she attended, instead Arabella lingered next to Aunt Maisy for the duration of the evening. But Arabella *was* happy for Miranda. In her own way.

"Quite frankly," Corbett continued in a candid tone, "you'll *never* do better. You are destined for spinsterhood, which wouldn't be so bad I suppose, if you brother remained unmarried or he married a girl you could actually tolerate. But *Jemma*? Your part in my mother's failed scheme to force Jemma back to Bermuda and marriage to me certainly won't help mend fences."

"I only told you when Jemma would be in the park. I never—"

Corbett continued as if she hadn't interrupted. "The Duke of Dunbar will *never* allow you to inhabit the same space as his *precious bride*. Your brother has made it clear your return to London is temporary."

"How would you know such a thing?"

You forget, Seagraves and Barker have been part of the duke's household and servants gossip. Your chambers are already being redecorated. You'll be sent packing again in no time. I believe a convent in Scotland was mentioned as your ultimate destination. The entire staff is placing bets on where you'll end up." Corbett picked a piece of lint of his knee. "Not that it matters where you go. Eventually, no one will even remember the duke has a sister. *Especially* not the duke."

A sickening sensation filled her, reminiscent of the way she once felt after eating fish that had spoiled. The ache caused her to bend at the waist, her free hand pressed against her stomach. "What a pretty speech, Mr. Corbett. How you flatter me."

My God. He was right. She would end up like Cousin Millicent. Rotting away in some ancient estate in Wales with no visitors for decades.

"Do you not *want* your revenge? Surely, revenge is a more desirable alternative than quietly agreeing to banishment?" He regarded her thoughtfully. "Or perhaps not. I thought you had more backbone."

His words had the desired effect and Arabella stiffened. "A

marriage of convenience? Or revenge, I suppose?" Her hand twitched mercilessly against her skirts.

"A business partnership of sorts." Corbett stroked his chin. "Marriage is the only way to ensure you are not subject to the whims of the Duke of Dunbar or his duchess. Wedding me will assure you'll have freedom. Your own household. You'll have a husband who gives your sister-in-law fits. You will never have to leave London unless *you* wish it."

"And what about your whims?" she countered.

A small smile lifted his lips. "Money, of course, is my primary objective. My family's fortunes, as you can imagine, are in ruin. You, on the other hand, have a very substantial dowry. One of the largest in London. In return, I'll settle a sum on you and be an absentee husband. I understand that's the best kind."

Arabella also had an additional inheritance in her own right, one that would come to her upon marriage, something she would not be disclosing to Corbett. Even if he absconded with every cent of her dowry, she would still be a wealthy woman. Once married, she would have freedom to do as she chose with no threat of being shipped off to Wales again.

"I must be assured that there will be no," she struggled to find the correct words, "*physical* aspect to our marriage. The marriage will be in name only." Dear God, his proposal actually had merit.

"I've no desire to bed you. I expect you are quite frigid." A toothy grin spread his lips to soften his insult. "Consider us to be...*business* partners. I vow to never cross the door of your bedroom. I do not plan to reside in London at any rate. My presence would be too tempting for your brother. Best I only show my face occasionally."

"What about my aunt? Our driver and groom?"

Corbett leaned over and took her hand and she resisted the urge to pull free. "No harm whatsoever will come to any of them. Seagraves will simply keep them with the coach for the next day or so. Then he'll take the horses and ride in the other direction. He's been well paid to do so. By the time your aunt makes her way to London we will already be wed."

She thought of her Grandfather cursing the traitor with his last breath, his eyes full of disappointment that Nick had not taken the promised retribution. Bitterness seeped into every corner of her body and she stiffened with righteous indignation. Miranda would soon have a passel of brats around her ankles with little time for Arabella, so what would she care? Aunt Maisy would grow tired of exile with her niece and who could blame her? Nick would never forgive her, but if she married Corbett she would never have to answer to him again. Alarm sounded loudly in her head but Arabella ignored the sense of doom preferring to focus on her indignation and rage. She was not to be trifled with.

"Fine." She clutched her hands to her lap. "I'll marry you."

🎿 4 🏺

Rowan jumped up the steps of the Duke of Dunbar's red brick home situated on one of the most prestigious streets in London, stopping to stare, as he often did, at the beauty of his cousin's residence. The massive structure took up the entire end of the street; wings on either side of the house curled as if open for an embrace. Acres of park land manicured into a twisting riot of gardens fell away to brush, having been allowed to grow wild with all manner of thorny plants and trees. The brush served as a natural deterrent to trespassers as did the high stone wall which surrounded the entire property. The impression was one of magnificence and powerful wealth, with just a thin veneer of danger, as if the rumors of witchcraft and pacts with the Devil and all the other gossip surrounding the Duke of Dunbar were true.

He rapped smartly on the door, hoping his cousin, Jemma and the duke had arrived home safely from their sojourn in Scotland. The couple's visit to the seat of the Duke of Dunbar was to only have lasted no more than a month, but then they had been there much longer due to concerns over

Jemma's health. Rowan hoped they were at home and only neglected to inform the family in order to rest.

The ball celebrating the marriage of the Earl and Countess of Kilmaire was to take place later that night, given by the Dowager Marchioness of Cambourne. Lord and Lady Dunbar, along with Rowan and his family, were all expected to attend. As was most of London. No one dared to disregard an invitation from the Dowager Marchioness, a grand dame of the *ton*.

Rowan would be there, of course, though he wasn't looking forward to it. Not because of Lord and Lady Kilmaire who were dear friends, but for other reasons. Reluctantly he admitted to himself the slight detour to his cousin's home was merely an attempt to avoid his mother, Lady Marsh.

As usual, the expectations of Lady Marsh were not in line with those of her only son.

Peabody, the Dunbar butler, opened the door wide. Once he caught sight of Rowan, his mouth turned down in dislike. "Baron Malden." He addressed Rowan by his courtesy title. "His Grace is not at home." The elderly servant began to shut the door.

"How odd. I would have expected them a day or so ago. Possibly His Grace will arrive at any moment." Rowan placed his hand on the heavy oak. "I'll wait a bit, if you don't mind."

Peabody sighed, rather dramatically, telling Rowan he *did* indeed mind. The door swung wide. "As you wish, Lord Malden. Your wait may be overlong. His Grace assured us he would arrive today, however—"

"The Dowager Marchioness of Cambourne is hosting a celebratory ball for Lord and Lady Kilmaire this evening and I can't imagine either my cousin or her husband would miss such an event. I'll wait in the drawing room and avail myself of my cousin-in-law's sideboard."

Peabody was too well trained to say anything more, but

his nostrils flared at the idea of Rowan drinking the Duke of Dunbar's scotch. "As you wish, my lord."

Snooty old bugger.

As Rowan made his way to the drawing room, he noticed the way the servants were bustling to and fro in anticipation of the duke's arrival. The entire foyer smelled of beeswax and the floor glistened beneath his feet. The drawing room was a massive, cavernous space with expensive furniture littered about in various groupings. The furniture was all heavy and masculine, dressed in reds and golds. A large stone hearth took up the majority of one wall, the fire inside popping and crackling, giving the room a warm glow.

Rowan made his way to the sideboard and poured himself two fingers of scotch before settling in a chair covered in deep burgundy brocade. He took a sip of the scotch and sighed in pleasure as the liquid slid down his throat.

A young maid slipped in to stoke the fire and add wood. Apparently, Peabody didn't mean for Rowan to catch a chill. The girl was small and cheerfully round. She bustled about her business shooting Rowan several curious gazes as she did so.

His eyes followed her as she moved, his gaze more on her clothing than the girl herself. He'd lately come into possession of a textile mill. Actually, several textile mills. They were in dire need of updating. The Newsome mills stood on several acres of land facing a river, once the primary mode of distribution for their goods. The river had been dammed making transportation from the mills prohibitively expensive, a problem Rowan was actively attempting to solve. He had plans for the mills, starting with the clothing the girl before him wore. Mentally he calculated the cost of her dress, apron, cap and wool stockings. What about an additional dress? She probably had only one, meant for church or her half-day.

The girl turned and caught him looking at her. Her cheeks

reddened but her eyes twinkled in invitation. "Will there be anything else, my lord?"

"No, thank you. That will be all." He gave her a polite smile.

Ready-made. The fast-growing class of tradesmen, merchants and shopkeepers had a hunger for ready-made clothing. The larger of the Newsome mills could produce such things. He already had in place an agreement to import cotton from America. The ships necessary to carry the cotton to England would be those of the Duke of Dunbar. His Grace was already actively engaged in trade all over the world, though few in the *ton* would care to disparage him over such a thing.

His parents, Lord and Lady Marsh, were horrified that their son would dirty his hands in trade. So upsetting was the thought to his parents that Rowan kept his business dealings quiet. He had no wish for them to know or understand his single-minded pursuit of building an empire of his own.

He turned his attention from textiles back to the scotch in his hand. His Grace seemed to have an endless supply of scotch, always of the highest quality. Carriages moved past the windows, the sound of the horse's hooves unable to penetrate the drawing room. It was peaceful here, much more serene then the scene doubtlessly playing out at the home of Rowan's parents. Lady Marsh was determined to play matchmaker for both her children, though he was currently bearing the brunt of her attention. Mother peppered Rowan with notes all week, begging him to attend her at his earliest convenience, which he had not done.

Guilt hung in his stomach. He took another sip of the scotch. Avoiding his mother was a rare outwardly show of rebellion, something his conscience usually kept in check. His parents wished him to marry, reminding them that had the fates not been so cruel, their home would already be full of the sound of grandchildren. Lady Marsh had even been so kind as to pick out the perfect future countess. Lady Gwendolyn White.

Lady Gwendolyn was a beautiful, well-mannered feather wit. He'd die of boredom before he could bed her.

One more finger of scotch was in order. He wasn't just avoiding his mother who had probably already invaded the bachelor apartment he kept. Rowan also had something of great importance to speak to the duke about.

Augustus Corbett.

His Grace was bound to become quite angry as Rowan related the news concerning Corbett. Very few men would be bold enough to remain in England after attempting to kidnap the future Duchess of Dunbar. Of course, Corbett had assistance.

A slow curl, a mixture of anger and desire, spiraled deep inside Rowan at the thought of the duke's sister, Lady Arabella. If she were standing before him, Rowan was certain he'd strangle her. Or lay her down, lift her skirts and take her savagely, something he fantasized about on a frequent basis. His feelings towards Arabella tended to be rather conflicted and had been for some time. How was it possible to be attracted to such a woman?

Rowan noticed his glass was empty. He stood and poured just a bit more and looked at the clock. Plenty of time before tonight's event. After settling himself, he thought back to the dinner he'd attended the night before.

Rowan had a varied and diverse circle of acquaintances and gentlemen he called friends. Mr. Gerald Wrigley was one of those acquaintances. A banker of some repute, Mr. Wrigley had been instrumental in assisting Rowan in past endeavors. More importantly, Rowan liked and trusted Wrigley, and his dinner parties were always entertaining. Unmarried as he was, Wrigley's older, widowed sister often played hostess at his events. Clara Wrigley Howard was utterly charming and made sure the wine and conversation flowed freely.

Also, Rowan was considering the possibility of an affair with Clara.

As he busied himself admiring Clara's daring neckline over dinner last night, he had listened to the conversation around him, carefully squirreling away bits of information he could use later. The gentlemen on his left was a young barrister named Jennings. Rowan was picking at his lamb when he overheard Jennings mention Bermuda.

Rowan only knew two people from Bermuda. His cousin Jemma and Augustus Corbett. He listened intently to Jennings' conversation with his dinner companion. The young barrister didn't care for his brother-in-law, a man who he saw as spoiled and lacking in character. Only a week ago, the brother-in-law had approached Jennings at his law offices and requested funds. Jennings was shocked, he'd said, because he'd been certain *Augustus* had left England some time ago.

Rowan nearly dropped his fork. There was no doubt in his mind Jennings was speaking of the very same man who'd nearly taken his cousin. After Jemma's aborted kidnapping, no trace of Augustus Corbett had been found. The only clue was a record of passage booked to Boston. The ship had already sailed but Nick sent his solicitor to Boston immediately to find Corbett. But if Jennings was to be believed, and there was no reason why he shouldn't be, Corbett had *never* left London. Nick's solicitor had been sent on a wild goose chase. Rowan had begun to make discreet inquiries but so far had discovered nothing more. Corbett had covered his tracks well.

Rowan sank deeper into the chair, sneaking a glance at the clock above the fireplace. Plenty of time left to make himself presentable. He'd be perfectly turned out. Smile at Lady

Gwendolyn, a woman he had absolutely no intention of marrying. Dance and be amusing.

He was so bloody *tired* of all of it. Especially of the perfection of women like Lady Gwendolyn.

Arabella wasn't perfect. Far from it. Maybe that was his attraction to her. Nick's sister was dour. Deceitful. *Unpleasant.* Yet something drew Rowan to Arabella's darkness. The urge to possess her was often an unwelcome feeling when he saw her. His desire for her confused him and had only grown stronger over time.

He took another sip of the scotch and closed his eyes imagining Arabella in his bed. She would be naked, the silken mass of her hair streaming over the pillows as he loomed over her. The image was incredibly arousing.

5

"He's taken her! Nick!"

Rowan sat straight up. Blinking to clear the sleep from his eyes he spared a glance at the darkened window. The moon was not quite up yet, but it was late. *Very* late. The glass of scotch he'd been nursing sat on the table next to him, no doubt put there by the annoyed Peabody. *Christ,* he'd fallen asleep.

A woman's heels clicked down the marble hallway towards the drawing room.

"Nick!" The voice was panicked. *Terrified.*

"My lady, His Grace is not here." Rowan heard the ruffled voice of Peabody echoing down the marble corridor. Peabody was *never* ruffled.

"Where is my nephew, Peabody?" Rowan recognized the voice of Lady Cupps-Foster, Nick's aunt. "Please tell me he has returned from Scotland."

Peabody said something to her in a low tone.

A cry of anguish echoed outside the door. "We'll never get word to him in time," she sobbed. "My God, he's taken my niece." The words dissolved into weeping. "Peabody, we must rouse the footmen. Someone. *Anyone*."

Rowan stood and moved quickly towards the door. Arabella was missing? *Taken?* She should be locked away safely in Wales, enjoying her exile and lamenting her sins. Opening the door wide, he startled Lady Cupps-Foster. Her slender form was shaking with exhaustion. Mud splattered her dark blue traveling gown. Bits of twigs and leaves stuck to her skirts. The spray of flowers on top of her bonnet lay wilted and torn to flap against her ear. Several strands of dark hair shot through with gray fell to her slumped shoulders. Her eyes were shadowed and wild, speaking to the terror she felt for her niece.

"Lady Cupps-Foster," he spoke gently trying not to frighten her, "what has happened?"

Confusion wrinkled her brow as she attempted to focus on Rowan. "Lord Malden?" Her hand immediately reached up to adjust her bonnet. "But what are you doing here? Is Nick with you?" Her body swayed towards the floor.

Rowan rushed forward, catching her before she fell face down in the hallway. Taking her elbow, he led her into the drawing room and settled her in the chair he'd vacated only moments before. Deciding sherry was in order, he poured her a glass from the sideboard.

"Lady Cupps-Foster, take a sip of this. It will warm you."

She looked askance at the sherry and shook her head. "Scotch or whiskey please. Though of the two, I'd prefer whiskey."

"Of course." Rowan didn't show his surprise as he brought her whiskey. He held the crystal cut glass to her lips as she took a sip of the amber liquid.

Suddenly she pushed the glass aside. "Oh, God. I've forgotten that John and Teddy Mac are still in the coach.

John's hurt. His head." She grabbed at Rowan's coat sleeve. "Please, you must have them retrieved at once."

Peabody went to the door, yelling for several footmen. "John and Teddy Mac are still in the coach. Bring them in and send for a physician."

"Teddy Mac?" Rowan didn't take his eyes off of Lady Cupps-Foster as he addressed Peabody. "The young boy who picked His Grace's pocket—"

"Yes." Peabody's voice shook. "He begged to go, and I felt it was safe enough. I sent out two footmen with the coach. Big, burly young men who—"

"The footmen." Lady Cupps-Foster took a large swallow of the whiskey. "Seagraves and Barker. They were in *his* employ." She gave Peabody a rather hostile look. "How could you send them to get us? How could you hire such men?"

"My lady—" The butler's throat bobbed in agitation. "They came with solid recommendations," Peabody said, barely above a whisper. His skin turned a deathly shade of gray. "His Grace wanted strong men to ride with the coach. I..." A devastated look crossed his face. "My God, I shall never forgive myself."

Lady Cupps-Foster turned from Peabody and stared into the fire, the glass of whiskey clasped in her hands. She was still shaking. "Teddy Mac is hungry." Her lips ticked up. "He's talked about food all the way back to London."

"Peabody, prepare a hot bath and a room for Lady Cupps-Foster." When the butler didn't move, Rowan growled. "Now, Peabody. And keep the staff away from the drawing room until I can sort this out. Get John comfortably settled. Take Teddy Mac into the kitchen."

Peabody jerked, as if he had only been waiting instruction to knock the inertia from him. Bowing to Rowan, he hurried from the room.

Nick's aunt rocked back and forth against the chair, dropping bits of mud on the expensive Persian rug beneath her feet. "Lady Cupps-Foster," Rowan knelt and took the glass from her. She'd long since lost her gloves and her hands were like blocks of ice. "Start at the beginning." He handed her the handkerchief from his pocket. "I will do everything I can to help as Nick has not yet returned from Scotland."

"The bloody rain. It's delayed him and with Jemma's condition...my nephew worries for her. Hopefully the rain will also delay that vile cur's abduction of my niece as well."

Nick was incredibly protective of his wife and given that Jemma was with child, he likely wouldn't want her bounced around on muddy roads which explained their delay in reaching London. They were either holed up at an inn or had found accommodations at some lord's estate along the way. Rowan thought the latter more likely. He should have assumed such when the duke didn't arrive earlier today. It would take time to locate the Duke of Dunbar. Cold fingers of dread caressed the back of Rowan's neck. Only one man would dare take Arabella. "Augustus Corbett."

"Yes. The very same. He's taken her." Hard, tear-filled eyes looked up at Rowan. "He must have been planning this for a long time, virtually since the time Jemma was rescued. Seagraves and Barker, the footmen, were in his employ for several months. They were with the coach on our journey to Wales." She shook her head. "Why didn't he take Arabella then? Why wait?"

Timing, Rowan surmised. Nick was still in London when he'd banished his sister and Corbett hadn't yet laid his false trail. Corbett wasn't stupid.

"A coach blocked the road to Camden. A dirty, shabby thing that looked to be in trouble. John sent Seagraves and Barker to see if we could assist the occupants or help in some way. Arabella thought it a mail coach on the way to London. John was hurt and Teddy Mac tied up." She sniffed in distress. "Seagraves, the larger of the two brutes climbed into our coach." Her mouth grew hard. "He dared to put his hands on me. On my mouth. He tied my wrists together and threatened to gag me."

"Corbett was mentioned by name?"

"Yes. When Seagraves left the coach for a moment, I overheard him speaking to Barker and Corbett's name came up several times. Seagraves was to stay with the Dunbar coach and us until at least the following morning. He drove us to a small shack off the main road. He'd packed food and water. Barker was to drive Corbett's coach." She blotted her eyes and clutched Rowan's hand. "Scotland. Gretna Green. Another sob escaped her. "Corbett is taking her to Gretna Green to be married. Seagraves said as much."

All things considered, Corbett's plan was actually quite clever. By planting the two false footmen in the Dunbar household, Corbett always knew the whereabouts of the Duke of Dunbar and Arabella, until he found the perfect time to strike. There was nothing between Twinings and Camden. No coaching station. Few inns. The road itself was not well-traveled. And the Duke of Dunbar was in Scotland. "How did you get away from Seagraves?"

Dark circles stood out starkly against the whiteness of Lady Cupps-Foster's skin. "Seagraves did not assume *me* to be a threat. I offered to cook." She lifted a brow. "I've never cooked a thing in my life. But the shack had a large cast iron skillet. Teddy Mac distracted Seagraves while I brought the skillet down on the top of his skull. I had to hit him several times before he fell to the floor. I untied Teddy Mac and together we managed to get poor John into the coach. Teddy Mac drove the horses." A tired sigh escaped her, and she wiped at her eyes. "I had no money. Corbett took my purse."

Her eyes welled with new tears. "I bought us some bread and cheese along the way with my silver buttons."

Indeed, she had. Rowan noticed that all of the buttons were gone from the front of her traveling cloak. Only the threads remained.

"Lady Cupps-Foster, why did you not summon the constable in Camden to chase after the coach? Certainly —"

"And what would I have told him? Arabella's reputation would be in shreds before I finished speaking. Her abduction would be public knowledge in the *ton*. My niece already suffers society's scrutiny for a variety of things that are not her fault. I suppose it was foolish." She sniffed. "Arabella's virtue may already be gone. But at least I can protect her from more gossip."

"My lady, I will go immediately to Bow Street and I can assure you of their discretion. I'll send a messenger to find His Grace and—"

"*No*, Lord Malden, it will be far too late." She closed her eyes and bent her head and clasped his hands. "*You* are an honorable man and a friend to my nephew. Please, you could go after her. I trust you to protect her reputation and shield her from gossip."

Rowan looked away from the pleading look in her eyes. "Lady Cupps-Foster, is there any possibility, *any at all*, that Arabella went with Corbett of her own accord? She did help him once." The thought occurred to Rowan all during Lady Cupps-Foster's recitation. He wouldn't put such a thing past Arabella.

Lady Cupps-Foster did not lift her eyes to meet his. Instead, her gaze remained focused on their clasped hands. "I watched Barker drag her kicking and screaming from the coach. She fought him. If nothing else, if Corbett manages to become her husband, he could use the opportunity to discredit your family, or worse. Please. I beg you. There is no one else. Neither of my sons are near enough to offer aid and who knows how long it will take to find my nephew."

Bloody Hell. Lady Cupps-Foster was right even though Arabella certainly deserved her fate. He should let her rot. But he couldn't.

"Very well. I'll go. I'll find Lady Arabella."

❧ 6 ❧

hank God.

Arabella breathed in relief as the coaching inn finally came into view. She was tired, damp and hungry. The rain, barely a drizzle as they'd approached Camden, had turned into a steady downpour that showed no sign of abating. Moisture pelted the coach relentlessly as the ancient vehicle labored in the general direction of Gretna Green. Corbett's coach was less than comfortable and in desperate need of new springs. Arabella was bruised from the constant jostling and exhausted from the non-stop travel. He had allowed only minimal stops, barely allowing time to relieve herself before they started off again. Barker deliberately kept the coach off the main road, but the action slowed their travel. Twice the coach had gotten stuck in the mud causing a delay of several hours. She'd been begging Corbett since early that morning to stop, if only to find relief from the constant rain.

Barker agreed with her, snapping at Corbett that the horses were exhausted and needed a rest. The footman, if she could call him that, had grown even more surly. He glared at

Arabella as if the entire journey was her fault. Which of course, in a way, it was.

Corbett finally agreed to stop at the next coaching inn.

Barker handed her out of the coach, his rough features hinting at the cruelty that lay within. "My lady."

Arabella refused to be intimidated, particularly by a man like Barker. Like the feral dog he was, Corbett's henchman would smell fear on her and attack. Shaking off his hand, she followed Corbett to the inn, head bent down, pulling her cloak tight. Truthfully, she *was* afraid. After being trapped inside that filthy coach with Corbett, she'd heard a constant litany of hatred directed at both her brother and Jemma. His handsome face would take on an almost maniacal cast as he crowed about his impending revenge. He also took every opportunity to touch her until Arabella found herself squeezed in the corner furthest from him. It had taken relatively little time for Arabella to determine that she loathed Corbett, but she forced herself to think of the freedom and revenge this marriage would bring her. Surprisingly, the prospect brought her little joy.

Corbett took her arm, leading her across the busy court-yard to step inside the inn while Barker disappeared, probably to see to the horses. Honestly, Arabella didn't care, relieved to no longer have to tolerate his smirking presence.

Stepping inside, Arabella saw the coaching inn was crowded with people making their way to London. The interior was dim, but she could make out a taproom to her left. The hum of dozens of voices met her ears as guests ate, drank and availed themselves of the fire blazing from the hearth.

She shivered, as much from the cold as from fear she'd be recognized. The inn was in Lancashire and a main stop on the way to and from London. She kept her head down, tugging the bonnet she wore to hide her face.

Corbett's grip on her arm was tight as he approached a

husky, red faced man holding two empty tankards of ale in one hand, wiping the sweat off of his brow with the other. Seeing Corbett, he stopped and nodded.

"Can I help you, my lord?"

Arabella's nose wrinkled. The man smelled as if he'd fallen into a bucket of ale.

"I'm in need of a room where my wife can rest for a bit before we continue our journey. We'd also like to have a bit of supper."

Wife. He called her his wife. Nausea filled her and she opened her mouth to object but stopped. *It will be true soon enough.*

"I do, my lord. One last room. A bit small and not our finest, but you can eat and rest. Lucky you came now. If the rain continues, you'd be fortunate to find even space in the taproom. He waved to a thin, harried girl who was making her way through the taproom. "Bess will show you up."

The sudden urge to flee was so strong, Arabella's feet actually moved back and forth.

Bess gave them a tired smile but led them up a flight of narrow stairs and down a poorly lit hall. She stopped in front of one door and swung it open to reveal a small, sparsely furnished room. A bed sat against one wall covered with a faded quilt. Even from the door Arabella could see the lumps in the mattress.

Probably full of vermin.

The center of the room held a scarred wooden table and three battered chairs. A chest of drawers stood against another wall holding a pitcher and wash bowl.

Bess hurried to the hearth, efficiently lighting the fire. She turned and bustled out of the room to reappear a moment later with hot water, towels and a bar of soap. Arabella pulled away from Corbett to approach the warmth of the flames ablaze in the hearth and hopefully chase the chill from her skirts.

"I'll send up something to eat for you milord. My lady." The girl bobbed, peering at Corbett from under her lashes. "Will there be anything else?"

"A bottle of wine as well." Corbett smiled in his charming manner and the girl giggled.

Arabella's lip curled. *Disgusting.*

Reaching into a side pocket, he produced a small purse heavy with coins. Pressing several pieces of gold into the girl's palm, he said something in a low voice before shutting the door.

The purse bore the initials M.T. *Marissa Tremaine.*

"Why do you have my aunt's coin purse?" Arabella made to snatch it from his hands and Corbett sidestepped her. "You promised she wouldn't be harmed."

"Lady Cupps-Foster is fine. I imagine she's on her way to London by now. Seagraves, while rather slow-witted, knows how to follow orders. I left plenty of funds to see dear Aunt Maisy home." He presented the same charming smile he'd given the maid. "I merely *borrowed* her purse. I'll repay her once we're wed. I promise."

He's lying.

The purse slid back inside his coat pocket. "I'll give you some privacy, my dear. Don't fret, I'll be back soon." He moved towards the door.

Arabella had never 'fretted' in her entire life. And she doubted Corbett gave a fig for her well-being. "I shall miss your delightful company." She took great satisfaction watching the smile fade at the scorn in her voice.

He slammed the door behind him.

Arabella's self-satisfaction dissolved at the click of the lock. Now that she was alone, without Corbett's constant presence, the unease which had been building since she'd agreed to this terrible bargain made itself known. What had seemed like an excellent way get back at everyone in her life for all the wrongs done to her now seemed the actions of a petulant and spoiled child. She would be stuck with Corbett, a man she now knew she detested, for the remainder of her life. Her family would despise her. Miranda would be forced to avoid her. She told herself she didn't care.

My actions are not those of an intelligent woman.

Grandfather had often praised her intellect stating that Arabella possessed more brains than most of the men in Parliament. She wondered what he would say of her acceptance of Corbett? The idea of marrying for revenge?

He would be ashamed and demand I fix the situation.

Carefully she untied the strings of her bonnet allowing it to fall from her head. She begged her hands to cease their shaking. Arabella had always considered herself to be rather fearless. One scathing look from her could freeze water. No one liked her, true, but neither did anyone in the *ton* risk offending her. It struck Arabella her fearlessness was born of the fact that she'd never been in *true* peril before.

Well, she was certainly in peril *now*.

"Dear God, I do hope I don't collapse into a fit of vapors," she whispered out loud. The thought of being at Corbett's mercy while unconscious and prone was incredibly unappealing.

Dabbing at her face with a towel, she carefully wiped away the grime beneath her chin. The action helped stall the cry of panic rapidly bubbling up her throat. She was very neatly snared in a trap she herself had willingly walked into.

I must find a way to escape Corbett and my own foolishness.

The lock clicked behind her and the door swung open.

Corbett was rather smug, his previous good humor restored. He waved in Bess who hastily laid the small table with fresh linens and steaming plates of food before bobbing once again.

Corbett pressed another coin in the girl's palm.

Shutting the door, he approached the table. "Mutton *my love*, with potatoes." Every word laced with false cheer and affection. "It smells delicious, does it not?"

Arabella turned, facing the bad bargain that was Augustus Corbett. A hasty agreement she'd made in anger. Corbett could not be trusted and the thought struck her that freedom would *not* be hers if she married him.

"It smells delicious," she lied.

While she'd had little to eat since leaving the Dunbar coach, only some cheese and bread Arabella doubted she would be able to eat. Her earlier hunger faded abruptly as she contemplated her future.

Corbett bowed low and pulled out the chair nearest to her. He motioned for her to sit. "My dear. May this be the first of many pleasant evenings together."

Perish the thought. The brush of his fingertips lingered against one shoulder and her stomach curdled.

"I was so very pleased when you agreed to our marriage, Arabella." He moved around the table, covering her hand with his. "So pleased."

She tried to move her hand away.

He slid his fingers through hers, gripping hard. "So cold and aloof. Is it any surprise no man will have you? Except *me*, of course." He sat himself across from her, the corners of his mouth twisting. "I like a challenge."

Arabella's heart raced wildly in her chest as panic escalated. She struggled to focus on her mutton, trying to ignore the bits of oil congealing around the bone. The potatoes, artfully arranged around the meat looked to have been harvested last fall. A bit of mush on the side of her plate may have been a vegetable of some sort. Possibly carrots.

Corbett poured himself wine, studying her before tipping the glass back to drain it. His eyes flitted to her breasts. "I shall ask you in the future to wear more appealing gowns, Arabella." He waved his glass in the direction of her bodice. "I like to see a bit of skin, possibly your neck would be a start. Or the tops of your breasts."

An unpleasant feeling clawed against her chest. "As we discussed earlier, your opinion of my clothing is of little consequence. I will continue to wear what I wish as my attractiveness holds little bearing in our marriage."

A hungry look entered his face. One that frightened her more than she cared to admit. He meant to take his husbandly rights. Stupidly she had believed Corbett when he claimed to not be interested in consummating their marriage. Of course he'd lied. Arabella looked down at the tines of the fork she clasped. It was the only weapon available to her. Lifting her chin she shot him a look that silenced twittering matrons at the fundraisers she so often hosted.

"Very *good*, Arabella. Do you use that look to put your servants in place? Perhaps frighten some poor girl who has offended you?" He threw back his wine and poured more.

"I'm afraid I've changed my mind. I've decided we don't suit." She was surprised at the firm tone of her voice as she was bloody terrified. "I shall arrange passage back to London on one of the coaches sitting in the courtyard."

Corbett giggled, slapping his palm against the table. Wine sloshed out on the tablecloth. "Oh, you *are* amusing, aren't you Queen Sour?" Patting the grease from his lips he glared at her from across the table. "The only coach you'll be leaving in is mine." He nodded to Arabella's untouched glass. "Drink."

Arabella stood on shaky legs. "You cannot force me to marry you."

"Don't be ridiculous. Of course, I can. Do you think I would allow you to just flounce out of here and go about your merry way? I made sure Seagraves informed your aunt of our agreement. I didn't wish her to worry."

Arabella paled. "She would never believe such a thing."

"Wouldn't she?" He tossed back the remainder of his wine and poured himself another full glass. "Sit down."

"I will scream." It was no idle threat. She wanted to scream her head off. Beat at the door. Surely someone would help her.

"You're given to fits, Arabella." His boyish face took on a mournful cast. "Delicate nerves and all that. I've already informed the proprietor you have delusions I've kidnapped you. My poor, *dear* wife. I fear you may be destined for the sanitarium." His mouth grew hard. "Have you ever been to a madhouse, Arabella? Even *you* wouldn't last long inside such a place. If you continue being disagreeable, I shall send you to one after our marriage. And we *will* be married. Now drink your wine like a good girl."

Arabella's mouth went dry at his words. Slowly she eased herself back into her chair, shaken to her very core. A sanitarium? Such a thing had never crossed her mind, for she'd never thought him so bold. As her husband, he would be within his rights to lock her away forever. "I don't drink spirits," she whispered.

"Well I think now would be the time to try, don't you? I've no desire to be married to a prude."

Arabella glared back defiantly as his blue gaze raked over her bosom once more. His interest had become more than passing. She pierced a tiny bit of mutton on the fork, studying the tines and wondering at their sharpness, before chewing the meat. Good Lord, the mutton was terrible. She laid the fork back down next to her plate.

"You *are* a prude, aren't you? Cold, like a block of ice. Not an ounce of fire in you. Perhaps I shall be the man to finally warm you."

"I doubt that." Her fingers ran over the knife beside her plate, testing the blade. Her heart sank. A dull butter knife, no sharper than the fork. She had only an ancient set of cutlery to defend her honor.

Abruptly, Corbett stood, as if something of import had come to mind. He circled the table until he stood behind her. His fingers dug into her shoulders and he leaned in. His breath was hot and smelled of sour grapes. "Well, I *do* like a challenge. Disappointment in the bedroom is certain, I fear. You'll lay there with no more animation than a gutted fish. Hopefully there's something appealing underneath this hideous dress."

She could barely breathe, afraid the slightest movement would set Corbett off. "Get away from me," she hissed.

One hand, clammy and slightly damp, circled the back of her neck like a vise, holding her firm. His other hand traveled down the front of her chest like an overly large spider, splaying across her bodice. The fingers squeezed as if her breast were a piece of fruit Corbett inspected. "Hmm." He sounded surprised. "Nicely endowed for a *shriveled* spinster, aren't you? Perhaps bedding you won't be the chore I expect it to be."

"There is no reason to continue, given my lack of appeal. Remove your hands." Her tone didn't hide the disgust she felt for him. "I'll see myself out." She tried to stand and his hold tightened.

"It's unfortunate you're prepared to give up your plans for revenge, however, I am not. I will have my heiress. Not the one I wanted, true, but a wealthy lady all the same. You are a consolation prize of sorts, Arabella. A sour, mealy apple when I wished for a sweet cherry." He found her nipple, twisting the tender flesh through the heavy folds of fabric.

"I plan on putting a brat in your belly *tonight*. Any child borne of our union will be very useful in keeping the Duke of Dunbar from killing me or annulling the marriage."

"You are insane as well as drunk." Her fingers fluttered over the table, resting on the fork.

"I'd have to be to bed *you*. I imagine a stone statue would be more welcoming."

Arabella's grip on the fork tightened.

$\bigstar$ 7 $\bigstar$

Rowan burst through the doors of the taproom, his boots leaving bits of mud scattering across the floor. Gloves slapping against his thigh in agitation, he was beginning to realize the futility of his quest.

I'll never catch them. Not at this rate.

Anxiously his eyes searched the taproom of the coaching inn situated in Lancashire and found nothing out of the ordinary. His stomach grumbled. When was the last time he'd eaten? Not since the morning or possibly even yesterday. It seemed ages since Lady Cupps-Foster had burst into Dunbar House and begged him to go after Arabella. Almost two days in the saddle with little sleep, only stopping to change horses. The only thing that gave him hope was that the rain would have been much more detrimental to Corbett in his coach than a man on horseback.

A young, harried barmaid brushed past, took a good look at him and turned to face him. "Greetings milord. You're welcome to sit." She jerked her head toward the crowded taproom. "What can I bring you?"

"Ale and a platter of those." He pointed at the small savory pastries. "And a fresh horse."

The barmaid nodded and walked away, yelling until a young boy appeared. Rowan tossed him a coin and the young lad ran outside to see to Rowan's horse.

He'd damn near been to every coaching inn on the main road to Scotland. At each inn he'd asked after a shabby coach, describing Arabella and Corbett. He inquired cautiously, mindful of the need for discretion. So far, his efforts had been in vain. No one had seen a woman resembling Arabella.

Rowan settled down at an empty table close to the main entrance so he could watch the door. Just in case. Maybe he would get lucky. This particular coaching inn sat at a cross-roads of the main road to Scotland but branched out into several less traveled routes. He suspected Corbett deliberately kept to the back roads, but the strategy would also slow his coach. Some of the roads would become impassable because of the rain. Even as he watched, hurried travelers struggled to finish their meals as two drivers entered the taproom to announce it was time to depart, least they all become trapped as the weather worsened.

A large, bulky man stomped through the front door, shaking the rain from his hair like some oversized dog; as he moved into the taproom his cloak flapped open wide and Rowan caught a flash of blue and silver. The colors of the Duke of Dunbar. The man glanced about the room, his dark eyes flat and emotionless, the coarseness of his features reflecting a brutal nature. He sat down at a table next to Rowan, scattering the previous occupants.

"Your employer informed me you won't need fresh horses until the morrow." The innkeeper passed by the man, handing him a mug of ale. "I believe he means to stay the night. I've room for you in the stables."

The man took a large draught of the ale and wiped his

mouth with his sleeve. "Fine by me. We barely stopped since we left Wales and it's a bloody long way away. And hellishly wet."

The innkeeper grunted. "Well, it'll be hellishly wet here as well."

Rowan chewed his meat pie, the savory mix of beef and vegetables turning to dust in his mouth. *Wales?* It had to be a coincidence. Or Rowan's luck had changed.

"He's told me his wife needs to rest. Poor lass. Given to fits, he's told me. That's a pity."

"Wife?" The man's brow wrinkled in confusion for a moment. "Ah yes," a snort of amusement sounded as he drained his ale. "Aye, his wife."

Rowan's dinner companion could be no other than one of the 'poorly turned out footmen' Lady Cupps-Foster had referred to earlier. Which meant Corbett and Arabella were upstairs.

༻✦༺

CORBETT TOYED WITH THE BUTTONS AT THE BACK OF HER gown. A popping sound met her ears along with the feel of her dress loosening as the button fell free, rolling beneath the table to land on the toe of Arabella's boot.

"None of my previous lovers found cause for complaint. You may find you enjoy my cock in you."

Wincing at the vulgar language, she shot back. "If your skill is so great, I wonder Jemma fled you at the first opportunity. How odd."

Hissing with anger, Corbett's hands pulled at the pins holding her hair, savagely undoing the tight bun at the base of her neck. The heavy mass twisted and writhed to fall over her shoulders.

"You've lovely hair, Arabella." Twisting the strands around

his fingers he pulled her head back and Arabella barely had time to struggle before a wet, drunken kiss was pressed to her mouth.

Her teeth tore into his lip until she tasted blood.

"Bitch!" Corbett released her hair to grab a napkin from the table to blot his lip. "I was going to be gentle." The hand circling her neck tightened. "But now I see there's no need. You are the type of woman who requires a firm hand. I will enjoy bringing you to heel."

Arabella wheezed, struggling to breathe as she lost her grip on the fork. Her arms swung in an arc across the table, searching for her weapon. Finally, she felt the stab of the tines against her fingers. Grasping the fork in one hand, she clawed against Corbett with the other. She swung the fork up and brought it down with as much force as possible against his neck, praying she'd hit an artery. Or possibly an eye. The fork jarred in her hand, sinking into his skin, just as he ripped the back of her gown away.

He shrieked in pain. "God damn you, Arabella!"

❧ 8 ❧

Rowan ran down the corridor. The man's voice could only be Corbett's which meant Arabella was here, somewhere. He stood still, his senses alert as he waited for Corbett to give away their location.

A thud, then a woman's muffled cry came from behind a door to his left.

Without another thought, Rowan slammed his shoulder against the warped wood. The door creaked but didn't open. Raising his foot, he kicked hard, the rusty lock falling free and the door opened.

As he stormed the room, Rowan silently thanked Lord Kilmaire for impressing on him the importance of being armed to the teeth, gentleman or not. Rowan was already a crack shot and didn't embarrass himself with a sword. But under Kilmaire's direction, Rowan had learned how to properly throw a knife. A large blade was even now tucked securely in his right boot just in case. He pulled his pistol from his coat. Nothing would give him greater pleasure than shooting Corbett between the eyes.

"Jesus," the word left his lips as he viewed the scene in the room.

Arabella flailed like a wild animal against Corbett, her dark hair spinning in a tangled mass over her shoulders. Her dress was ripped down the back, the material opening to reveal the startling bright red of her chemise.

Corbett was holding her by the arm, viciously shaking her. She spun, twisting and contorting in an effort to free herself. Her face turned towards the open door. Arabella ceased her struggle, shock stamped on her features. Blood dribbled from her split lip and the red marks of Corbett's fingers stood out against the pale skin of her neck.

"Lord Malden?" Her sable brows knit together in confusion.

"Get your hands off of her." The sight of Corbett's hands on Arabella incensed Rowan. He'd never wanted to kill a man so badly.

Corbett caught sight of Rowan before tossing Arabella to the floor. A fork protruded from his neck, a trickle of blood spilling from the wound.

Good girl.

"Arabella," Rowan didn't take his eyes off of Corbett. The man was practically frothing at the mouth like a lunatic. "Get behind me."

Arabella stared at him, blinking like a confused owl.

"*Move*, Arabella." His hands clutched the pistol as she finally heeded him, scuttling like a crab across the floor.

The fork in Corbett's neck bobbed as he twisted to look at Rowan.

"Who the bloody hell are you?"

A COPPERY TASTE FILLED HER MOUTH AS SHE SWIPED AT THE

blood from her split lip. The entire side of her face throbbed from Corbett's harsh treatment. But had she hit her head? She must be hallucinating because Lord Malden, her sister-in-law Jemma's cousin and member of the same traitorous family stood before her, in the middle of the room, a pistol pointed at Corbett. Lord Malden and she were not friends. He rarely spoke to her unless it was to say something annoying. A well-known rake, he was handsome and amusing, the perfect heir to the Earl of Marsh, Jemma's uncle. And he didn't like Arabella. Not one bit.

What was he doing here?

He stood like a shield between she and Corbett, his large body tensed in a protective stance. Malden was travel stained, his once fine clothes rumpled and his expensive boots covered with muck. Dark brown hair curled around his ears and collar from the rain. And he smelled distinctly of horse.

It was at this *most* inappropriate of moments, as she took in Malden, that something very dark and wicked stirred in Arabella. The feeling, given the current situation, was completely unwarranted.

"Get out." Corbett's words slurred. "She's *my* heiress. You'll have to find your own. This is none of your bloody affair, whoever you are. My wife is prone to fits. I'll likely have her committed." He shot Arabella an evil leer.

"She's not your wife." Malden spat out.

"Are you deaf? *Get out.*" Corbett reached up and pulled the fork out of his neck with a groan. He glared at Arabella and tossed the fork towards her place on the floor. "You're going to pay for that, Arabella."

Rowan stalked towards Corbett with intent, his face hard and determined. He flipped the pistol around and cracked the butt against Corbett's nose. "*That* was for my cousin."

A horrible crunch sounded before a streak of crimson

burst from his nose. Corbett shrieked, grabbing his nose with both hands as blood spurted between his fingers.

"Cousin? *You're* Jemma's cousin?" He backed up a pace and grabbed a napkin off the table, his eyes narrowed. "How is the traitorous little tart?"

"I should shoot you where you stand." Malden sounded nonchalant as if he were just considering what to order for dinner. "She's not your wife." He repeated.

"She will be shortly. We're on our way to Gretna Green to make things legal. I didn't kidnap her. She came of her own free will. She's agreed to marry me."

"Is that why her dress is torn? Because she's agreed?" Malden barely looked at Arabella as he spoke, but she could sense the tiny bit of doubt that bled into his words.

"He's insane." Her voice trembled, knowing if he didn't believe her Malden may well leave her to the mercy of Corbett. "He took me from the Dunbar coach and threatened my aunt. Kept me prisoner in that coach. Locked the door to this room. Attacked me over dinner. Does that sound like I'm here of my own free will?" She shivered and the torn arm of her dress fell over her shoulder.

Malden's eyes shot back to her with startling intensity.

"She's lying." Corbett spat.

"I am so willing I stabbed him with the only weapon I had at my disposal," She hissed. "A fork." Arabella looked up at Malden.

Please believe me. Please.

A cry of rage escaped Corbett's mouth at her words. He flung the bloody handkerchief at Malden's face before he put his head down like an enraged bull and charged, taking Malden by surprise. The pistol fell to the floor and Malden managed to kick the weapon away. Corbett bellowed in frustration as he flung himself at Malden and attempted to grab the pistol.

A flash of silver fell out of Malden's boot, spinning in an arc until it landed near Arabella.

A knife. She reached out, her fingers wrapping around the hilt before concealing the blade in her skirts.

A cry of triumph escaped Corbett. He stood, clutching the pistol in his hand.

Malden was on his knees before Corbett, his body taut. "Run, Arabella." His voice was soft and low. "Run."

Corbett shook his head and cocked the pistol. "If you leave, dearest, I promise to shoot your friend here."

Arabella grabbed the knife tighter and shook her head. "No. You will not."

"On second thought, I believe I'll shoot him anyway. How delightful it will be to celebrate our marriage while Jemma is in mourning, her eyes red-rimmed with grief." He looked down at Malden. "You really shouldn't have come after Arabella. She's not worth it, you know." Corbett shot her a look of dislike.

"Do you really believe you can shoot me and walk out of here unscathed?" Malden sounded matter-of-fact. "The entire taproom saw me. I'm a lord. A baron who is heir to an earldom. I'm related by marriage to the Duke of Dunbar." He shrugged. "*You* are the son of a traitorous and little remembered former Governor of Bermuda. How is your father, by the way? I've heard he's reduced to sitting in a chair with drool coming off his chin."

"Shut. Up." Corbett's voice shook and his right eye twitched.

"I met your brother-in-law, Jennings. He doesn't care for you. I doubt you'll see another penny from him. Also, there is the problem of *her* brother." Malden jerked his head in Arabella's direction. "He may not want you dead for her sake, but he will for Jemma. Particularly if you shoot me."

The pistol lowered a fraction. Beads of perspiration formed on Corbett's upper lip.

Malden tensed, ready to spring.

Suddenly a grin split Corbett's face. "A shame the pistol went off accidentally. Yes, that's it." He nodded his head slowly. "I thought you were an intruder. Or perhaps *you* were trying to kidnap my betrothed. In either case, my wife will not be able to give testimony against me as I plan on having her committed shortly after the wedding. She has fits. It's all very neat."

Arabella didn't think, allowing her anger and fear to guide her. She gripped the knife and flew at Corbett, aiming for the small marks left in his neck from the fork. The knife sank into his flesh much more smoothly than the fork, spraying Arabella with a fine mist of blood. She stumbled back as Corbett reached for her.

"You bitch." He reached up, his free hand struggling to grab the hilt of the knife. As he did so, the pistol fired. The shot of the pistol went wide and swung Corbett's body back against the edge of the table, spraying the room with mutton, blood and crashing dishes. His foot slipped on one plate of greasy mutton and his arms began to flail as he fell backwards against the window. The sound of shattering glass met her ears, then Corbett disappeared from sight.

"Arabella!"

A dull thud, the sound of cracking bones, came from the ground below.

Arabella shook uncontrollably, rooted to the spot, wiping furiously at the drops of blood that lay scattered on her skin. She put her hands to her ears to stop the awful screaming that filled the room.

The screams were coming from her.

56

"The fall broke his neck, though to be truthful, your blade hit his artery. He would have bled to death had he not fallen." The constable scratched away at a pad and glanced at the crumpled form of Augustus Corbett.

"I had no choice." Rowan shot a glance at Arabella who sat against the wall, her arms wrapped around her knees. He'd decided the moment Corbett fell from the window he would take the blame for the man's death. There was no reason for Arabella to ever know Corbett's death was assured the moment she stabbed him. At least she'd stopped screaming.

"I'm sure you didn't, Lord Malden." The constable, MacLauren, had arrived shortly after Corbett fell from the window at the summons from the inn's proprietor who'd heard the sounds of struggle.

"Mr. Corbett said his wife was mad and given to fits." The innkeeper said in a concerned voice as he stepped carefully around the damaged table to the broken window. He looked down at Corbett and gave a gasp. "He never said his wife was violent."

"She is not his wife." Rowan snapped. "Nor his betrothed."

MacLauren gave him a studied look. "Lord Malden, you've not explained your relationship to the lady, only that you came to her aid. Conveniently. Are you her brother? Cousin? Or something else? I don't even have her name."

The constable was suspicious. He couldn't blame MacLauren. The inn as well as the small village several miles to the east from whence the constable came were situated on the way to Gretna Green. The constable had likely witnessed many such incidents, though probably none as dramatic. Rowan could easily be the jealous lover trying to wrest an heiress away before another man claimed her.

"Her name is Lady Arabella Tremaine, sister of the Duke of Dunbar." His words laced with a sharp patrician accent left no doubt as to Rowan's station should MacLauren have any doubts. "She was kidnapped and taken from the Dunbar coach as it traveled to London. I am here at the behest of her brother whom I am related to by marriage. You can verify the truth with His Grace if you wish, though I would ask for your discretion regarding the events that have transpired out of respect for the lady's reputation."

The innkeeper's eyes grew as large as saucers. "She's the Devil of Dunbar's sister? Oh, saints alive."

"Ah." MacLauren stroked his mustache as he studied Rowan. "I believe I'll send word to His Grace. And I'll need a sworn statement from you, milord."

"Of course." Rowan gave the constable the address of the Dunbar home as well as that of his own lodgings.

MacLauren raised a brow. "You said he had an accomplice, but I can find no sign of the man you described. The coach looks to be abandoned except for a small valise and a trunk, though one of the horses is missing. He's long gone, whoever he is, though I will send word to my counterparts in the area."

Rowan spared a glance at Arabella, who sat huddled into a small ball in the far corner of the room. The heavy mass of her hair streamed down her shoulders in disarray, hiding her features from view. He'd seen only a blur of skirts as Arabella leapt in front of him, the silver of the knife flashing in her hand, not an ounce of fear on her face. He was wise not to tell MacLauren the truth. Though Rowan had asked for discretion, the inn and taproom had been crowded. The proprietor of this fine establishment didn't look especially trustworthy, but the man seemed fearful of the Duke of Dunbar. Perhaps that fear, along with several gold coins would buy his silence.

Rowan had promised Lady Cupps-Foster discretion and Arabella *had* saved his life, though, he considered ruefully, it could be argued his life wouldn't have been in danger had he not been sent to rescue her in the first place. She'd been brave and defiant right up until Corbett fell from the window. A horrible, low keening sound came from her as he fell and Rowan had the impression she wasn't seeing Corbett, but something else.

He tried and failed to ignore the red chemise flashing beneath the remains of Arabella's staid, mud-colored traveling dress. Given the situation, the color of her underthings, along with the sensations they aroused, should have been the last thing on his mind.

MacLauren glanced at Arabella and nodded. "I'll make arrangements for the body. I'll be as discreet as possible."

"Both myself and His Grace are most appreciative. If there's nothing else, I need to return Lady Arabella to London as soon as possible."

"Of course, Lord Malden." MacLauren dipped his hat, shooting Arabella another glance before leaving the room.

"While I make arrangements for our journey, do you have

a place Lady Arabella can rest and change her clothing?" Rowan addressed the inn keeper. "I'll also handle all the damages to the room, where the accident occurred."

"Of course, my lord. I'll have my own wife attend her in our private quarters." He bustled off to find his wife. Rowan heard him calling for water to be heated.

Assured the man was gone, Rowan walked to Arabella. Kneeling down, he took her hand, flinching slightly at the coldness of her fingers. "Arabella, do you have a change of clothes? A trunk?"

"I—" Her voice was low and scratchy. "I have clothes." She cleared her throat. "His—I mean *Corbett's* coach should have my things." She pulled her hands away and pushed up from the wall, declining his help. Her eyes were dark, fathomless pools, so brown they appeared black. "I'm fine, Lord Malden. *Perfectly* fine."

He wasn't sure what he'd expected. Maybe some expression of gratitude? An acknowledgement of what they'd just been through together or some indication she needed comfort?

Red chemise or not, Arabella was *still* Arabella.

❧ 10 ❧

"**A**re you ready to leave? The coach is just outside."

Arabella smoothed the skirts of her dark gray traveling dress. It was slightly wrinkled, but clean and high-necked which would hide the worst of the bruises left from Corbett's fingers. With her hair brushed and braided along with a change of clothes, it was easier to pretend the last few days of her life had only been a bad dream. Or a nightmare. She certainly felt very different from the woman who had agreed to marry Corbett out of revenge.

"I am."

Malden stared back at her, a concerned look lingering in the depths of his hazel eyes. He looked large and protective, and Arabella had the urge to throw herself against the breadth of his chest and snuggle against him for safety.

She turned away, slightly embarrassed by her train of thought. It was natural, she told herself, to feel some sense of...*connection* with Malden.

The knife slid into Corbett's flesh as if his neck were no more than a pad of butter.

She'd said those words to herself as she watched Corbett flail against the knife protruding from his neck.

Corbett is dead.

Hands shaking, she pulled on her gloves as Malden watched her, his brows knit together in concern. "I am anxious to return to London." His attention to her well-being made her uncomfortable as no man, outside of her brother, had ever truly given a care for her welfare. Arabella reminded herself that she did not like Lord Malden, regardless of his aid.

"As am I." Malden moved closer.

Her skin immediately prickled as he neared. His clothes were still in deplorable condition and he was in desperate need of a shave. The soap he'd used to wash smelled fresh and clean although it did little to wipe away the horse smell lingering about his broad shoulders. His eyes were hazel and tilted at the ends, something she'd never noticed before. Nor had she ever taken note of the high cheekbones and slash of his nose. He had the look of a Viking. Or at least, what she imagined a Viking to look like. The dark brown hair curling around his ears was the exact shade of fine French brandy.

Dear God.

Completely unsettled, she walked around Malden and headed outside to the courtyard. A large comfortable looking conveyance with matched bays awaited them.

A snort sounded behind her. "Lady Cupps-Foster insisted you'd be overcome with gratefulness should I come to your aid. I knew better." He held out his arm to assist her into the coach, his lips twitching as if he held back a smile.

"You do not know me at all." An odd pressure filled her chest. The same as she'd had when he'd rushed in to save her from Corbett. "My apologies if I appear ungrateful. I am most appreciative for your intervention, Lord Malden." She allowed him to help her into the coach.

"Rowan," he said softly. "And I will call you Arabella."

No, that would not do. She wished to only think of him as Malden. "I do not think—"

"Arabella," he drew her name out. "I have ridden all over England in the last few days looking for you. I'm tired. Filthy—"

"Yes." She wrinkled her nose deliberately. "You smell of horse. Perhaps you should ride instead of joining me in the coach."

His lips tightened just a bit, drawing her eyes to his sensual mouth. Something dark flashed in his eyes. "I've earned the right to call you Arabella, and I *will*. You've had a very traumatic experience, though since you are not weeping hysterically or fainting in my arms, I have to assume you are sufficiently well. I'm not sorry Corbett is dead. Had he not broken his neck I would have done it for him." He climbed in behind her. "So *please*, stop hissing like a cat." He took the seat across from her and crossed his arms. "And I'm bloody tired. If you don't like the smell of me perhaps *you* could ride up top with the coachman."

Before she could utter a scathing retort, he'd closed his eyes.

❧ 11 ❧

Arabella *snored*.

Not loudly, mind you, but just enough to be annoying. He'd been in the throes of the most amazing dream. Arabella was dressed only in the red chemise, and her hair was down, spilling over both of them as he moved between her legs. He awoke aroused with his stomach grumbling.

Jesus.

Another unladylike rumble met his ears.

Staid. *Cold.* Those were words anyone would use to describe her. How odd Arabella would wear such a scandalous garment beneath her matronly attire. He'd always suspected she hid something behind her tightly braided hair and sour disposition. Not just the chemise. Rowan had glimpsed the curve of her breasts, full and high, beneath the ripped dress. When she'd stabbed Corbett, he'd witnessed the sleek, pale expanse of her back.

Now he couldn't stop thinking of what *more* her proper clothing hid.

Sexual desire was not the same for everyone. What

attracted one person might leave another cold. Rowan appreciated passion. A challenging intellect wrapped around a sensuous nature. *Red underthings.*

He looked at Arabella, sleeping rather peacefully, blissfully unaware that every fiber of his being told him to claim her like spoils after a war.

Wickedness.

Arabella held a glimmer of darkness along with the red chemise which seemed in need of taming. Every curt word or sneer she bestowed upon him did nothing but stir his arousal. He wished to wrap the sable mass of her hair around his wrist as he thrust into her, naked beneath him. Hear her moan his name and rake her nails down his back. If nothing else, the last few hours had made Rowan aware of an inescapable truth.

He wanted Arabella. Every deceitful inch.

ॐ

SOMETHING HEAVY FELL AGAINST ARABELLA'S FOOT AS THE coach rocked to one side. Half-asleep, she wondered if it was the hot brick she'd asked for as they left the coaching inn. Except hot bricks didn't fall against your entire leg.

Arabella's eyes snapped open. *Not* a hot brick.

Malden was sleeping, his long legs stretching out in front of him. The coach, while nicely appointed, was not terribly large and his boots, his *very muddy boots*, had fallen against her skirts. With a hiss, she pushed his leg away.

The leg flopped back against her skirts. She tried to push it away again and found the leg, as well as the foot attached to it, wouldn't move.

A small sound of amusement came from Malden. His lips turned up at the corners though his eyes remained closed.

He was awake and annoying her deliberately.

"Stop this instant."

A grin moved across his lips. Lashes fluttered against the high cheekbones as his eyes slowly opened. "Stop what? I've been asleep. You sound like an enraged fishwife."

Malden had the loveliest eyes. Light brown shot with green and gold framed by lashes that any woman would envy. The rough shadow of a beard clung to his jaw, the hair a shade or two darker than that on his head. He had tiny creases at the corners of his eyes a sure sign he laughed often, something he was struggling not to do at the moment.

"You snore," she countered. A fluttering rose up and caressed her breasts as those hazel eyes surveyed her.

"As do you." He didn't sound the least put out.

"I absolutely do *not*. I would never." She turned to peruse the passing scenery. There wasn't much to look at. Drizzling rain. Muddy roads.

"You do. Like a bear coming out of hibernation. We should talk about Corbett."

The quick change in topic sent a dull throb to her stomach. "No. I've told you I'm fine. There is nothing to discuss." How quickly his concern would dissipate should he find out the truth. She didn't wish to speak of Corbett. Her discomfort was all centered on the guilt of Malden nearly dying because of her and her own stupidity. She gave little thought to Corbett. Which probably made her a monster.

"I've no need of your ministrations." She refused to look at him.

"Ministrations? I can see you are determined to remain stoic and show not a shred of weakness. Most women—"

"I am not," she choked out, "*most* women."

"That is an understatement." He shot back.

Arabella's jaw clenched. "I am not like the giggling women who surround you in the *ton*, fainting if they so much as see a spider. I beg you, stop hovering about me like an overzealous nursemaid. I do not seek comfort from you, nor would I wish it if you offered." Did he hear the lie in her words? She wanted nothing so much as to crawl into Malden's lap and wedge herself inside his coat. Horse smell or not. The feeling was *most* unwelcome.

"Why? Why not me?" Confusion lit the hazel eyes.

"You know why, Malden."

"As you wish, Arabella." He put his hand up to stop her from saying more. "No need to bore me by reciting all the things you dislike about me, my family, my cousin, your family's honor and whatever additional ills you seek to leave at my door."

Arabella inhaled sharply. It was time to put their familiarity with each other to an end. Perhaps the distance would staunch the constant fluttering of her chest when she looked at him.

"*Lady* Arabella. I've given you no leave to speak to me so informally."

Malden snorted with laughter. "I think given the fact I rode over nearly half of England for you, I've earned the right to call you by your first name. *Arabella*."

"How," she tried to sound imperious, desperate to regain her control, "much longer to London? I am anxious to be out of this coach and—"

"Away from me?" One hand flew up to his heart. "I'm wounded." He gave a shake of his head and shut his eyes before she could say more.

<hr>

ROWAN WATCHED ARABELLA FROM BENEATH HIS LASHES NOT surprised to see her scowling at him, before turning to look out the window. She raised a hand to brush a wisp of hair off her forehead, her fingers trembling. Her dark eyes held the sheen of tears and her bottom lip quivered briefly as if she would weep.

Rowan resisted the urge to climb across the seat and pull her into his arms whether she wished comfort or not. Clearly, Arabella was distressed but he sensed any attempt to offer her solace would be met with a scathing remark. He shut his eyes and forced himself to relax despite Arabella's presence. An impossible task.

12

Rain beat against the walls of the coach, the window panes shaking as thunder sounded in the sky. The horses slowed as a small coaching inn came into view, it's courtyard empty but for one other coach. The storms had intensified, the rain giving way to sleet and gusting wind.

The coach slowed to a stop. Malden opened his eyes, barely sparing her a glance before he exited the vehicle. She could hear the muted tones of the coachman speaking to Rowan.

A bolt of lightning snaked across the darkening sky.

The door to the coach flew open and Malden's dark head popped through, raindrops dotting his hair and shoulders. "We need fresh horses and something to eat."

"No. We should push on. My aunt will be concerned as will my brother. We can't afford to stop." Aunt Maisy *would* be concerned. She wasn't so sure that Nick would be.

"We're stopping and for longer than it would take to only change horses. The roads are becoming dangerous. Hopefully the storm will pass us by as we refresh ourselves."

"I think we should press on. I'm not hungry." In truth, her stomach had been grumbling for hours but she didn't wish to be in Malden's presence any longer than necessary. Her thoughts were jagged. *Sharp*. And she'd been thinking of her parents which she never welcomed.

"I insist." As if to make Malden's point the wind gusted up and the coach rocked. The light was beginning to fade, and more thunder grumbled somewhere in the distance. He held out his hand to assist her out of the coach. "Besides, the driver refuses to continue in this weather no matter how much I pay him. Come, let's make the best of things."

Rowan was not wearing gloves and the sight of the large masculine hand held out to her caused Arabella to shirk back.

"As you will." He shook his head in disgust and turned from her. "I'll be inside, Arabella. When you decide you'd like to get out of the rain and have something warm to eat, then you are welcome to join me. Your mood is as foul as the weather. Should you decide to continue your sour attitude you may stay in the coach."

She opened her mouth to reply but Malden was already out of hearing, and rapidly disappearing from view. His coat, worse for the wear, stretched against the breadth of his shoulders as his long legs churned up the muddy ground between the coach and the inn. The riding breeches he wore were dirty and seemed pasted to the muscles of his thighs.

Indecently tight.

Arabella blinked and shook her head. Exhaustion was making her delirious. She didn't give a fig for the cut of Malden's breeches.

The wind intensified, slamming the door of the coach closed.

"My lady?" The driver, his cloak whipping about his form, forced the door back open. "I need to see to the horses." He held out a hand to help her down.

"Yes, of course." Taking the driver's hand, she nodded, silently cursing Malden for abandoning her so quickly. Clutching her own cloak tightly, Arabella struggled against the wind as she made her way inside.

"WE WILL HAVE TO STAY THE NIGHT, UNFORTUNATELY." Malden stood before her in his rumpled clothes looking as disappointed as she was that they were destined to spend a night in each other's company. She'd assumed Malden meant to drive all night to reach London, but that was impossible now. The storm prevented further travel.

Arabella looked out the window of the small common room she found herself in. The wind had picked up, tossing tree branches and leaves against the inn. She could barely make out the barn.

"I see." She pushed back the cup of weak tea she'd been nursing.

The common room smelled of damp and spilled ale, the fire barely able to keep the chill from the room. An older woman, wisps of gray hair hovering about her temples, moved among the tables, carefully stacking empty plates in her arms. The common room must have been quite busy earlier.

"I hope that you do," Malden snapped, before taking a deep breath. "The inn has no more rooms to let. As you may have guessed, this establishment typically only feeds travelers, as close as it is to London. Few stay the night. The lone guest room is occupied."

Dear God, she'd have to bed down on the floor before the fire. She looked down at the dirty floor. There were bound to be vermin hiding somewhere in the corners. "Full?"

"An elderly couple traveling to London to visit their daughter. The only other room belongs to the owner and his

71

wife." He nodded towards the woman stooping to sweep the floor. "I would not presume to ask either couple to vacate their lodging." The look he gave her brooked no discussion on her part. Deep shadows were etched under his eyes and his hair stood on end. He still smelled vaguely of horse.

Arabella found him absolutely breathtaking.

"The owner has *graciously,*" Malden emphasized the word, "offered us the use of his parlor. I'm sorry you won't have a bed, but under the circumstances, it's the best we can do."

"That's very kind." If he thought she would throw a fit over sleeping in a parlor after all that had happened, Malden would be sadly disappointed.

A tiny frown etched his lips. "You don't mind?" He sounded a bit incredulous as if he expected an argument from her. Possibly had they been here prior to her running off with Corbett, she may very well have objected. Her comfort, given the circumstances of the last few days, no longer seemed of the utmost importance.

"It is better than the barn, where you will be. Or are you planning on sleeping in the common room?" She asked sharply, panicked at the thought of having Malden in her direct vicinity. Arabella had hoped for some privacy.

Malden came up so close to Arabella their noses nearly touched. She could see the bits of gold and green circling his irises. The rough stubble of his chin was clearly visible.

"I am sleeping in the parlor. There are two chairs. You need not be concerned for your virtue. It will be quite safe." He stood back and walked from the room not sparing her a backward glance.

13

Arabella held her hands out to the roaring fire in the small parlor the inn's owner had led her to. Sparsely furnished, the room nonetheless was spotless and smelled pleasantly of lemon and beeswax. A vast improvement over the stale smell of the common room. Before the hearth sat two overstuffed chairs, the fabric covering them faded. Stuffing hung out the back of one and she saw the hint of a spring poking out of the other.

After bringing a basin of hot water, soap and a towel, the owner's wife departed leaving Arabella in peace. The soap smelled vaguely of lye and the towel rough, but it was wonderful to feel somewhat clean. She longed for a bath, but such a luxury would have to wait.

Not certain when Malden would return, she hastily claimed the chair without the spring poking out. Despite the way the chairs looked, hers was remarkably comfortable and she sank into the cushions with a sigh. The fire was warm and cast a beautiful golden glow over the room. As she held out her hands to the flames Arabella had the most horrible urge to cry. She rarely cried, but then she was not herself.

Perhaps that was a good thing.

Corbett had terrified her. If he had succeeded in his quest to marry her, whether willingly or forced, Arabella had no doubt she would truly have put her in a sanitarium. She hugged her arms to herself, shivering at how close she had come to such an existence. Even more horrifying, she'd nearly condemned her sister-in-law to the same fate. All in her bid to protect her brother. How smug and self-righteous she'd been in assuming she was qualified to decide Nick's fate for him.

"I've asked for dinner." The door opened to reveal Malden. He stepped into the parlor wearing a clean shirt, still wearing his indecently tight breeches. She caught only a faint whiff of horse, but the aroma was mixed with soap. He hadn't bothered to shave.

"I believe it will be roast. The innkeeper's wife says there's enough to go around." He clapped his hands together in anticipation. Moving towards her, he spied the coiled spring sticking out of the empty chair.

"Comfortable?" A smile tugged at the corner of his mouth.

"Very." She returned her gaze back to the fire deliberately stifling the urge to grin back at him. She wished Malden weren't so attractive.

"I would have given you the better chair by the way." A dark brow raised as he nodded at her. "You need not act so smug you've bested me somehow."

Arabella relaxed, allowing herself to sink further into the deep hollow in the cushions, a testament to years spent sitting in front of the fire. What would that be like, she wondered, to spend a lifetime with someone? It was something she'd never truly considered.

I shall never know. The best I can hope for is not to be sent back to Twinings.

"Hungry?" Malden asked.

"Famished."

A knock at the door was followed by the delicious odor of roast and freshly baked bread.

"I hope you'll find the room comfortable." The innkeeper entered the parlor followed by a buxom girl carrying two trays. In his arms he held two quilts. "Between these and the fire, you'll be toasty warm my lord."

"We are more than comfortable," Malden said graciously. "I wish my own sitting room were half as welcoming."

The man beamed at Malden's praise. "It is my pleasure, my lord. There's plenty of wood." He nodded to the pile next to the fireplace. Polly has brought you something to eat." He dipped his head in the direction of the girl bustling about to lay out the trays. "Roast is a specialty of my wife. And the bread is fresh baked. I hope it pleases you."

"It smells wonderful," Arabella interjected.

The innkeeper bowed and the girl dipped before bidding Arabella and Rowan a good night.

Rowan turned with a surprised look on his face. "Your courtesy surprises me."

"I can be kind," she insisted.

"Can you?" The words dangled in the air. "I've yet to experience such a thing."

Did he truly find her so lacking in common decency? The thought pained her. She shouldn't care what Malden thought of her. "I've heard stories of your charm and appeal amongst the women of the *ton*. I fear it has been drastically over-inflated."

He sighed and pinched the bridge of his nose. "I'm too tired to spar with you tonight. I reserve the right to trade insults with you on the morrow once I'm better rested." A grunt sounded from him as the spring found its target. "Not a word, Arabella."

A bottle of wine sat on the table next to the food and Rowan poured each of them a glass.

"I don't drink spirits," she informed him with a sniff.

The broad shoulders shrugged. "Well I certainly do. I asked for scotch, but I suppose this will need to do." He held up the bottle. "I'm hoping it doesn't taste like vinegar." Taking a sip, he smiled and turned his attention to the food.

Beef, potatoes and peas graced two large plates. The food was not fancy in the least, but it was plentiful. A loaf of bread and a crock of butter completed the meal. Lifting the glass of wine in a mock toast he said, "Here's hoping you don't like your roast and the peas find no favor with you."

Arabella stabbed at the roast, his cheery mood annoying her. "I adore roast. *And* peas. I am also fond of bread."

Shooting her a mischievous glance, Rowan sliced off a hunk of the still warm bread, slathering it with butter before handing it to her. "I am relieved to find some things find favor with you."

His tone was teasing, but the comment struck another nerve. Corbett too had mentioned the same deficit in her personality. No wonder she lacked popularity amongst the *ton*. She had a distinct lack of positive character traits.

"Thank you," she whispered as she took the proffered piece of bread. Eyeing the wine, she thought of the mountains of empty bottles her father would trip over in his study. Perhaps her father had also been filled with self-loathing.

Before she could stop herself, she grabbed the glass of wine from his fingers and took several swallows before setting the nearly empty glass back down. The taste, akin to some fruit gone sour lingered on her tongue. Not completely unpleasant. A warm, fuzzy feeling burst from her stomach and spread down her limbs.

"You just told me you didn't care for spirits." Malden sipped at his glass. "You are very contrary, Arabella."

She ignored the comment, too engrossed in the light fluffiness filling her head. She admonished herself for enjoying the liquid, fearing for a brief moment that she would lose all control and instantly become a drunkard like her father. Ridiculous, of course. Nick drank spirits and was certainly not a sot. Besides, was her reputation of such importance? No one truly liked her anyway so she doubted drinking wine would make things worse.

They ate in silence for some moments before she reached across and poured herself more wine. The glow now spread through her entire body. No wonder her parents had been so enamored. Wine was synonymous with euphoria.

She snuck a look at Malden, who had fallen upon his plate like a ravenous beast and was now eyeing what was left of her roast.

Feeling emboldened, she took another sip. "Do you find me dour?" She pushed the remainder of her roast towards him.

He didn't answer for the longest time, only stared at her intently considering how to answer. Heat suffused her cheeks and it wasn't because of the fire. Or the wine. It was the way he looked at her. Pleasure twisted low in her belly and mixed with the wonderful feeling the wine gave her. Arabella had the sudden urge to curl around Malden like a cat and beg to be stroked.

"Dour women," he leaned back in his chair, hooking one long leg over the arm, "do not wear," he sipped his wine, "the undergarments of a courtesan. Particularly, a red chemise."

Her cup trembled as it met her lips. The deep baritone of his voice caused a delicious sensation to waft across her body. Her toes actually curled at the sound. Then his words sunk into her wine fuddled brain.

Dear God, he'd seen the chemise.

"Do not drink so much or so fast." His eyes ran over her form. "Are you wearing it right now? The red chemise?"

Her breath caught. "This is an improper conversation and I—"

"It's a simple question, Arabella. Yes," the length of his fingers stroked the stem of his glass, "or no."

The way he touched the wine stem was fascinating. What would it feel like to have him touch her in such a way? Long ago, during her debut, there had been one or two gentlemen who dared to touch her. She'd allowed both a kiss but found she remained unmoved. Her lack of reaction caused one man to declare she was frigid. Corbett's touch had disgusted her.

Instinctively, Arabella knew Malden's would not.

"Yes. I'm wearing the red chemise." She held out her glass for more wine. "I suppose you find that odd, given that I am so dour and unpleasant."

"Indeed, I do."

Arabella rarely spoke about herself to others, but the wine loosened her tongue. "I assume you are familiar with my parents?" At his nod, she continued. "My mother, the illustrious Charlotte, was fond of such undergarments. As a girl I'd often watch her dress for an evening out. She always chose such lovely materials and colors." Her mother's underclothes had been nothing short of scandalous and Charlotte wore them for her numerous lovers. Shortly after her mother's death, Arabella had wandered into Charlotte's dressing room. Her mother's maid had rifled through Charlotte's dresses but left the decadent underthings to Arabella. She supposed that had been the start of her affinity for such garments.

"We should not be speaking of such things," Arabella mused in a soft voice. The entire night felt surreal. Perhaps she was dreaming and none of this was real.

"No. We should not." He peered at her over his glass.

"Why did you come for me?" The question had plagued

her since he had appeared brandishing a pistol at Corbett. "You don't even like me."

"Not in the least," Malden admitted as he studied his wine.

Affronted, she snapped. "It's a simple question." She mimicked the words he'd used earlier. "I suppose it was for Nick's sake."

He drained his wine glass and faced her with a hungry look.

Arabella's heart thudded dully, and the tips of her breasts puckered beneath her dress. *He likes me just a bit.*

"It was most assuredly not for Nick." He shrugged, his eyes not leaving hers. "I've been obsessed with punishing you for your deceit. Possibly it was for that. Punishment." His voice had lowered to an erotic growl that played across her skin.

"I'm not sure how I should reply to that." Dark wicked images filled Arabella's head of Malden. Touching her. Stroking her skin.

"Perhaps it's best you don't."

Malden's leg hung over the arm of the chair, so close she could run her fingers over the sculpted muscles of his thigh if she wished. And she *did* wish to.

Arabella turned and looked back into the fire, ashamed at the direction of her thoughts. Perhaps a love of scandalous undergarments wasn't the only thing she'd inherited from her mother. Charlotte had been terribly flirtatious, which was a polite way to say Mother was a bit of a whore. She'd often heard her parents arguing about Charlotte's behavior.

"Why did you do it?" Malden murmured.

There was no anger in his tone nor accusation, just simple curiosity. For a split-second Arabella thought he was speaking about her agreement to marry Corbett. He wasn't. Malden wished to know why she'd helped Corbett in his failed attempt to take Jemma back to Bermuda. She stayed silent for the longest time, and just stared into the fire, wondering how to explain her motivation. How does one rationalize assisting in the kidnapping of one's future sister-in-law?

Finally, Arabella said, "Have you ever considered how difficult it is to be one of the Devils of Dunbar? No," she shook her head before he could answer, "I don't suppose you have. You'd never understand unless you were born to it. There are such expectations, you see, and not all of them good."

"I am familiar with expectations." A small trace of bitterness tinged his words, but he didn't elaborate.

"The Duke of Dunbar and his family *must* serve the Crown. This is not lip service, Malden. It is part of our family history, along with the tales of witchcraft and such." She gave a snort and waved her hand. "Nick's parlor tricks aside, to have our loyalty questioned was more horrible than you can imagine. My parents died because of the rumors. My father shot my mother and then turned the gun on himself. Oh, I know," her words slurred a bit, "my parents would have probably come to a bad end on their own. At least that's what Aunt Maisy says." She took a deep breath. "After, it was only me and Nick."

Treason. Suicide. Her adored older brother treated as if he were the devil because his eyes were two different colors. Even Mother had never looked directly at Nick, horrified she'd given birth to a monster. The entire *ton* held their breath in anticipation of Arabella making the slightest misstep. Flirt too much at a ball. Dance with abandon. Laugh at an innuendo. Become the whore her mother was.

She did none of those things.

The only small joy she allowed herself was silken undergarments, whispering against her skin while she dressed like an elderly matron. A small remembrance of the mother she both hated and desperately loved.

"You did not know Nick when he mourned Jemma, thinking her dead," she continued. "You did not despair he would drink himself to death and leave you alone in the world." Arabella turned back to the fire and sipped her wine. "I wished her never to hurt my brother again. I wished her to disappear."

14

Bloody hell.

Part of him hadn't wanted Arabella to prove herself human. Far easier to resist a devious woman with no conscience, though his cock seemed not to care either way.

Damn.

He found himself enraptured by the way the fire lit the pale oval of her face, her eyes dark like coal. A bruise had darkened against her cheek from Corbett's harsh treatment and Rowan had to push away the rage he felt. He admired her beautiful hands, so slender and elegant, moving in a nervous fashion against her skirts as she spoke about her parents. The lustful nature he saw that Arabella kept trapped beneath the somber attire.

"We should speak of what happened with Corbett." He found himself saying.

"I do not need you hovering about demanding I allow you to soothe me. She stood abruptly almost tipping over the small table laden with the dishes from their meal. "How many times must I tell you?"

"That's just as well." His hand went to reach for her skirts least she topple into the fire.

An offended puff of air left her lips. "Perhaps *I* should sleep in the stables."

The glass of wine sloshed a bit, sprinkling Rowan with red drops. Swaying on her feet, she reached out a hand for balance and Rowan trapped her neatly between his legs.

Her eyes widened. "What do you think you are doing? Release me this instant."

"No." Rowan hooked his leg around her hips, pulling her closer. Taking the glass from her hand, he tugged Arabella down into his lap. She was softer than he'd imagined, her bottom lush against the arousal in his breeches. The front of her dress, a hideous high-necked atrocity he longed to strip from her body, hid the rounded curves of her breasts, but he felt their fullness pressing against his chest.

Arabella's lips parted, the simple act drawing his attention to the gorgeous red of her mouth. She looked too shocked to speak. But she didn't swat at him or slap his face. Nor attempt to get away. "I am not in need of comfort," she said quietly.

"Maybe I am." He set his glass down before cupping her face between both his hands. Gently he stroked the line of her jaw, pausing over the bruise and cursing Corbett.

A soft, feminine sound of approval came from Arabella as she tilted her chin into his hand and lifted her mouth.

When his lips met hers, Rowan groaned. The taste of her was exquisite. Darkness and vulnerability mixed with innocence and the heady taste of wine. Her lips were pliant beneath his, offering no resistance. Arabella's inexperience was obvious as she seemed not to know exactly how to move her mouth. Knowing another man had not kissed her thus aroused him more.

Arabella pressed herself closer, unknowingly twisting her

plump bottom in a teasing motion against his already aroused cock. A soft mewling escaped her lips.

Rowan held her more firmly, drinking deeply of Arabella. He wanted more of her. All of her.

She arched, her lush curves molding against the lines of his chest. Her hands wound through his hair, raking her nails against his scalp. *Closer*, she seemed to urge.

His hand moved to cup one rounded buttock, squeezing gently, kneading her soft flesh, before running down the length of her thigh. He demanded her lips to part, to surrender to him, as his tongue found hers.

Arabella shivered at the uncertain invasion. But after only a moment of coaxing, her tongue curled around his, mimicking his actions. She was moving gently back and forth against the hardness in his breeches. A whimper came from the back of her throat.

He cupped one breast, tracing the outline of her peaked nipple, imagining the nub pushing against the red silk of the chemise. If he touched Arabella between her legs, she would be wet. Ready for him. A growl escaped him, and he pulled his mouth from hers. He'd forgotten himself.

I'm about to take her on this chair.

Dazed, Arabella looked at him from underneath the dark sootiness of her lashes, her lips swollen and slightly parted. The black pitch of her eyes blinked. "Rowan?" Her voice was low and sultry, the sound of a woman who wished to be bedded. His cock twitched madly, urging him to take her. "Why did you stop?"

He closed his eyes, struggling to get his breathing under control. "Arabella—"

Almost immediately her body stiffened. The delicate hands went up against his chest to push him away. A hurt look flashed across her face before the lush mouth once again looked as if she'd sucked a lemon. Her chin tilted arrogantly even as a wounded look filled her eyes.

Rowan tightened his arms, refusing to release her. She was so quick to anger. "Stop, Bella. I would not dishonor you."

She froze at the sound of her pet name. "How fortunate it must be for your family to use their honor only at times deemed suitable."

Angered at her words, and detesting her tone, Rowan grabbed her hips and forcefully pushed her down hard against the arousal that threatened to rip the seams of his breeches. "You may put your fears of rejection aside."

Her mouth widened in shock, but her features softened. "Vile." The word sounded almost affectionate. "I should never have offered you an ounce of gratitude or comfort." Her voice had lowered again to a husky whisper. She gave a futile, tired struggle before curling herself upon his chest all the while hissing out her dislike of him.

Rowan closed his eyes, pressing a kiss against her temple, enjoying the feel of her in his arms and the sound of her voice. Her hair smelled slightly of bergamot, a strong scent more suited to a man than a woman. Somehow that fit her.

"Goodnight, Bella."

⚜

SHE WAS IN GRANDFATHER'S COACH. HIS COACH WAS wonderful. It smelled of leather and pipe tobacco. Just like Grandfather. Arabella laughed as she popped another sweet in her mouth. Her brother, Nick, sat across from her. The Duke of Dunbar was in residence for the Season and she and her brother had spent the afternoon in the park with Grandfather before His Grace reluctantly sent them home. She often thought that even though he was a duke, Grandfather was lonely sometimes. Especially since Grandmama went to heaven.

Arabella missed Grandmama.

The coach pulled up to the town home her parents inhabited. It was much smaller than Grandfather's and the staff not as well turned out. Papa and Mama rarely took she and Nick to the park. Her parents would certainly never buy them sweets. She hated this house. Just the sight of the dull gray brick filled her with a heavy foreboding.

'Please Nick. Let's not go in. Please. Let's go back to Grandfather's. I don't wish to go in. Truly." Something was wrong. She could feel it.

"Don't be a cow, Bella." Her brother gave her an annoyed look. "I bet Cook is making cherry tarts."

Cherry tarts were Arabella's favorite.

The coach stopped and Nick helped her out, grabbing her about the waist and swinging her to the ground before the footman could even put down the step. Her brother was big already and didn't need the step.

She flung open the door and ran down the hall. Several of the maids were gathered together, their pails and mops set aside. "Sluggards!" Arabella trilled as she ran through them, scattering the maids like a flock of birds. One reached out to stop her, grabbing at her clothing. 'Lady Arabella. Stop, I pray you.'

But Arabella didn't stop. Instead, she burst into Papa's study, Nick on her heels. She skidded to a stop at the sight before her, the lemon drop she sucked on falling out of her open mouth.

Blood everywhere. A rifle in Father's mouth. Her mother lying on the floor, still clutching a cup of wine. A horrible screaming sounded, like the wild banshees the Irish cook told her about. It wouldn't stop. It was coming from her.

'Bella!"

She awoke with a start, shaking as the remnants of the dream left her. It had been years since she'd relived the nightmare of her parent's deaths. Her mother's outstretched hand grasping a goblet of wine even as a pool of blood widened around her. Father, with the back of his head gone, a crimson splatter behind him on the wall. Nick had flung her over his shoulder and run from the room while she screamed. Her brother must have taken her to the drawing room, but Arabella had no memory of him doing so. What she remembered next was Peabody kneeling beside her while Grandfather spoke to the staff. Then nothing but black. Every dress had been black for what seemed years until a pair of unkind girls began to caw like crows when she neared them while walking in the park.

Grandfather had told her not to worry, for those girls would bother Arabella no longer. Every little girl, he said, had a father or mother with secrets and Grandfather knew them all.

Arabella hadn't known what Grandfather meant by that at the time; she'd thought he was only comforting her. Of course, now she knew exactly what he had meant.

She lay still, listening to rain batter the windows. The parlor was dark, the fire in the hearth beginning to dim. The wind continued to howl, but not as loudly. Arabella wiggled and stopped. Warm muscles lay beneath her cheek, accompanied by the steady beat of a heart. Rowan's heart. She was curled up in his lap.

Her head moved slightly with the rise and fall of his chest. When Arabella tried to move away, his arms tightened around her.

"Malden?" she whispered. When he didn't reply, she lifted her head, taking the opportunity to study him up close. The strong lines of his nose and cheekbones stood out starkly against the fading light of the fire. She wished to run her fingers along the seam of his mouth. Touch his lips.

He's beautiful.

The tip of her finger scraped against his jaw where the line of stubble was rapidly filling in. He'd have a rather nice beard if he went much longer without his valet. The shirt he wore was unbuttoned just enough to expose a small triangle of flesh at his throat.

"Malden?" She waited again for him to respond. Assured that he would not wake, Arabella boldly touched the exposed skin. The flesh beneath her finger was warm and smooth. Sneaking one more look at him, she touched the tip of her tongue to the same spot, tasting salt and heat. He was delicious. She shivered and not from the chill that permeated the room.

Foolish. I am foolish.

In the cozy little parlor, cuddled in Malden's arms, it was easy to forget the outside world. Corbett, Jemma's treasonous father, her brother's anger and her own bitterness all faded away. At this moment, here, in Malden's lap, she was safe from all of it. Closing her eyes again, she burrowed into his chest, inhaling deeply of his scent. Tomorrow would come soon enough. Tonight, she would only allow herself to feel the pleasure of this moment.

❧ 15 ❦

Arabella opened her eyes to find herself in the chair, with one of the quilts given to them the night before tucked around her. She looked to the other chair but found it empty. No rain beat against the windows.

And she was quite alone.

Sour wine clung to the inside of her mouth. Water was an immediate necessity. And her tooth kit. Gingerly she moved her head, careful least she intensify the pounding headache behind her eyes. Sunlight streamed through the window across from her, shining on a field of wildflowers. Birds darted by, singing their morning song. A bloody bucolic scene. She truly detested the country.

Well, I couldn't have behaved more like a wanton last night. Mother would be impressed.

"Stop your singing," she spoke out loud to the warbling birds. She was irritated. Her head hurt and she was more than a little ashamed of herself. The coach ride back to London with Malden sitting across from her would be unbearable.

A timid knock on the door was followed by the older woman from last night, carrying a tray with tea and toast.

"His lordship said you'd be wanting something to eat this morning." A crock of butter and jam lay next to the plate along with a steaming pot of tea. "He said you'd want something light." She gave Arabella a knowing look.

Wonderful. In addition to feeling rather immoral, the innkeeper and his wife thought her a drunkard. She'd managed to become her parents within the space of a few hours.

"Thank you." She stood and threw off the quilt. "Please leave the tray."

The woman bobbed and left the room. "I'll bring you water to wash."

Arabella waited until the woman left before flouncing back on the chair. Perhaps she'd dreamt the events of last night. Maybe this entire journey was nothing but a nightmare brought on by eating spoiled fish. She would wake up in her bed at Twinings wondering when Nick would allow her to come home.

No. This was no dream. She'd nearly married Corbett and she'd kissed Malden.

More than that, you nearly allowed him further liberties.

Arabella moved to the tray and took a piece of toast, slathered it with butter and munched away. She was starving and wished there was something a bit more substantial on the tray. And the tea was weak.

Tasting the jam and deciding it suitable, she spread some on top of her remaining piece of toast. Apparently, she wasn't frigid, which was a bit of a relief. She was certain her attraction to Malden was only because of the situation they'd found themselves in, not because of any genuine feeling. Except Arabella didn't feel especially distressed over recent events and what of Malden?

Arabella wasn't naïve, and she didn't consider herself to be quite as innocent as most unwed ladies. Her parents were not discreet, and she and Nick happened upon them having sexual relations often, and very rarely with each other. Once, she'd needed to retrieve a doll mistakenly left in the family's private drawing room and interrupted Mother and one of her lovers. The man had been nonplussed at the sight of Arabella, only giving her a sly grin before walking out of the room, naked, his clothes bunched in one hand.

Arabella knew exactly what had been pressed against her bottom last night.

She set her cup of tea down with a clatter, spilling some on the tray. The tea was terrible. She didn't even bother to wipe it up. Instead, she stood and began to pace around the room. Nothing like what occurred last night must ever happen again. Ever. She would avoid Malden like the plague, insisting he ride on horseback for the remainder of their journey. If he brought up her previous lapse in judgement, she would pretend ignorance.

Satisfied, Arabella began to search through her things for the tooth kit.

SHE NEED NOT HAVE WORRIED ABOUT AVOIDING MALDEN.

He was waiting for her in the courtyard, solid and handsome, with nothing more than a polite look on his face. There was no hint of the passion he'd displayed for her the night before. Had she not known better she would have thought them meeting for the first time.

"Good Morning, Lady Arabella. I trust you slept well?"

She searched his face for some hidden innuendo and found none. Arabella wished to reply that no she hadn't slept well. His lap hadn't been at all comfortable. Nor had she cared to be kissed senseless then left wanting more.

"Yes, quite. Thank you, Lord Malden."

He assisted her into the coach, waiting patiently as she settled her skirts over the warm brick he'd procured. She felt his eyes on her the entire time as she pulled the rug over her lap and finally clasped her hands.

"It's a fine day. I believe I'll ride the remainder of the journey and leave you the coach. I'm sure you'll be more comfortable." Malden was the very epitome of politeness.

How annoying she found his manners today. "I appreciate your courtesy."

"We'll be in London by nightfall." Malden's eyes lingered on her for a moment longer before he turned and shut the door. She heard him speaking to the coachman and the jingle of reins as he mounted his horse.

Malden stayed slightly ahead of the coach for the remainder of the day, not even allowing himself to ride along-side, probably to avoid any opportunity for her to speak with him. When they stopped briefly to change horses and she saw to her own needs, Malden stayed with the coach.

Coldness settled over her. This is what became of letting your guard down. She completely disregarded the fact that her intent had been to avoid *him*. Rejection was a feeling Arabella knew well. She just didn't like it. All things considered, Malden's manner was for the best. If he ever realized she had lied about Corbett, his rejection would become full blown hatred.

Arabella must have dozed off because when she awoke, the light in the coach had turned to the dim mistiness of twilight. The coach moved slowly, winding through London's evening traffic. As the noise of the streets filtered into the coach, she allowed herself a small smile.

I'm home.

Lights twinkled in the windows of the rather imposing town home which took up the entire back section of the cul-de-sac. The London residence of the Duke of Dunbar was massive and bespoke of great wealth and power, but to Arabella, the brick structure was home. As the coach slowed, a sense of urgency filled her. She wished to be safely inside where she could allow Peabody to fuss over her. Tired and dusty, she longed for a bath in the sanctuary of her own room.

As the coach rolled to a stop, Arabella was surprised to see Malden open the coach door. She had honestly wondered if he still traveled with them. His tall form had been absent from view the entire afternoon. The waves of his dark brown hair blew about his face and curled about his ears. His cheeks held a touch of red owing to the days spent riding outside. He looked so vital, so masculine and unbearably attractive that Arabella had trouble looking at him.

I've touched that skin. Tasted him.

The brief touch of his fingers jolted down her arm. Immediately she shook him off and moved quickly towards the steps leading to the front door.

Malden gave a small sound of frustration as she shook him off.

"I'll inform my brother of your assistance and he will reimburse you for any monies owed for my care and travel." Arabella marched up the steps without looking back at him. "I'm certain you wish to be on your way so I will bid you goodnight. I appreciate your care in seeing me back to London."

Legs brushed against the back of her skirts causing her skin to prickle deliciously.

"I'll see you in."

The door was flung open to reveal Peabody. He took one watery look at Arabella and clapped his hands as a look of utter joy suffused his craggy features. "Lady Arabella! Thank the heavens!" The butler's hands shook, too well trained to hug her.

"Peabody." She took hold of the butler's hands, much to his surprise. "I am so *very* glad to see you." How often she'd taken Peabody for granted, a man who'd seen to her well-being since she was a child. Arabella wasn't certain she'd ever touched him before.

The butler smiled at her regard, the tops of his cheeks pinking. "We are most glad you are home, Lady Arabella."

She was suddenly so exhausted Arabella thought she would faint at the butler's feet. "A bath, Peabody, please, then something to eat." Malden still stood behind her, but she ignored his presence, wishing he would leave on his own. She moved towards the stairs. "Please see Lord Malden out."

"There you are." A deep, husky voice boomed from the direction of her brother's study. "I was wondering when my sister and her *betrothed* would arrive. I insist you and Malden join me."

Her brother Nick, the Duke of Dunbar was home.

❧ 16 ❧

His Grace, Nicholas Tremaine, the Duke of Dunbar had lingered in his study after dinner, expecting his sister and Malden to arrive at some point this evening. According to gossip, the pair weren't terribly far from London, and he thought only bad weather had delayed their return. The same he and Jem had experienced while traveling from Scotland.

After dinner, Nick ordered his pregnant wife up the stairs to bed. Well, ordered being somewhat of a stretch. One did not order Jem about. She'd wished to stay with him to await Arabella's return, even attempting a bribe in the form of a fencing challenge. If he won, she would bow to his wishes and go to bed. As with most things concerning his duchess, there was a catch. Jem would fence only in her chemise, which guaranteed his loss. He wouldn't be paying the least bit of attention to his form, only to *her* form.

Nick reminded her, rather sternly, of her delicate condition. He would join her in a bit after speaking to his sister and Malden. Jem and Arabella detested each other and if they were both present, any discussion was bound to dissolve into a fight. And Nick wished the truth for the situation was beyond comprehension.

Then there was Malden.

The news of his sister's abduction greeted he and Jem as they alit at Dunbar House. Jem was beside herself as they'd missed the ball celebrating the marriage of Lord and Lady Kilmaire. They'd been forced to stay an extra day at the home of Baron Kelso, Nick's cousin, due to Jem's aversion to the bouncing of the coach. Spence was not in residence but in India, nonetheless, Nick commandeered the place, worried for Jem and the baby's health.

Peabody greeted he and Jem, tearful and wringing his hands like one of those plump matrons who'd lost their dogs in Hyde Park. He was surprised to find that Aunt Maisy was also in residence. His dearly loved aunt floated down the stairs just in time to collapse into a fit of tears. She babbled and sobbed, her words making little sense until she said 'Corbett'. Nick surmised the rest.

Peabody, hands shaking, produced a note from Malden, Jem's cousin. Malden had conveniently been visiting at the time of Aunt Maisy's arrival, apparently to warn Nick that Corbett was still in England. According to Malden's note, he'd had no choice but to go after Arabella in Nick's absence.

There were constables, bow street runners and Dunbar solicitors aplenty. Malden did *not* have to go after Arabella himself even with Aunt Maisy begging him. No sane man would. The fact Malden *had* gone after Arabella was particularly interesting to Nick. Malden was one of the sanest men in London which made his behavior all the stranger.

As Nick sought to comfort his weeping aunt and Jem took Peabody's hand to calm the older man, Nick caught the eye of his wife. Understanding passed between them. Arabella *could* have orchestrated her own kidnapping. She was nothing if not consistent in her machinations. But Aunt Maisy denied such a thing. Arabella had *fought* against the footman, Barker, as he'd pulled her from the coach. And she'd had to beg Lord Malden to go after Arabella. A bow street runner could not be trusted with such a delicate operation. Discretion was necessary to protect Arabella's reputation.

Apparently, Malden had *not* been discreet enough if the torrent of cards left by callers was any indication. The gossips in London were whispering that Arabella was quite *ruined*. And by *Malden* no less.

"Nick. You're home." His sister looked exhausted but otherwise unharmed. Arabella halted as she walked in the study, frowning as she considered his greeting. "Betrothed?" She snuck a look at Malden who followed her slender form at a distance. "Whatever are you talking about? If you are attempting to be amusing, you've missed the mark."

"Miss Lavinia Woodstock." Nick sucked the whiskey through his teeth. He did so enjoy whiskey.

"Lavinia Woodstock?" Arabella's brow wrinkled. "I don't —"

"Come now, don't you remember her for she certainly recalls you." He was deliberately being vague with Arabella, wondering how she would explain herself.

"Oh, yes. From school. A terrible girl. Something was always wrong with her skin for she itched constantly. I caught her stealing the cream Aunt Maisy sent me to keep me from getting freckles. What has she to do with anything?"

"She has announced your betrothal to the *ton*." He took pleasure in watching his sister's face redden. "Or rather, your *ruination*. Miss Woodstock observed you and Malden at a coaching inn together. You were in a disheveled state and wearing Malden's coat around your shoulders."

Malden gave Nick an exhausted look but seemed otherwise unbothered by the accusation.

"Corbett...he...ripped my dress." Arabella choked out.

"Thankfully, Miss Woodstock was oblivious to your...*abduction*. At least from Corbett. There was absolutely no mention of him."

Betting at White's had been brisk on the reason why Lord Malden, one of the most eligible bachelors of the *ton* would be spotted in the company of Lady Arabella Tremaine. No one could fathom Malden in a scandalous liaison with Arabella.

Nick couldn't imagine such a thing himself.

Malden, a man whom Nick considered a friend and who rarely lacked a smile, was not smiling now. "How nice to see you, Your Grace. I did my best to protect your sister's reputation. I assume you've come up with an explanation to keep the *ton* at bay?"

Nick nodded. He would discuss the details with Malden in a moment. "I assume Corbett is dead?"

Arabella entered the study, her body folding down into the leather couch across from him, like a tiny ship whose sails were suddenly devoid of wind. "Everyone thinks that Malden and I..." Her face reddened further, and her hand twitched against her skirts.

Nick studied his sister carefully. Something was *different* with Arabella, for she wasn't arguing with him nor flinging insults around the room. Most disturbing of all, there were no death threats to Miss Woodstock.

"Corbett is quite dead, Your Grace. I saw the body." Malden looked as exhausted as Arabella, perhaps even more so. Dust covered his coat and bits of muck fell from his boots. "I long to take credit for his demise but cannot. The idiot fell out the window and broke his neck. The constable, MacLauren, has filed a report. He will likely seek you out to confirm my rescue of Arabella was with your blessing and I had not kidnapped her myself." Malden ran a hand through his hair and Nick watched, fascinated, as his sister's eyes followed the movement. "I asked to have him buried. I will leave it to you and Jemma whether you wish to inform Corbett's sister."

"Nick—" Arabella whispered looking nearly as lost as she had when their parents died.

He held up a hand. "I wish to hear the story from Malden. You have a habit of garnishing the truth, Bella."

His sister's eyes narrowed, but she did not snap at him. Nor argue. Completely out of character for Bella. Arguing was how he and Arabella communicated.

Malden gave a weary nod towards the sideboard. "Do you mind?"

"As long as you pour me another as well." He held out his glass, wondering why Malden wasn't defending himself against the accusation of ruining Arabella. Or running from the premises at the thought of a betrothal.

Malden took the glass from Nick's outstretched hand and moved towards the decanter of whiskey. He passed Arabella and somewhat deliberately did not look at her. After pouring each of them two fingers of the dark amber liquid, Malden settled himself in a chair.

"How would you like me to begin?" Malden seemed unconcerned with being interrogated by the Devil of Dunbar.

"The *ton* is rife with speculation about you and my sister." Nick growled back at him. He'd long suspected Malden was not at all the delightful scamp he appeared to be. He certainly wasn't if he had the slightest interest in Arabella, which Nick was beginning to think was the case.

Malden didn't flinch, but he downed his whiskey in one swallow. "Your sister was an unwilling victim of Corbett. He kidnapped her somewhere outside of Camden, I think."

That much Nick knew from Aunt Maisy. "*Were* you unwilling, Bella?" He peered at his sister over the rim of his glass.

"Of course. I didn't go with him of my own accord. Don't

be ridiculous. He tore my dress. I had to stab him with a fork to protect my virtue." Her voice and fingers trembled as she spoke. His sister looked on the verge of tears, something that rarely happened.

"Go up to your bath, Bella." He watched as her features contorted in protest. "You and I will discuss things tomorrow." Taking pity on her, for he did love her dearly no matter their estrangement, Nick stood and enveloped her in a warm embrace, kissing her temple. "I am glad you are safe. I would not wish for anything to happen to you."

Arabella clung to him, shaking, and began to sob quietly into his coat, like the lost child she had been and likely still was. "I am truly sorry, Nick. For all of it."

"All will be well, Bella." The tears frightened Nick. Arabella was well and truly distraught by her adventure. Gently he pushed her towards the door to the waiting Peabody, nodding for the butler to take her upstairs. Shutting the doors to the study he turned to face Malden. "Start with how you found my sister."

❧ 17 ❧

"**A**re you *mad?*"

Nick smiled slyly over his cup of tea, set it down and proceeded to tear into a rasher of bacon. He was starving and he loved bacon.

"I would like the answer to that as well." Jem, in the presence of her barely tolerated sister-in-law, looked ready to attack him with the pot of honey sitting next to her plate.

Snatching another piece of bacon, Nick crunched away. "I've spoken at length with Malden. He and I are in agreement. The scandal is monumental. I would not have my sister become a pariah nor have you upset in your condition."

"I was not aware how fragile you thought me." Jem slathered honey on a scone, the pastry crumpling beneath the pressure of her knife.

"This entire conversation is ridiculous," Arabella spat.

"Bella, your name has found its way into the betting book at White's. The odds are four to one that you bewitched poor Malden and he came to his senses too late. No one can believe he ran away with you of his own volition."

"Because he *didn't.*" A hurt look passed over her face.

"There are three to one odds I've threatened Malden's life should he *not* marry you."

"What about the scandal if I go mad and murder my husband?" Arabella turned back to him, a snarl on her lips. "I can barely tolerate his company for the measure of a coach ride and you expect me to endure Malden for a lifetime?"

Jem slammed her knife down on the table making the footman behind her jump. "You ungrateful—"

Nick held up his hand. "My love, please. It is apparent that your family has a penchant for rescuing mine."

He waited for Arabella to launch into a tirade about Jemma's treasonous father but surprisingly, she did not. Her hands were clenched tightly against her sides, probably to keep herself from pummeling Jem.

"I will not do it. I will not marry Rowan."

Nick raised his brow at Malden's given name, doubting his sister realized she'd used it. He also doubted she was indifferent to Malden. "You will, sister, else you find yourself scandalized and sent back to Twinings. Perhaps you like Wales."

Arabella's face fell. "No, I beg you. Please do not send me back there again."

"Can we not," Jem had picked up her knife again, "just say that a mistake has been made with assurances from both parties that nothing improper occurred?"

Good Lord his wife was frightening when she had a weapon in her hand. It was incredibly arousing. "You, more than anyone, know what gossip does to a woman's reputation. And this is London, not Bermuda. Far worse. Also there is the matter of Corbett and his death. I would prefer no one go looking too closely at what *actually* happened at that inn."

Jem glared at him, biting into her scone.

"My love, I am aware of my sister's failings, in particular towards you, but surely even you can see that this is the only way, else Arabella will be doomed to live out her days at Twinings or somewhere else far away."

The flicker in his wife's eyes told him Jem would like nothing more than to have Arabella as far from London as possible. While Jem wished Nick to forgive his sister and repair their relationship, she had not gone so far as to actually wish Arabella to be in her presence. As for himself, Nick was *trying* to forgive his sister.

"Have either of you bothered to look at today's newspaper?" He opened the paper and laid it on the table for both women to see. "This morning's edition contains a cartoon. All of London is supposed to guess who the cartoon refers to, although I think it clear."

The cartoon showed a snarling woman with snakes on her head instead of hair, dressed in a gown at least twenty years out of fashion. She was clinging to a handsome man who bore a striking resemblance to Malden. The artist was very good.

"A terrible likeness, don't you think?" he asked his wife. "I don't think Arabella looks nearly that sour."

"I'm Medusa?" Arabella sounded rather angry. And stricken. "God, look what I'm wearing."

"Bloody Hell." Jem cursed and buttered another scone.

"Can't you silence them?" Arabella turned to him. "You're the bloody Duke of Dunbar. What good is it to be considered the Devil if you can't force people to bend to your will? Surely you can—"

"There is also worry any scandal will hinder Petra's chances of a good match." Petra was Malden's younger sister who had made her debut only last year. It was on the tip of his tongue to tell both his wife and sister that while Malden didn't appear overjoyed at the turn of events, neither did he attempt to wiggle out of the situation. "Malden agrees that he must do the honorable thing for both Arabella's sake and his sister's."

"And my delicate condition, no doubt." Jem's eyes had grown thoughtful.

He could see his wife had come to the same conclusion he had. "We will put out the story that the two of you were on your way to Scotland to seek my blessing for the wedding before going to Gretna Green. You were overcome by your affection for each other and didn't wish to wait. Such was your passion."

A horrible noise came from Arabella.

"I pleaded with you to return to London and be wed properly. Which you will be." The cartoon was terrible, but all things considered, the match was a good one. Malden had his fingers in a handful of business ventures and had a talent for making money. His father, Lord Marsh didn't approve of a future earl being in trade, but Nick thought Malden quite astute. No doubt Malden had already decided an alliance with the Duke of Dunbar and his fleet of ships could be most profitable.

Arabella sputtered and stomped about the breakfast table, terrifying another one of the new footmen. Curses, many of them directed at Malden, were uttered under her breath. Without a backward glance at either he or Jem, Arabella flew out of the breakfast room probably to hide somewhere and sulk. She bumped into the footman, a young lad from Surrey who shrunk back further, probably frightened out of his wits.

He made a mental note to have each and every servant thoroughly investigated again. Knowing Corbett placed two men in his employ, and beneath his nose, infuriated Nick. Some of the blame for this incident fell in his lap. He had been so concerned with Jem and his newfound happiness he hadn't adequately protected his sister.

Once Arabella's footsteps had receded, Jem said, "My uncle is most distressed that his heir likes to dirty his hands in trade and I'm sure he'll be less than pleased to know

Rowan has some sort of plans for your ships and would marry your sister to gain access to the fleet."

"I would give your cousin the use of the ships anyway. He does not need to marry Arabella to have my backing."

"True." His wife reached across and ran her fingers across his scarred knuckles. "I know my cousin better than most. Rowan rarely does things without a distinct purpose. He would not marry Arabella without a good reason."

"Mmm." Nick pretended to mull over that bit of information. Malden had a reputation for being single-minded in his pursuit when he wanted something. One might even call him ruthless. But Nick suspected he knew what Malden wanted and it had nothing to do with business.

"He plays the charming scamp for my aunt and uncle's benefit, though he's less and less inclined these days. If Arabella thinks she will lord over Rowan, she is sadly mistaken." Jem looked at her empty cup of hot chocolate and sighed in disappointment. "Drat."

Nick knew Malden's secrets, or at least some of them. Jem's cousin was more than a match for Arabella. "Your aunt and uncle will be less than pleased over this development."

With barely a sound, a pot of hot chocolate appeared at Jem's elbow as if by magic, brought by the ever-present Peabody. The butler fussed over Jem, constantly seeing personally to her well-being and comfort. Nick was beginning to find all the attention somewhat annoying.

"Good Lord, stop mooning over my wife, Peabody." His teeth tore into another piece of bacon. "It's disturbing."

The butler ignored Nick and instead asked quietly if Her Grace wished for anything more before shooting his employer a bland look and leaving the room.

"I should have him sacked, the old bugger. He's constantly making cow eyes at you. Anticipating your every need. I live in fear he will trip me as I go down the stairs so that he may have you all to himself."

Jem laughed merrily and reached out to take his hand. Turning it over, she pressed a kiss to his palm, her eyes full of love for him. "Don't worry, husband. I will rescue you."

$$\text{❦} \quad 18 \quad \text{❦}$$

"Your mother is in a state and has taken to her bed over this whole affair. Lord White is furious, and Lady Gwendolyn devastated."

The Earl of Marsh accepted the glass of scotch from Rowan as he settled himself on the leather sofa. "That will be all," he intoned to the butler. "Shut the door behind you."

"Delicious." Rowan sipped at the amber liquid. "Dunbar has something similar."

"His Grace was kind enough to share his last shipment with me. Which I appreciate. But that does not mean I am happy over these developments. What is this about? I know you weren't suddenly overcome with affection for the lady."

"Corbett is dead."

The Earl paused, his glass of whiskey still just shy of his lips. "I see." Lord Marsh finally took a sip. "How—"

"He abducted Arabella as she left Wales determined to force her into marriage. I went to retrieve her," Rowan stated. "I found them at an inn on the road to Scotland."

"Why?" his father snorted. "Surely any number of other gentlemen could have gone after her."

"Because I was asked to." Rowan didn't wish to try to explain his reasoning to his father when he wasn't so sure himself. It was easy to rationalize he'd had no other choice, not with Lady Cupps-Foster sobbing into his shoulder, but that wasn't entirely the truth.

"Would have served her right had Corbett succeeded. After what she put your cousin through, marrying Corbett would have been a most fitting punishment for Arabella."

"Not even Arabella deserved Corbett," Rowan said in a low voice.

His father raised a brow at Rowan's answer. "She is an unpleasant young lady."

"What's done is done, Father. We were seen together and assumptions were made. While the story His Grace put out may not be easily believed and slightly scandalous, it is better than the alternative. Questions about Corbett would not only reflect poorly on Arabella but would ultimately lead back to the Duchess of Dunbar. Would you have Jemma gossiped about as well? Or Petra?"

"Why should you be punished for doing the lady a service? Arabella is a termagant and in light of her devious nature her reputation would be ruined eventually in some other way. I'm not sure I've ever seen her smile. Lady Gwendolyn is a much better choice for you."

"Because you and mother chose her?" Rowan said lightly.

"There is an understanding in place with Lord White." His father looked away.

"I agreed to no such understanding. *You* did. I am a grown man with no need for you to dictate my choices." Anger slowly unfurled within Rowan's belly. It was always this way with his parents. He was surprised it had taken his father so long to mention their grave *disappointment* in him. His entire life had been lived under the cloud that he could not possibly live up to their expectations, expectation that his older brother would have satisfied had he not perished.

"If James—" Lord Marsh started.

"Do not pretend that James would have made a wiser choice than I, for you have no idea what he would have done. Or wanted."

"James was a good lad who would have grown into a fine man. He knew his duty to his family and the earldom."

Rowan grit his teeth. His father had castigated him many times with this speech. "James has been gone, Father, for nearly fifteen years. I am sorry that you are stuck with me as your heir and not my brother. Sorely aggrieved that I cannot be what you wish, that I cannot be perfect as James was. Lord knows I've tried."

Lord Marsh took a sip of his drink and turned his gaze to the window; his face grew shadowed and pained. "Do not remind me of that day."

Rowan and James had gone swimming, but only James had caught a fever. Two days later he was dead. While Lady Marsh wailed, Lord Marsh glared with accusation at his remaining son, for it had been Rowan's idea to swim in the icy pond. He'd been trying to atone for that mistake ever since, working so hard at being the son his parents wished. Trying to be James, Rowan had nearly lost sight of who he actually was.

"I will speak to His Grace. You can't seriously mean to marry the chit."

"You will *not*," Rowan's voice grew taut with anger, "speak to His Grace. Take a moment, Father, and try to see the advantages of my marrying Arabella. Becoming my wife assures us nothing concerning the treasonous activities of Jemma's father, *your brother*, will ever come to light. The Duke of Dunbar holds one of the most powerful and wealthy duchies in England."

"And the most infamous," Lord Marsh interjected. "Besides we are already aligned to Dunbar through your cousin."

Rowan raised a brow. "The match is much more advantageous than that of Lady Gwendolyn and you know it." Rowan wanted Arabella with a burning intensity that bordered on obsession. On their return to London, he chose to ride horseback rather than share a coach for fear he wouldn't be able to control himself. The merest glimpse of her bare wrist or curl of hair filled him with indescribable lust. But Father would never understand his attraction to Arabella. Rowan wasn't sure he could explain it himself.

"She had your cousin *kidnapped*. Jemma could have been killed or worse." His father's lip curled in distaste. "Lady Arabella is a deeply troubled, spoiled child who was given too much leeway by her overindulgent brother."

"Arabella did *not* kidnap Jemma, Corbett did. She deeply regrets her actions." Rowan gave a small sigh. "I do not condone what she did to Jemma, but I understand why she felt it necessary."

Lord Marsh made a grunt of disbelief. "You are making excuses for her?"

"I'm not. I only said I understood her reasoning. Besides, this entire affair has been punishment enough. I don't imagine she appreciates being forced into marriage either simply because the gossips have maligned her."

"Yes, because gentlemen have been lining up to court her. Really, Rowan, she constantly sports a frown, wears dark, unflattering colors, is deceitful in the extreme and is not to be trusted."

"I didn't realize you took notice of Arabella's dress." Rowan shifted as his breeches grew tight. Just the thought of taking Arabella out of those staid garments to caress the skin beneath aroused him.

"Your blessed mother does, I do not." His father looked askance at him. "You do not need to sacrifice yourself for her honor. She has none."

"I've signed the betrothal agreements. They'll be sent for you to review as a courtesy."

His father's posture reflected his blatant shock. "I can still salvage things with Lord White." Lord Marsh blinked in confusion.

"I am marrying Lady Arabella, Father. I am sorry you and Mother aren't pleased." Rowan stood. "But I'm wedding her, not you. You'll have to come to terms or family gatherings are bound to be awkward."

A sputtering sound came from his father. "While I have grown fond of His Grace —"

"You are *afraid* of the Devil of Dunbar. It is not the same as being fond of him," Rowan snapped, delighted when his father's face reddened. "I bid you good day, Father. Thank you for the drink."

"I am *beside* myself. What is your brother thinking in marrying that girl? Even if she hadn't gotten herself involved with," Lady Marsh lowered her voice, "Corbett and his mother, she is still unacceptable. Lady Gwendolyn took to her bed upon hearing the news. I would express my disappointment to Rowan, but he has yet to appear before me."

Jemma sipped her tea and cast a sideways glance to her cousin, Petra. She loved Aunt Mary dearly, but her dramatics were beginning to grow tiresome. Granted, no one could blame Lady Marsh for her ill-concealed horror at the prospect of Arabella as a daughter-in-law, but Rowan's mind was set. And after speaking at length to Nick, Jemma thought she understood the situation better. "Rowan is a man of nearly thirty years, Aunt Mary. I am sure he knows his own mind. I assure you, Nick did not coerce him in the least."

Aunt Mary shot her a doubtful look. "No one will ever believe Rowan was simply overcome with passion for the girl."

Jemma nibbled on a sugared biscuit. Aunt Mary and Petra

were both informed of the true reason Rowan and Arabella had been together, or at least the pertinent points. "Does it matter? Perhaps they will assume Rowan wishes to marry her for financial reasons. Her dowry is enormous. I am married to her brother. When you look at things from that perspective, their betrothal makes sense."

"Arabella is not who I would choose as a sister-in-law." Petra stole a small cake from the tray. "She terrifies me. Always has. Rowan should beg off and Arabella can be banished again. Wouldn't we all be happier?"

Aunt Mary clapped her hands. "A brilliant idea. Jemma, surely you can discuss such with His Grace? You, more than anyone, should wish her gone."

It was true, she didn't care for Arabella, but neither would Jemma dictate to her husband abandon his sister. "I would never ask him to do such a thing. Regardless of her actions, Nick loves her dearly. And she has begged his forgiveness."

"She's a sour spinster. I would think gossip that she's been ruined would do nothing but enhance her reputation." Petra was rarely so unkind towards another.

"That's a bit cruel, Petra." Jemma had wondered at Rowan's behavior toward Arabella since the first time she'd seen them together nearly a year ago. The air fairly crackled between the two with animosity, which on reflection, Jemma though may be something else. Attraction.

No wonder he agreed to go after her.

"You can't mean to say that you approve of this marriage?" Lady Marsh dabbed at her eyes with a tissue and her lips trembled as she spoke.

"I am as shocked as you are, Aunt Mary, however, I do sense a change in Arabella. Her time with Corbett forged a connection between she and Rowan." Jemma shrugged. "I do not pretend to understand, but I do not think Rowan is easily manipulated. He knows his own mind. You do not have to like his decision, but you should respect it." She gave both women a pointed look. "Nick loves his sister. I will not have him hurt over your disapproval else you answer to me."

Aunt Mary sat back, her unhappiness clear. "Your meaning is taken, niece, though I doubt His Grace is in need of your protection."

Jemma shrugged. "You'd be surprised."

❧ 20 ❧

"**G**ood Lord, taken by that vile man Corbett. I was rather put out when you didn't arrive at my wedding celebration, but it appears you had a good excuse. Or a terrible one." Miranda whispered in Arabella's ear as they walked out of hearing range of the groom who had accompanied the carriage. The day was beautiful and sunny, if a bit chilly and she and Miranda had opted to visit the park, even though Arabella wished to avoid the thinly veiled curiosity of London society. She simply couldn't hide in the house any longer and was in desperate need of some exercise and fresh air. Besides, Arabella detested cowardly behavior.

"Chester," Miranda addressed the groom, "we are taking a turn about the path. You stay with the carriage. I promise we won't stray too far." Miranda bent her head to Arabella. "I wouldn't wish him to lose his place. I know he's been instructed to follow us about." She shot the groom a brilliant smile before turning back to Arabella.

"When you didn't arrive at the ball, I had.the ridiculous notion that you were upset with me for marrying. I should have told you about Colin years ago, but I couldn't, you see." The emerald of her eyes glittered at Arabella. "Colin was my secret. I'd told no one. Not even Grandmother. He'd left me so long ago and..." A rustle of silk followed the slight shrug of her shoulders. "I'm sorry I didn't tell you sooner."

Arabella squeezed Miranda's hand. "I wish you had told me." She'd never considered that Miranda had been heart-broken for years, always assuming her friend, who was forever cheery and good-natured, had few cares in the world.

"I was a bit ashamed of myself for thinking such a thing. That you wouldn't attend just to be spiteful."

Arabella gave her dearest friend a wan smile. She *had* been upset. Angry. Filled with desolation that Miranda had found love and Arabella would be alone. "Perish the thought. I am thrilled for you."

"And then to have that horrid little gossip spread such tales. Lavinia Woodstock of all people. I'm grateful she didn't catch wind of the true situation. Thank goodness Lord Malden went after you, else there is no telling what Corbett would have done."

He would have married me as I agreed. What would her friend think if she told Miranda the truth? "Yes, I am grateful as well."

"Did you know Rowan has been a frequent dinner guest of ours? He's helping Colin with some recommendations on how to modernize Runshaw Park. Colin is in dire need of direction. There is so much to be done at the estate." Miranda waved her hands about as she spoke. "Just the other night he visited to discuss wool of all things. Well, I suppose Colin can give an educated opinion on such since he helped run his Uncle Gerald's sheep farm. At any rate I missed most of the conversation as a box of books had just been delivered. A surprise for me from Thrumbadge's Booksellers from my darling husband. Did I ever tell you that I have a very soft spot for Lord Malden? He would always dance with me when no one else dared approach me. Because of the *incident*." Miranda had lowered her voice. "Though now that I'm married I—"

"Miranda." Arabella came to a complete stop. "Would you like to know the remainder of the story or will you continue to chatter on?" Her friend had an endearing and somewhat annoying habit of prattling endlessly, her conversation madly jumping from one topic to the next.

"Oh yes. Quite right." Laughter floated out of Miranda's lips. "I do apologize. I'm just so happy to see you and know you are unharmed. I've missed you dreadfully."

Arabella squeezed her friend's arm. "I've missed you as well." Since her return to London, this was the first opportunity Arabella had to speak to Miranda privately. She'd thought to confide her shame to her friend. Tell her she'd agreed to go with Corbett out of some misguided idea of revenge. But looking at Miranda's happy face, so beautiful as the morning sun glinted across her features, Arabella lost her courage. Miranda loved her, true, but she would never understand how Arabella could consider a marriage for revenge.

At the time it seemed like a capital idea. I simply wanted to hurt everyone.

A pair of gentlemen walking together shot Miranda an appreciative glance, but Miranda barely noticed. Gentlemen always stared at Miranda, even with her tarnished reputation she was still one of the most beautiful women in the *ton*. Arabella often felt like the dull brown duckling next to a magnificent swan. Miranda seemed not to care a bit for her looks, or at least didn't care for the attention they garnered.

As they strolled, arm in arm, along the bank of one of the small ponds along the path, Arabella finally spoke. "I stuck him with a fork, Miranda. And then a knife."

Miranda did not take her eyes off the path. "I assume you are speaking of Corbett."

"He tore my dress." Arabella swallowed, remembering Corbett's hands on her. The way her skin crawled as he touched her. "Malden told the constable *he* stabbed Corbett, but it was *me*. I didn't even tell Nick the truth. I had no choice, you see. Corbett's pistol was pointed at Malden's head and I couldn't allow it. I ran at him and pushed the knife into his neck. When I stabbed him, he tripped and fell from the window. I—"

"My poor Bella." Miranda put her arm around her. "I never met the man, but if anyone deserved stabbing, it was certainly Corbett. Besides, what were you to do? Stand by and allow him to shoot Lord Malden? Don't upset yourself. You did not kill Corbett. He fell from the window and broke his neck. A *fortunate* accident. It is never appropriate to find happiness in another's death, even when it is deserved. But you had no other choice. I know well of what I speak."

Arabella nodded. Miranda had faced her own scandal for the shooting of Archie Runyon, her mother's cousin. She was still whispered about.

"I am never sorry that I shot Cousin Archie. He tormented my family for years. I am also not sorry he is dead. Not in the least." A shadowed look crossed her lovely face. "I'm glad Lord Malden told the constable that he stabbed Corbett for it would do your reputation no good if it were known you wielded the knife. Society frowns on such antics, though were you a gentleman, they would applaud you. At any rate, in addition to being ruined, you would be deemed slightly mad or dangerous if the *ton* knew the truth. I should know. You do not need more scandal heaped upon you. Your betrothal is scandalous enough."

"I've a mind to just flee to Scotland, or perhaps go abroad. Maybe I should visit America," Arabella muttered. "Or perhaps travel the continent. Spence is in India. I could go there."

"Fleeing London would solve nothing, and your cousin would not welcome your intrusion in India. Besides, you care greatly for your reputation and your family's honor. Isn't that what began this whole mess with Corbett?"

Arabella stiffened. "I am well aware of my fault in all that has transpired. And the Dunbar family honor leaves much to be desired."

Miranda shook her head. "I'm not placing blame, Bella. What's done is done."

"This entire situation is ridiculous. I've no more desire to marry Malden than he does me, yet we are betrothed. I cannot fathom how Lavinia Woodstock spied us at the inn. My betrothal is now in the betting book at White's. It's horrifying." She'd spent years trying not to draw unwelcome attention and within the space of less than a month Arabella had found herself in a maelstrom of gossip and innuendo. "I've not even seen Malden since the night he returned me to my brother."

A small lie. She had dreamt of Malden, which wasn't at all like seeing him in person though the effects were the same on her body. Awaking in the middle of the night, her heart would race and her skin prickle as a distinct shameful wetness seeped between her thighs. She could still feel the press of his lips against hers.

"Rowan could not be forced into marrying you should he not wish it." Miranda's voice was firm.

Arabella gave a bitter laugh. "*Please*. Malden is known as an amusing, charming, *honorable* gentleman. He's rather perfect for all that he's a bit of a rake. I'm sure he spends his days considering the cut of his newly tailored coat or losing his fortune at one of London's finer gambling establishments.

He squires his mother and sister about Bond Street like a proper son should."

"You make him sound quite boring." Miranda lifted a brow. "The man you describe would not have ridden to your rescue, I'm sure. That man would have sent a constable or bow street runner rather than miss a ball." She paused, as if unsure how much to say. "Did you know your future husband holds the markers of some of the wealthiest men in London?"

Arabella shook her head and gave a choked laugh. "Surely, you're joking. Malden?"

"Malden is rich as Croesus, Arabella. Not from gambling, though Colin tells me Malden pretends to be a poor player to catch the other players off guard. He's made several investments on Colin's behalf which have nearly doubled in value. I'm not sure why he's holding so many markers, but there's several gentlemen who will be ruined if he ever calls them due. He sounds rather ruthless to me. You would be wise to watch your step."

"I do not think we suit," Arabella stated firmly.

"I doubt Lord Malden cares for your thoughts on your mutual suitability for apparently he's made up his mind. Besides, it is much easier to be happy, don't you think? And you are not indifferent to him."

Arabella started to throw a scathing denial at her friend when Miranda began waving madly. "Oh look, there's Miss Lainscott. I must say hello. Come, you must meet her."

Arabella shook her head. "I think I'd like a moment to gather my thoughts, if you don't mind. You've given me much to consider." She had no desire to meet Miss Lainscott, at least not today.

"You wish to pout." Miranda gave a frustrated sigh. "Very well. But you and I will call on Miss Lainscott before I leave for Runshaw Park. The poor girl is in the care of Lady Dobson and any distraction is most appreciated. Perhaps you two will find something in common and become friends." Miranda hurried over to a slender girl wearing an overlarge bonnet who was waving to her in excitement.

Arabella sincerely doubted Miss Lainscott had any desire to be friends with her, no matter what Miranda imagined. She wandered over to the edge of the pond where the thickness of the trees increased and leaned against a large oak tree, bending her head back to look up into the canopy of leaves above her head. Taking off her gloves, she ran her fingers over the gnarled truck of the oak, enjoying the roughness beneath her hand. Marriage. She'd always thought if she did marry, it would be to some elderly gentleman who would only require Arabella to do her duty in providing an heir and then leave her alone. Someone she would see on holidays and perhaps during the Season but nothing more.

'I did not come for you for Nick's sake.'

Heat rippled down her body to her core as she remembered his words and her eyes fluttered closed. A strange yearning for Malden struck her.

"I wondered if I'd ever find you alone, *Lady* Arabella."

Shocked, her eyes snapped open at the familiar voice.

Barker stood, not two feet away, his bulk hidden in a tangle of flowering vines. As he stepped closer, she hastily pressed her gloves to her nose. Barker was in dire need of a bath.

"Do I offend your precious sensibilities?" A sneer accompanied his words. His eyes were stony and full of dislike even as they ran knowingly over her body.

Arabella took a step backwards. "What do you want?" She glanced towards Miranda, but her friend was engaged in an animated conversation with Miss Lainscott and paying Arabella no mind. The groom who'd accompanied she and Miranda wasn't looking her way, his attention taken by two young maids who spoke to him while their mistresses gossiped several feet away. Surely if she screamed, someone would hear her. "If you are found in London—"

"You're the reason Corbett's dead and I haven't been paid." Barker cleared his throat and spit near her feet.

Arabella felt the blood drain from her face. "How dare you. You took me from my coach by force. You helped Corbett kidnap me." She turned to wave at the young footman. "One scream from me and you'll be arrested."

Barker gave an ugly laugh. "That's rich. You weren't screaming when I drove the coach away. Didn't even try to escape, did you?"

"I was concerned you would harm my aunt." Every fiber in her body urged her to flee. How had Barker found her?

"You agreed to marry Corbett and when that toff showed up, you changed your mind, so you stabbed him. Killed him dead. Probably pushed him out the bloody window."

Arabella shook her head viciously. Her hand began to twitch against her skirts. "He tripped and fell out the window and broke his neck. I wasn't anywhere near him at the time. He died from the fall." How could Barker know *she* stabbed Corbett? Rowan had taken responsibility. "Not that it's any of your business."

Barker gave her a speculative look. "That's where you're wrong, Lady Arabella. I wasn't paid for services rendered."

"I hardly see how that is my problem." But she could see it was *going* to become her problem. And Barker wanted money to go away.

"I'm sure your brother, the duke, won't see it that way. Nor that fancy toff."

Arabella swallowed. Her brother would never forgive another deception. And Malden? He would hate her and break the betrothal. Did she want Malden to view her with disgust? Or have her brother banish her to parts unknown?

Resigned, Arabella reached into her reticule, pulling out

what funds she carried. "This is all I have." Allowing herself to be blackmailed went against everything Arabella believed in but what other choice did she have?

Barker chuckled and snatched the coins from her hand. "I knew you'd see reason, Lady Arabella."

❧ 2 1 ❧

Rowan told himself, as he sat discussing his acquisition of a textile mill with the Duke of Dunbar, that he wouldn't attempt to see Arabella today. Twice before he'd tried to call on her only to have Peabody politely, but firmly, rebut him. Such a show of cowardice was unlike Arabella. Surely, she had something to say about their betrothal and approaching marriage. Even if she didn't, Rowan had quite a lot to say to her.

"How precipitous that you are to become my brother-in-law, as it seems you will need my ships. Cotton, I assume, from America. Wool perhaps? You know, I've heard an interesting story as to how you came into possession of the textile mills."

The Duke of Dunbar was one of the few noblemen in England who openly engaged in trade. The family had become enormously wealthy as a result of their shipping empire and brought goods to England from all over the world. They hired only the best captains, paid the crews well and sailed to faraway places few others would attempt.

Luxury goods, especially things not available anywhere else were brought by the duke's ships to London. Even if Arabella hadn't entered the equation, Rowan would have approached Nick.

"Have you?" Rowan gave his friend a bored look.

"Ah, Malden. You know that I have."

Rowan didn't doubt it. The Dunbars not only dealt in shipping but also in information. "The fool should not have gambled what he could not afford to lose," Rowan bit out, then he smiled. "He was fortunate that it was I who he nego- tiated with and not another who would not have been so kind. Besides, I'm not sure I've gotten the better part of the bargain. The Newsome properties are in poor shape and will take a great deal of investment to modernize."

Nick shot him a veiled glance, the pewter ring he always wore on his thumb, dull and pitted with age, caught the light. "You have become more interesting over time, Malden."

A great bubble of laughter erupted from inside his chest, as he wondered how much he should confide to his future brother-in-law. "I am glad you think so, Your Grace."

A flash of gray outside the window caught Rowan's eye, appearing as it did amongst the brilliant red of the rose bushes. Either the Dunbar residence was home to an enor- mous mourning dove or Arabella, dressed in her usual staid garments was walking about the gardens.

The duke's lips twisted in a smile. "I fear your attention has wandered, Malden, and is no longer on our conversation. I did so wish to ask you about your winnings of the other night."

Rowan didn't so much as widen his eyes at the comment. He had found, over time, that it was best to keep a poker face when dealing with His Grace. The man had an uncanny ability to decipher a person's thoughts.

When he didn't answer, the man across from him turned and looked out the window. "Is there something in the garden that interests you? Perhaps my collection of topiaries?"

"Possibly." He saw the knowing look on the duke's face. "Would you excuse me, Your Grace?"

"She likes to take the path around the weeping willow. Watch your step as that part of the garden is murky and a bit ferocious, much like my sister. Be careful, Malden. Arabella has been known to bite."

Rowan stood. "Like most wild things, Your Grace. Give Jemma my love."

THE DULL GRAY OF ARABELLA'S DRESS WASN'T DIFFICULT TO make out amongst the riot of color in the garden. Flashes of gray popped in and out of the brilliant spray of red roses and the deep green of the trees and grass. As he followed the path, Rowan came up behind her, enjoying the gentle sway of her hips as she walked. Her dress was devoid of any decoration, as he expected, and more appropriate for a governess than the sister of a duke. Her glorious hair was once again brutally tortured into a fat braid that was then curled at the base of her slender neck.

Rowan's fingers itched at the thought of taking apart that braid.

"Hello, Bella." He used the shortened version of her name purposefully. Doing so annoyed her and he did so delight in annoying Arabella. "I am relieved to see you've survived your illness."

She turned and for a moment, he saw a flicker of joy at the sight of him in the depths of her dark eyes. Recovering quickly, her lips curled into a frown. "I've not been ill."

Rowan imagined the red chemise covering her generous curves beneath the staid dress she wore. He'd thought of little else since leaving her with her brother a fortnight ago. He craved Arabella as a thirsty man craves water. "How odd. I've called twice this week and in both instances Peabody assured me that you were unwell."

"I don't suppose you considered I'd no wish to see you, Lord Malden." She was so stiff from displeasure Rowan thought her neck would likely snap from the effort of holding herself like a pike.

"Of course you wish to see me." He ignored the small hiss of irritation she made. "And I thought we agreed that I was to be called Rowan. My reward for riding all over England searching for you."

"You decided. I did not. Riding all over England is a bit of an exaggeration don't you think? There is truly only one main road to Scotland." Her lashes lowered to fan the pale skin of her cheeks before raising her chin to glare at him.

Rowan wanted to laugh at her waspish retort but instead he deliberately rested his gaze on the rise of her bosom. "I detest you in gray. Brown is barely tolerable."

Arabella sucked in her breath, which only served to push her ample breasts forward, straining the fabric. Even though the dress was ridiculously high-necked, Rowan still felt the sting of arousal. She could be dressed in a nun's habit and he'd still want her.

"What is it you wish to speak to me about? I'm sure you didn't seek me out just to attack the color of my clothing. Perhaps you've reconsidered?" She turned from him as the words tapered off and she pretended to study one overlarge bloom.

"No. I've not reconsidered. Do you want your reputation ruined?"

"Miranda has survived a blow to her reputation," she countered.

"True. But she had the Dowager at her side and even then," he shrugged, "Miranda often found herself a wall-flower. You would not be admitted anywhere in London."

She spun about to face him. "I've a mind to visit Italy. Or perhaps I'll travel to India." Her eyes narrowed. "No one in London truly believes the story of our mutual affection which resulted in our being spotted at the inn. Not even Lavinia Woodstock who *actually* saw us." Arabella shook her head.

Rowan couldn't take his eyes from her lips. Lush and full, Arabella's mouth was the color of ripe berries. He wanted to kiss her senseless and run his hands over the curves of her body. He had no intention of breaking off their betrothal.

"There is also the past to contend with," she sputtered.

"Oh dear, shall we revisit that again, Bella? Ancient history." He knew Arabella would come back around to Uncle William, Jemma's father. The man *had* committed treason. And he'd framed Arabella's father for the deed. They had all suffered enough for the sins of his uncle, but that was in the past.

"I do not think your family is quite so cavalier and will welcome me with open arms. I—" She cleared her throat as if the words were painful. "Wronged your cousin."

"You did. And that's a rather polite way to admit to being an accomplice to kidnapping." There was no point in denying it. Arabella had done a bloody *terrible* thing. The only difference between then and today was Rowan now understood *why* she'd done it.

Her dark eyes flashed with anger at his quick agreement. "Think about it, Malden. You said you wished to punish me. What better way than to discard me and have me branded a ruined woman?" A harsh laugh left her. "Surely that is what your family would want rather than have you marry me out of some sense of misplaced honor. You should marry whom you wish."

Difficult, contrary Arabella. She was right of course, on all points. He should leave her to flail in the wind and salvage what she could of her reputation before disappearing into obscurity. But he couldn't. "How do you know I am *not* marrying whom I wish?"

She turned from him, whipping her head around abruptly. The look of fear and horror on her features had been so comical Rowan smiled to himself.

"I wish you to leave." Her fists clenched at her sides as she kept her gaze focused on the garden.

"You are not fleeing to the continent." He walked closer, sniffing at the bergamot scent she wore. No rose water or scent of lilies for Arabella.

Leaning forward, he brushed his lips across the back of her neck. His hand trailed slowly down her spine to the base of her back, watching in fascination as Arabella's body arched against his touch. Unwillingly, he guessed. He'd been aching to touch her since the night at the inn.

"Your behavior is unwelcome, much as it was before. Stop."

"Never." His mouth moved along the slope of her neck, grazing his teeth against her skin. Unfortunately, the high neck of the gown didn't allow him to explore further. "I don't wish you to think my attentions before were merely the result of eating too much roast and enjoying the wine."

"I refuse to marry you." Her voice lowered, a throaty seductive sound. "You come from a nest of traitors." She shivered slightly. "It shall never—"

"Enough, Bella." He nipped the sensitive skin beneath his lips. Bending her head back toward him, his mouth fell on hers, ravenous and hot. One hand circled her waist, the other cupped her face, pulling her back tightly against the length of him.

Arabella whimpered and her free hand pulled at his hair, drawing him closer to her until they were melded together.

Rowan wished to devour her. Lay Arabella down in the grass and take her beneath the willow tree. Lift the drab dress to her hips and taste her. He wondered if Nick could see them from the library and found he didn't care.

"I'm not marrying you for honor or your brother's bloody ships, Arabella." His voice was rough and hard against her mouth. "Nor am I so honorable to marry you to salvage your reputation."

She pushed away from him, eyes slightly dazed and reached up to touch her swollen lips. "Then why?"

"I want you."

Her eyes widened and she took a step back, shocked at his confession. A bit of sable hair slid free from its braided restraint and fell upon her cheek.

"It's insanity, I know."

But as he looked in her eyes, dark pools of ebony that shone like brushed velvet, a rush of intense longing crept across his heart, a sensation no other woman had ever invoked in him.

She felt it too. He could see it in the way her body leaned towards him, lips parted.

Jesus.

"The opera," he whispered across the small distance between them not trusting himself to touch her again. She was still close enough that he could smell the bergamot that hovered in the air around her. "Tomorrow night. My family's box. Your brother and Jemma will also be in attendance."

"I will not." The words trembled from her lips. "I detest the opera. All that warbling in a foreign language gives me a headache and sours the stomach. And I refuse to be paraded around for the *ton*'s amusement. You cannot command me to do your bidding. I—"

Rowan's arm snaked out to wrap around her waist. Arabella's eyes were nearly black, the pupils barely discernable. Gently this time, his lips pressed to the corner of her mouth.

"Do not be late." He hesitated. "And do not dress like an elderly matron."

❧ 22 ❧

Malden had a *horrible* affect upon her. Her breath would seize up whenever he neared. Her heart would race and her hands would tremble. And his arrogance was not to be born. Dictating she attend the opera, an event she had little interest in? Who did he think he was?

As he stalked away from her, his boots churning up the granite path, Arabella's hands curled into fists. She wanted to shriek out her dislike of this whole situation. The only thing that kept her silent was her refusal to give Malden the satisfaction of seeing her ruffled by his presence.

Slowly she turned back to the roses overflowing from the carefully manicured beds. The warmth licking up her body was not caused by the small patch of sunlight she stood in. Even now her legs were still unsteady, and her breasts ached from his visit.

Her wanton nature, bestowed upon her by the illustrious Charlotte, had been brought to the surface. By Malden, of all people. His kiss made her want to press her bare skin to his and wrap her body around him like a vine. It took all her strength to pull away for she hadn't any real desire to do so.

He's to be my husband.

Taking a deep breath to still her beating heart, Arabella turned and walked deeper into the garden. In some odd way, she felt connected to Malden. Perhaps it was the shared experience of Corbett, or possibly that kiss at the inn. Whatever pulled her towards him unnerved her. Unsettled her. As did the constant urge to yield to him. The worst was the fear. Not of him, but of the way he made her feel. What had happened to her?

Malden. Malden happened to me.

Arabella sat down on a curved stone bench beneath the large weeping willow. This was her thinking spot, a place she retreated when bothered or distressed. Something about the tree comforted her. She proceeded to draw a pattern in the crushed stones of the path with the toe of her shoe, musing over her present situation and wondering if she should just flee to Italy. As she was planning her escape a large shadow appeared, blocking the rays of the sun.

"Ah, there you are."

Her brother looked down at her from his great height, his mis-matched eyes, one blue and one brown, twinkling in the light filtering through the trees. She knew most of London feared her Nick and indeed her entire family. All those old stories of witchcraft and selling one's soul to the devil. The mis-matched eyes were considered the mark of Old Scratch himself. Once she'd even seen an elderly woman make the sign of the cross when he approached, declaring him the devil. But to Arabella, Nick was her adored older brother. The only person in the world who truly knew who she was and still loved her. Protected her.

My brother deserves to be happy.

And Nick *had* found happiness, despite her attempts to

ruin that joy because she didn't understand it. Or wish to share him. The Duke of Dunbar's honor had only been part of why she'd acted so horribly.

What a terrible person I am.

The thought stung. How could anyone want her? Especially Malden?

When Arabella didn't answer, Nick frowned and plopped down next to her, sliding up and butting against her shoulder as he had when they were children. Nick was in a good mood. Cheerful. A mischievous smile cut across his face. Perhaps he was beginning to forgive her.

"I've received the bad news that I'm to attend the opera tomorrow night. Doesn't anyone realize I detest the opera? Reminds me of a bunch of cats wailing. Jem must be put out with me to demand such a thing."

Arabella shoved him back. "I've also been commanded to appear."

Her brother raised a brow. "Commanded? You? How interesting. I've never known anyone to order you about; not even Grandfather dared. Is that why your cheeks are flushed? From being ordered about?"

"I'm overwarm." Nick was far too perceptive by half.

"It's quite chilly out here despite the sun shining." The big body quivered as if he were freezing. "Not a trace of warmth. Perhaps you're coming down with something. Are you trying to get out of attending the opera? Don't you dare. If I must suffer, so must you."

"Send me to the Continent, I beg you, Nick. I'll study the ancient buildings of Rome and learn to paint."

"You detest painting. Your poor teacher... what was his name?"

"Mr. Sebastiani."

"Didn't you dump your oils over his head in protest to

drawing a bowl of fruit? Your lack of artistic talent is only trumped by the absence of any musical ability."

"The piano was never properly tuned. It wasn't my fault."

Laughter boomed out of her brother, his large form shaking with merriment. "Oh yes, I remember well. My poor piano. It never recovered from your ill treatment and stayed out of tune for years."

Arabella sighed and grasped her brother's hand. "Malden owes me nothing, especially not marriage. No one dishonored me. I can refuse."

Nick squeezed her fingers. "The world is not kind to a woman who is perceived to be ruined. I am grateful it is only your association with Malden that has come to light. Any mention of Corbett and his death and you *would* be banished to the Continent, mayhap for the rest of your life. Left to an apartment in some obscure Italian city until you grow old and fat. You don't even like the Italians. And I won't be able to visit."

Arabella looked at him in question. "You won't?"

"You know how I feel about warm sunshine and pleasant people." A sigh escaped him as his gaze held hers. "Society is unforgiving to any woman in this predicament. Doubly so for you. How ecstatic the *ton* will be to devour another scandal from our family."

"You fear for Jem." It was hard to keep the bitterness from her tone.

"And you." He looked away from her for a moment. "I've never told you that Jem's reputation was ruined in Bermuda. Completely destroyed. Because of me. We were seen together," he cocked his head, "although in my case, I *did* thoroughly ruin her." He shoved against her shoulder again. "Don't be shocked."

"Good Lord, that I *could* be shocked. Do you not remember who our parents were?"

"Point taken, Bella." A sorrowful look crossed his strong features and Arabella could hear the pain in his voice when he continued. "When I left Bermuda, Jem was shunned. *Cast out.* Treated no better than a *whore* by people who'd known her all her life. People who claimed to love her." He looked Arabella in the eye. "And Jem was the richest heiress Bermuda had ever seen. The cream of island society. I would not have that for you, Bella."

"You never told me." She couldn't miss the regret in her brother's eyes. And Nick was right. The *ton* would fall on her like a pack of wolves and enjoy tearing her to bits. She'd lately been reminded of how few friends she truly had. "Nick, I am deeply and truly sorry for what I did. I hope you can find it in your heart to forgive me for I behaved quite terribly."

"I do forgive you, Bella. It's the forgetting that is difficult."

They sat in silence for the longest time with nothing but the sound of the birds chirping in the trees. Finally, Nick said, "Malden is a very interesting man, wouldn't you agree? The longer I know him the more intrigued I become."

"Indeed?" Arabella was becoming more intrigued as well.

"I sense a mercenary beneath his polished and charming exterior. One would never guess given the cheerful rake he pretends to be. He is skilled at cards but allows himself to be fleeced. Until he doesn't."

"I wouldn't know for I've never played cards with Malden. I will let you know if I ever do." She pushed a rock around with her toe. "I'm sure he only wished the use of your fleet, though why I'm not sure." Arabella gave Nick a curious look. "You know why though, don't you?"

"I suspect there are several reasons. But you may perish the thought he only wishes an alliance. I've told him he will have the use of the ships and does not need to marry you to do so. Rest assured I did not coerce Malden. He wishes to do the right thing and his reasons are his own."

He threw an arm around her and pulled her close in a hug before standing. "I am a great believer in fate. I also believe there is something between you and Malden. Do not be so anxious to discard it." Nick pulled her from the bench. "Come. I asked Cook to make you cherry tarts. Your favorite."

23

A circus freak would receive less attention.

Arabella lifted her chin in defiance, determined to ignore the dozens of eyes watching as she made her way to the box of the Earl of Marsh. Whispers and the snapping of fans followed her every move, though in all fairness she supposed some of the gossip was directed at her brother and sister-in-law.

As she followed demurely behind her brother, she reminded herself that no one attending tonight knew anything about her association with Corbett. Not a soul knew she'd agreed to being abducted. A carefully placed word here and there assured all of London she and Rowan were merely overzealous lovers who'd wished the Duke of Dunbar's approval. Let them murmur in confusion that no one had ever seen them together or knew of their mutual affection. Many doubted such a thing, preferring to think Rowan was forced to marry her. Or perhaps she'd tricked him into ruining her. No one thought Rowan could *actually want* to marry her. Especially Lord White, who by all accounts was quite angry Rowan would not be wedding his daughter.

It had all the makings of a Greek tragedy.

The Duke of Dunbar, resplendent in black, hovered protectively over his still slender duchess while Arabella followed a step behind. The crowd parted around them, keeping back a respectful distance, the ladies nearly toppling over in an effort to give a proper curtsey. The gentlemen bowed politely, some even greeted the duke in a friendly manner, but not many. Arabella felt a surge of pity for Nick, though after so many years he was probably used to such treatment.

The Duke of Dunbar wore a tiny smile on his lips as if amused by the blatant show of fear and respect showered upon him. Jemma was not nearly so entertained. For every remotely insulting look the duke received was returned tenfold by his duchess. Jemma tilted her head arrogantly, allowing herself to dangle in a reckless manner from her husband's arm, a chilling look of warning given to anyone who thought to disparage Nick.

Arabella watched her sister-in-law with renewed respect. She had spent so much time convinced Jemma was merely a fortune hunter who wished to use Nick for her own ends, she'd never truly considered the depth of her sister-in-law's feelings. Those feelings were on display this evening. Jemma *loved* Nick.

I very nearly took her from him. Regret and relief mingled inside her that she had not succeeded. Because of Malden.

She smoothed down the rustling silk of her skirts hoping Malden would understand the dress was a peace offering of sorts. Created of deep indigo, the gown's color was so dark it appeared black. Tiny bits of brilliants had been sewn into the skirt, sparkling beneath the lamps until Arabella appeared to be lit by blue fire. The heart-shaped bodice clung to her curves, pushing up the swell of her breasts. Honestly, she felt a bit naked with so much of her skin exposed but in comparison to many of the gowns worn by the other ladies in attendance, hers would still be considered prim rather than daring. The thick strands of her hair had been piled atop her head in a series of luxurious waves, with several curls left to dangle down her back. A pair of sapphires hung from her ears, a Christmas gift from Grandfather. She'd never actually worn the earrings before tonight as her usual wardrobe didn't require jewels. The earrings went perfectly with the gown, she thought, and had nothing whatsoever to do with pleasing Malden.

Liar.

Entering the box, her eyes searched the small area, but his tall form was nowhere to be seen, only Lord and Lady Marsh, along with Lady Petra, Malden's sister seemed to be in attendance. Arabella's stomach dropped.

Malden was not here.

Perhaps he'd finally come to his senses and decided to end their association. That would be rich. Her first instinct tonight had been to plead a headache and stay home safe in bed. Or wear a gown of pewter satin.

Nick and Jemma greeted Lord and Lady Marsh with smiles and warm hugs. Petra even giggled at something Nick said. When the trio turned to Arabella they looked askance as if she might suddenly attack them.

"Lady Arabella." The Earl of Marsh took her hand politely, his eyes flat and suspicious upon her.

"Lord Marsh. Lady Marsh." Arabella tried to keep her features serene and pleasant. "Thank you for the invitation this evening." Her manners were flawless. She could feel her brother's approval.

"Goodness, what a lovely gown, Lady Arabella. The color is magnificent." Lady Marsh was equally polite although her dislike of Arabella bled into her voice. "We are so pleased you could join us."

Arabella nodded, lowering her eyes. She'd no wish for Lady Marsh to notice the twitching of her lips. The woman's abhorrence for Arabella was blatantly obvious. Apparently, the affection Lord and Lady Marsh felt for Nick was not to be extended to his sister.

A small frown crossed her brother's lips. He too noticed Lady Marsh's attitude.

Jemma gave his arm a tight squeeze and a look passed between them.

"Lady Arabella." Petra, Malden's sister, dipped into a perfect curtsey, her dark blonde hair glowing in the lamp light. Petra was heartbreakingly beautiful, with her lovely oval face and rosebud of a mouth. Her words were polite but her gaze no less hostile than her mother's.

"Lady Petra." Arabella wished to ask after Malden, but fear kept her from doing so. What if he *had* begged off? The thought was not appealing. His family detested her, that much was clear and her typical method of dealing with such...*censure*, would be a well-placed scathing remark.

I promised Nick I'd behave.

Lady Petra was clearly *appalled* at the thought of Arabella sharing the Marsh box and unable to maintain her polite demeanor, took Jemma's arm and moved away. The Marsh box was situated to the left of the stage on one of the balconies with a spectacular view of the stage. If Arabella had cared about the opera in the least, she would have been thrilled at the view.

Petra led Jemma to the first row of seats closest to the railing. She giggled and clasped Jemma's hands, obviously happy to see her cousin. Lady Marsh barely gave Arabella another glance before joining Jemma and Petra. Lord Marsh asked Nick something in a low tone and they moved to the far corner of the box.

Lord Marsh was probably trying to convince Nick to send her back to Wales.

Arabella clasped her hands behind her back and wandered over to the railing, as far away from the giggling Petra and her mother as she could get. She pretended great interest in the swirling mass of society that filled the theater below, only pushing back when she noticed several women openly watching her.

I wish this bloody evening was over.

"You look beautiful." The curl dangling just beneath her ear batted against her neck as if teased by a gentle breeze. The briefest brush of fingertips moved against the small of her back.

She arched automatically, her body softening as it sought to be caressed. A delicious tremor followed in the wake of his touch, lighting her skin with awareness of Malden's presence.

"You are late, my lord." She announced waspishly.

"Were you worried, Bella?" He moved to stand beside her, his eyes glinting with green and gold lights as they roamed in appreciation over her bodice.

The temperature in the room increased as heat washed up her chest.

"Of course not." How did he become more attractive each time she saw him? Malden was breathtaking in his dark formal clothes. The sharp lines of his face were clean shaven above the snowy white of his cravat. He smelled of shaving soap with just a hint of tobacco. It was a thoroughly masculine scent, one Arabella found she liked even more than the aroma of cherry tarts baking.

No wonder few women in the *ton* could resist him. Though based on rumors she'd heard, few women actually *did* resist. The thought was rather disheartening.

"Bella, you're clenching your teeth. You must be

distraught I'm late." He was smiling at her, the fine lines around his eyes crinkling in amusement.

"Perish the thought." She shivered as his hand fluttered against her waist, wishing her heart would stop racing. For God's sake, he'd barely touched her.

"I am sorry I'm late. There was some business I needed to take care of personally and it was unable to wait." He brought her hand to his mouth, turning her wrist and kissing the spot where her pulse beat madly. "I'm sorry I worried you, Bella."

"I wasn't worried in the least. But it was rude to keep me waiting and I—"

"I will not change my mind." His voice lowered to a murmur only she could hear. He was still holding her hand, far longer than polite. Even for a betrothed couple.

Arabella looked down at her gloved hand clutched in his, then back to his face. "Release me."

"Never." His thumb massaged the base of her palm. But he winked at her and let her hand go, only to take hold of her arm and lead her to the row of seats behind Lady Marsh.

The small, polite touch of his hand on her elbow created a low throb across Arabella's mid-section and seeped down her limbs. It annoyed her, the way her body reacted to the mere appearance of Malden, for she had no control over the delicious sensations.

After seating her, he exchanged greetings with his mother, sister and Jemma. The women laughed at something he said, and his mother took his arm.

Arabella sat quietly, not attempting to join the conversation. What could she say at any rate? Both women delighted in Malden's presence. He tensed at his mother's fawning, the tightening of his shoulders evidence of his discomfort especially since his mother seemed reluctant to relinquish her hold. He joked easily with Petra, teasing her about her newest beau. The two were obviously close.

Arabella wondered if Petra thought about making her disappear as she had once done with Jemma.

Probably.

Nick passed her on his way to sit next to his wife and paused, leaning down with a smirk. "The wailing of cats awaits us. Pray do not run from the box when the soprano starts."

Arabella allowed a small smile to cross her face. "I shall wait until the tenor begins, Your Grace." That small gesture by her brother meant the world to her and strengthened her resolve to get through the evening intact. Straightening her spine, she composed her face into polite snobbery, as she had done many times in her life. One did not sit through tedious luncheons for a multitude of charities without knowing how to reflect bored reserve.

Lord Marsh stopped to greet his son, barely sparing Arabella a glance before moving to sit next to his countess.

Malden settled into the chair next to her, the muscular length of his thigh mere inches from her skirts. It was difficult to maintain her stoic manner when he sat so close. Heat flowed from him to curl around her ankles and slide up her skirts. The feeling he produced both calmed and aroused her.

A satisfied smile played upon his lips, but he did not turn to face her, though he leaned closer.

Arabella nearly swatted him with her fan. He clearly suspected the effect he had on her.

As the lights dimmed and the music began, her skirts rustled. A leg moved discreetly into the folds of her gown before stopping. A foot nestled securely next to hers.

She didn't move. Her heart beat madly in her chest telling herself if she did move, she might well risk tearing her gown. She regarded Malden discreetly from beneath her lashes. He appeared oblivious to the location of his foot against her slipper.

He seemed transfixed on the soprano warbling onstage.

Deliciously tortured by Malden's presence, Arabella remained still, not willing to have the warmth disappear. She hadn't realized how cold she'd been before Malden, possibly she'd been freezing for years. Sometimes she thought of herself as a small, starving plant finally receiving the sunlight needed to thrive. That she had become so dependent on him in so short a time alarmed her.

Since his appearance in the garden yesterday, Arabella became determined to summon up some semblance of her former anger and bitterness, seeking the emotions as protection against her growing feelings for Malden. Her outrage remained absent. Instead she felt an unraveling panic over the lie about Corbett and the fear Malden would find out. She could opt out of this betrothal very quickly by confessing everything to her brother.

But I would lose them both.

"You're frowning again. I'll admit that Balderez is not the best tenor." He nodded to the stout man tottering around the stage. "I fear he will do nothing but enhance your distaste for opera." Fingers stroked slowly across the top of her hand, tracing the hollow between her thumb and forefinger.

A delicious melting sensation slid down to pool low in her belly at his touch and it took Arabella a moment to respond. "My brother likens the opera to the wailing of cats. I've only ever attended before because Aunt Maisy declared that I must. I suppose opera is an acquired taste."

"I don't particularly care for opera either, but I thought it best we make a public appearance together." Malden nodded towards his mother. "Has Lady Marsh behaved herself thus far?"

"Yes, my lord. Lord and Lady Marsh have been most welcoming." It was only a small fib. Malden knew his family would be less than enthusiastic about their union and

Arabella didn't find it necessary to admit to his mother's obvious dislike. Besides, with Malden beside her, she found the opinion of the Marsh family, at least this evening, irrelevant.

"You're a poor liar." He studied her intently for a moment before the fingers of his hand threaded through hers.

I'm actually a very good liar. The truth lay on the tip of her tongue.

As the opera dragged on, Malden said nothing more, but he did not release her hand. He continued to move his leg into her skirts and intermittently stroke the base of her thumb with his. Malden's subtle attention drew Arabella into a heightened state of awareness. Her body hummed softly, in tune with the masculine presence next to her. She kept staring at the curve of his ear and the tiny bit of his neck she could see above his collar.

Arabella startled as the lights came up to signal intermission. She'd been so focused on Malden she'd quite forgotten the opera. A steady stream of gowned ladies accompanied by gentlemen in their formal wear entered the booth to give their regards to the Earl of Marsh and his family. The small space rapidly filled with the press of bodies.

Her brother's tall form loomed over everyone in the box. She watched as he wrapped his arm protectively around Jemma and led her to the door. As they passed, she caught sight of Jemma's face, which had turned a sickly green color.

"Air." Nick muttered to Arabella as he moved swiftly towards the door. "Possibly a bland biscuit of some sort is required."

Arabella watched as her brother led Jemma out and she turned to see a distinguished looking gentleman coming towards her. His craggy face and lips hinted of distaste as he approached. The man stopped before Malden. "Malden."

Malden stood abruptly, the wry, amused look he'd sported

for most of the opera disappeared. "Excuse me for a moment, Bella." He stood to follow the older man who was standing before Lord Marsh.

Without thinking, Arabella clung to his hand, filled with momentary anxiety. Which was ridiculous. She'd managed to navigate the *ton* without Malden for years. She released his hand, ashamed of her sudden weakness.

The hazel eyes softened on her. "I will not leave you to the wolves, though I am more afraid for them rather than you."

Her lips twisted into a sneer. "You've nothing to fear, Malden. I was thinking how bored I will be while you are gone. Your company is better than none, after all."

One side of his mouth ticked up. "Of course. What was I thinking?" Gently, he brushed the line of her jaw with his knuckles before leaving her.

THE LOSS OF MALDEN'S PRESENCE WAS AKIN TO A CANDLE being snuffed out, leaving one in complete darkness. Arabella cursed her sudden fragile nature, blaming him. If she didn't stop this nonsense, she would soon become a wailing, needy milksop of a girl. Exactly the type of young woman she despised. Lifting her chin, she spied a pretty girl with ash-blonde hair speaking to Petra. The pair drew their heads together and shot glances in Arabella's direction before the girl moved to greet Lady Marsh.

Arabella picked up the playbill Malden left in his seat and leafed through the small booklet. What did she care if no one greeted her or spoke to her?

"Are you enjoying the opera, Lady Arabella?" Petra flounced down next to her, a false smile on her pink lips.

"Yes. Thank you." Arabella wished she would go away.

Petra annoyed her. She was too delicate. Pink-cheeked. Innocent. Petra had attended one of the teas Arabella hosted for the Anchor Society, a charity supporting the widows of sailors. Lady Marsh must have been there as well, but Arabella couldn't recall. Tea had been held in the gardens. Petra had spent the entire afternoon hiding from Arabella behind a series of flowering bushes. The girl lacked a spine, though she was certainly a great beauty. If Malden were wise, he would marry someone exactly like his sister.

Arabella ignored the slight pain in her chest thinking of Malden with another woman.

"Honestly, Mother and I weren't certain you would join us this evening." Petra regarded her with no small amount of curiosity. "Not because you don't like the opera, but because you don't like *us*." Her voice lowered as if imparting a confidence. "Though I assure you, the feeling is mutual."

Arabella stiffened. Apparently, Malden's twit of a sister had grown some claws since she had played hide and seek at the Anchor Society tea. Perhaps that would make Petra less dull. "Then we are in agreement." Arabella raised a brow. "I'm certain you didn't make your way to my side just to tell me of your dislike. Do go on."

"The current situation is appalling. Lady Gwendolyn is beside herself."

Lady Gwendolyn White. She suspected Lady Gwendolyn was the ash blonde Petra had been whispering with. It was rumored Malden was about to offer for her when Arabella had ruined everything.

"Lady Gwendolyn's distress is really none of my concern. Just as I am not your concern." Where was Malden? Petra deserved a scathing retort and Arabella's resolution to not be insulting was weakening in the face of the girl's attitude.

Petra sat back and clasped her gloved hands. "You are a *horrid* person."

Arabella blinked and stiffened her spine. True, she *was* a horrible person, or at least she had once been. Before Corbett. *Before Malden.* Now Arabella thought of herself as merely unpleasant. She was striving to become likeable and Petra was making her efforts more difficult.

"I will not allow you to harm my cousin again. *Ever.*" Petra's voice was full of determination. "Why Rowan agreed to this marriage rather than sending you somewhere far away, as you deserve, is beyond my understanding."

"I'm sure most things are beyond your understanding," Arabella snapped.

Petra had the decency to redden. "I see nothing to recommend you." She leaned closer. "This marriage is akin to inviting a large snake into our midst and hoping it does not decide to swallow us all whole."

Arabella carefully spread her fan upon her lap and waited for the boiling rage within her to subside. It was not often that one was compared to a snake. She was surprised how much Petra's words hurt, for she cared nothing for the girl or her opinion. Again, it occurred to her that she could simply tell her brother or Malden everything. Arabella would be outwardly declared unredeemable and she could avoid unfortunate conversations such as these.

"My apologies, Lady Petra, all this *wailing,*" Arabella allowed the double meaning to sink into Petra's pea brain, "has upset my delicate constitution. Of course, I mean the opera." A brittle smile molded her lips. "I fear I am not an admirer."

Petra reddened further. At least she wasn't so stupid as to not recognize an insult.

Arabella stood, enjoying the shocked look on Petra's face. She refused to sit quietly and be insulted by a girl whose greatest daily challenge was deciding what ribbon best matched her dress. The Dunbar coach sat parked just outside. Malden be damned. She'd done her best.

"Excuse me, Lady Petra. I bid you a good evening." Inclining her head slightly, Arabella made for the door.

❧ 24 ❧

Rowan headed back towards his father's box leaving Lord White to sputter from his rebuke. The conversation had been long overdue. White's arrogance in assuming he could walk into the Marsh box and openly show his distaste for Arabella was at an end. He had made things perfectly clear to White. Now Rowan's anger was directed at his parents. His mother in particular. Didn't either of his parents wonder at Lord White's insistence Rowan marry his daughter Gwendolyn?

He kept such things from his parents.

Rowan sometimes purchased the markers of gentlemen he thought might prove useful to his future business dealings. He rarely told the gentlemen in question he held their markers, preferring to negotiate through a third party. When the chance came to purchase Lord White's debt, Rowan did so. White was well respected in Parliament despite his lack of financial sense and he was a friend of Rowan's father. Friend of his father's or not, Rowan didn't care for White. He'd had a number of the man's markers for years. Somehow White found out Rowan held his debts, so large a sum that if called due, White would be ruined.

Which was why Lord White had ingratiated himself with Lady Marsh. His determination to have Gwendolyn wed Rowan was nothing more than a bid to have his markers *forgiven*.

I should call them all due immediately and bankrupt him. But he wouldn't. Rowan rarely made decisions out of anger and White could still prove useful someday.

Nick had interrupted Rowan's discussion with White to inform him he and Jemma were taking the Dunbar coach. She was unwell and indeed, upon seeing his cousin's face, Rowan became concerned. Jemma was pale and shaking and Nick's face creased with worry. He assured Nick he would see Arabella home.

Arabella.

He'd been in a constant state of arousal since he'd spotted her, shocked to see her in a gown of *color*. True, the deep indigo could be mistaken for black, but all in all, the gown was a vast improvement over the browns and grays she typically favored. And he could see the graceful curve of her neck and the swell of her breasts pushing against the bodice. Rowan could not take his eyes from the expanse of lovely pale skin. The sable mass of her hair was not braided or subdued into an unflattering hairstyle but had been allowed to spill over her shoulders in artful disarray. He had inhaled bergamot, wanting desperately to nuzzle beneath her ear and nibble at the nape of her neck.

Desire, so fierce he'd nearly tripped approaching her, radiated throughout his entire body. He couldn't seem to stop touching her, deliberately seducing her with soft whispers and the press of his leg against hers, forcing the lush body next to him to soften. He'd been about to ask the color of her chemise, but the lights came up.

While no one else seemed to be anxious to see him wed to Arabella, possessing her was all Rowan could think about.

Entering the Marsh box, he made straight for the seat where he'd left Arabella. The chair was vacant. The box had emptied of guests and only his mother, father and sister remained.

"Where is she?" He spoke without pretense.

His mother pretended ignorance. "I believe the duke has taken her for a stroll around the terrace. I'm sure she'll be right as rain in a few moments. She was in dreadful need of some fresh air. Poor lamb."

Besides the fact his cousin Jemma would violently object to being called a 'poor lamb', Lady Marsh was being deliberately evasive.

"The duke and duchess have gone home as I'm sure you've guessed. *Arabella*, Mother. Where is she?" He cast a sideways glance at his sister.

There was a reason Petra didn't play cards for every emotion showed on her face. And just now, she looked rather guilty.

A hint of a smile graced his mother's lips.

"She left." Petra interjected. "A headache. She doesn't like the opera and compared the singing to wailing."

Rowan pinched the bridge of his nose in frustration. "You allowed her to leave? Alone?" Of course they'd allowed Arabella to leave by herself.

His mother placed a hand on his sleeve. "Let her go, Rowan. It was clear she wasn't enjoying herself. And now that His Grace has left it would have been awkward had she stayed. Lady Gwendolyn has promised to return to our box and—"

He shook off his mother's hand. "If anything has happened to her you will be held responsible, Mother." He turned and said over his shoulder. "Enjoy the rest of your evening." He was furious. Bloody furious. First Lord White and now this. He'd coddled his parents for far too long. Because of James.

I am not James. James would have married Lady Gwendolyn happily whether he wished to or not.

He searched the thinning crowds of the refreshment area, looking towards the terrace in case Arabella sought out her brother instead of leaving. She would not know Nick had taken the Dunbar coach and Rowan didn't care for the thought of Arabella wandering down the dark line of coaches where she could be easily accosted. Or worse, hire a hackney.

Rowan hurried down the sidewalk. Several couples mingled about, enjoying the night air. He could hear throaty laughter somewhere to his right. But no Arabella. Perhaps she'd gone back inside to look for him.

A slender woman, the folds of her cloak flashing open to show the brilliants lining her skirts, walked from between two coaches. She put her hands on her hips, turning to look up and down the street as if searching for something.

Arabella.

Instantly he walked to her side before she could try to elude him. "There you are. I didn't realize Balderez had the effect of making one ill. Or induce ladies to run from the theater." He took her arm and turned her to face him.

A sheen of tears coated the dark velvet eyes. Arabella was clearly upset. She twisted away from him. "Let go. I'll see myself home. You are relieved of your duty to me," she said, the militant attitude she often assumed on clear display.

"It is not duty and I did not mean to abandon you." The sight of her distress unexpectedly tugged at his heart. His fingers closed over her elbow. "You should have waited."

Her chin lifted defiantly. "Perhaps I didn't care to be treated to Lady Gwendolyn sneering at me from across the room. And your sister has all the personality of a tea cake. I would have enjoyed my evening more had there actually been cats wailing onstage."

So, it hadn't been his mother, but Petra who'd caused Arabella to flee. A possibility he'd not foreseen. He wondered what his dear sister, who had the most pleasing of personalities when permitted to be anything other than demure, had said to upset Arabella. Rowan fought back the urge to defend his sister. But he was infinitely happier with Arabella's insults than the horrible wounded look he'd first seen in her eyes.

"Come. I'll see you home." He started to lead her towards his own coach.

"As I said, I can see myself home. Direct me to the Dunbar coach if you please, and I'll be on my way."

"Jemma was feeling ill. Your brother and she have already left and taken the coach. You are left with me to see you home safely." A curl had fallen from her coiffure to land on her cheek and without thinking he reached out and tucked it behind her ear.

"No, thank you, Malden." She shied from his touch and tried to get closer to the street. "I shall hire a hackney."

Obstinate woman. "Rowan. Stop calling me Malden with that dismissive tone you like to use. My name is Rowan." He gripped her arm and half-led, half-dragged her down to his waiting coach ignoring the stares of the few people they passed. "Unless you wish to add to the gossip about us, you'll cease your dramatics."

"Dramatics?" Her cheeks puffed out in outrage.

Finally seeing his coach, Rowan placed both hands on Arabella's waist and shoved her into the interior. He instructed the driver before climbing in himself and latching the door.

The coach started to inch down the street, surprisingly thick with evening traffic.

Arabella glared daggers from her place on the leather

squabs. Her struggles had caused more of her hair to spill down one side of her face. Deep, angry breaths erupted from her, forcing her breasts to nearly spill from the gown.

Rowan found her glorious to behold.

"*I will not marry you*. I don't care if the entire *ton* spits at me as I walk past and am reduced to growing fat in an obscure Italian city."

Rowan wasn't sure, exactly, why Arabella should grow fat in Italy, but he didn't interrupt.

"You are much more suited to a woman of Lady Gwendolyn's stature, whom your sister was kind enough to inform me actually desires to wed you. A simpering pea-wit who will obey your every whim and call on your mother for tea and needlepoint."

"My mother doesn't needlepoint." He leaned forward. "You're jealous."

Arabella swatted at his shoulders. "I am not jealous. I resent being abandoned." *And hurt.* "You arrogant—"

The rest of her tirade ceased as his mouth fell firmly on hers. Grabbing her roughly, he trapped her, pushing her back against the squabs. With a groan, his hands slid beneath her cloak to wrap around her waist as his lips moved possessively over hers. There was madness in the kiss, the insanity of his desire for her. He nipped at her full bottom lip.

Arabella whimpered softly, the sound of her surrender. The lush lines of her body molded against his chest as her arms wound seductively around his neck.

Then she nipped him back.

❦

SHE SIGHED IN PLEASURE AS SHE WRAPPED HERSELF AROUND Rowan. The kiss was merciless, demanding she yield to him. Arabella did so gladly, her ire turning to desire for Malden.

Her senses swam as his lips moved over hers, willing her capitulation. Tentatively she opened her mouth as he'd done to her before and touched her tongue to his.

A deep growl came from his chest.

Hands slid through her hair, loosening the carefully placed pins. Tiny pinging sounds met her ears as the pins fell to the floor of the coach. The kiss became more urgent. Commanding. She was locked in an intoxicating battle of wills Arabella most certainly would lose.

I want to lose.

His larger body covered hers, all muscle and heat, dominating the small space of the coach. Insanity gripped Arabella as it always did at Malden's touch. A deep yearning filled her for him. Physical, yes. But also something more. She wished desperately to belong to him.

His mouth left hers to toy with the sensitive skin of her neck before falling to the tops of her breasts. Warm. Soft. Lips skimmed over the delicate flesh and pleasure radiated down her body. She shivered, arching against him. Her nipples tightened painfully beneath the silk of the indigo gown.

"Rowan—"

Her breath caught as a finger slid down the front of her bodice, followed by his hand. He deftly popped out one breast, caressing the tip of her nipple with his thumb.

"Do not ever call me Malden again." The tip of his tongue touched the hardened peak. "I mean it, Bella."

"No." She moaned softly. "I won't. I will wait and call you Marsh when you are earl."

His teeth grazed her nipple, punishment for her remark. "*This* is why I came for you." His tongue circled her nipple, deliberately torturing her with every flick. "You need never doubt again. I *want* this marriage. I want *you*."

At his words a flood of wetness seeped between her

thighs. Her skin felt raw all over, the silk of her gown chafing against the most sensitive parts of her body. Arabella was a virgin, but she also knew what was happening between them.

I want him to touch me. Put his hands on me.

"I'm a wanton. Like my mother," she gasped as the heat of his mouth covered her nipple, suckling her. "I've always been afraid her nature would become mine."

The weight of his hand moved underneath her skirts, stroking the sheer silk covering her legs. He lingered over the hollow of her knee before his fingers found the space between her thighs. Settling her astride his lap, he wrenched up her skirts.

"But only for me." The possessive rasp came from him. "Only me."

She could feel the cool air of the coach against her stockinged legs as he found the slit of her underthings. "Part your legs, my love." His voice was rough.

My love. More wetness. The hard length of him pressed with determination beneath her buttocks. Deliberately, Rowan rotated his hips, rubbing his arousal against her.

"This is very uncalled for," she whispered against his mouth. "Most improper." She pushed back, the feel of him at once easing and increasing the mounting pressure between her thighs.

"This," his voice was low and heavy with desire, "is most called for." A light touch wound through the soft hair covering her mound, before a finger pressed against the slick wetness of her flesh, moving with purpose through her folds. He seemed in no hurry, teasing and caressing the hidden bundle of nerves.

"Please." Arabella clung to him.

Two fingers filled her, thrusting inside with gentle force. The sensation was unlike anything she'd ever felt. Her muscles tightened against his hand, wanting more. Her entire lower body ached. Need built with each stroke against her flesh.

"Kiss me, Bella."

She did as he asked, lifting her lips to his, while his hand continued to move in a deliberate fashion. The ache grew, spilling the pleasure down her legs to her toes. As his fingers continued to move inside her, his thumb flicked lightly against the source of the ache. Shamefully she tried to force the lower part of her body more firmly into his hand.

Her entire body coiled tighter and tighter, each caress of his thumb and fingers threatening to undo her. The urge to lose control was frightening. And wonderful.

"Let go, Bella." The press of his thumb became more insistent.

Arabella moved her hips, panting and begging as Rowan stoked the tension only to retreat. Frustrated she tugged at his hair to urge him forward. His mouth fell to her breast, sucking the nipple fully into his mouth as he pressed down with his thumb.

Arabella cried out, before Rowan pressed her face to his coat to muffle the sound. She bucked violently as waves of the most magnificent bliss she'd ever experienced coursed through her. His fingers continued to milk her, stroking and teasing until the last of her tremors ceased.

He held her close as she lay limp and gasping against him, whispering dark, beautiful things that had she been more aware, would have brought a blush to her cheeks. As her breathing returned to normal, he nuzzled her cheek and kissed her gently.

"The carriage is slowing."

Carefully he straightened her skirts and pulled up her bodice neatly tucking in her breast before placing Arabella on the seat beside him. He moved to pick up the pins from the coach floor and handed them to her, watching her intently.

Hands shaking with the intimacy of what had just occurred, Arabella took the pins and tried to give her hair some semblance of order.

A soft chuckle came from him as his lips brushed her temple. Then he pulled her close to him.

Arabella clutched at the buttons of his coat, the sense of loss at parting from him nearly as profound as the pleasure she'd just experienced. Her thoughts ran wild at her behavior. At the first opportunity she'd allowed almost complete ruination. In a *carriage,* of all places.

"Don't, Bella." Rowan murmured, likely sensing the tension in her body. "You are not your mother." He kissed her cheek, then took her hand and pressed a kiss to her palm. "You are *magnificent.*"

Arabella sucked in a deep breath and nodded, not trusting herself to answer. When the coach came to a stop, she reluctantly pulled away from him.

The warmth of his hands brushed the top of her breasts as he straightened her bodice and Arabella's body flared to attention again. God, what was happening to her?

Rowan stepped out of the coach and stood with his hand outstretched to clasp hers. He moved to walk her to the door but Arabella abruptly released his fingers. "Good night, my lord."

Telling her legs to move forward, Arabella made it up the steps just as a footman swung open the door. She did not look back.

❧ 25 ❧

The stunning brunette smiled back at Arabella and turned sideways, smoothing her skirts. It was amazing what a new hairstyle and fashionable clothing could do for a person. At Aunt Maisy's insistence, Arabella had accompanied her to Madame Moliere's, one of the most well-known modistes in London. Arabella had tried to beg off, insisting she already engaged the services of a lesser known dressmaker.

Aunt Maisy was remarkably persistent.

"My lady, you are a vision, if I may say so." Edith, her new lady's maid, clapped her small hands in delight. Edith was another new addition at the behest of Aunt Maisy. She was to be married, Aunt Maisy explained, and needed a new wardrobe as well as a proper lady's maid. And Edith did wonderful hair.

Arabella allowed a tentative smile. She'd felt beautiful the night of the opera, but that had been a special occasion. "You may, Edith."

Dressed in a walking dress of deep green, with her hair in a lose cluster of waves at her back, Arabella nearly didn't recognize herself. After so many years dressed in brown and gray, she had yet to get over the shock of seeing herself in colors. Aunt Maisy went a bit wild, choosing fabrics in a variety of hues Arabella might not have considered otherwise. Nothing high-necked, though aside from a ballgown, most of her dresses would still be considered demure. No browns or grays. No questions about Rowan, either. Whatever thoughts Aunt Maisy may have had in that regard, she wisely kept to herself.

Arabella had resigned herself to marrying Rowan and stopped protesting or making plans to leave the country. Which was a good thing. The banns had been read. She and Rowan were to be wed at his parent's home under the same wooden arch used only a short time ago for Jemma and Nick. At her request, the wedding would be small. Only family as well as Miranda and her husband, the Dowager Marchioness of Cambourne and Lord and Lady Cambourne in attendance.

"Here my lady," Edith handed her a small reticule made to match the dress. The maid cocked her head, examining Arabella for any small flaw in her attire. Satisfied, the maid nodded in approval.

Arabella gave Edith a stern look. "I suppose I should go down."

The maid bobbed and her eyes twinkled as she looked up at Arabella. "I did hear a carriage arrive."

Heart racing with anticipation, Arabella carefully made her way downstairs, telling herself she'd been to Gunter's, purveyor of flavored ices and all things epicurean, dozens of times. There was absolutely no reason for her to feel such excitement. Except today she was going to Gunter's with Rowan.

Arabella hadn't spoken to Rowan since the night of the opera. Not intentionally, though she had made plans to put him off should he call the following day. When he did call, she was still abed. She assumed he planned his visit on purpose, knowing she wouldn't be awake. Instead he left word he had to leave London for a few days on business. That had been a fortnight ago. Rowan had an unfailing ability to guess at her moods, assuming correctly Arabella needed time to think after what had happened between them.

He'd only sent her one note, accompanied by a lovely box of the most exquisite cherry tarts from Gunter's.

'I'm taking you for a ride in the park and then to Gunter's tomorrow for a lemon ice. I beg you to wear something that is not appropriate for a nun to take her vows in.'

It occurred to Arabella that she could refuse. Or accept his invitation and wear something horrid and brown. But she took one look at her old wardrobe and decided against dressing like a drab matron. Nor did she have any desire to refuse him by pointing out his invitation was actually more of a command. It was exhausting to constantly be at odds with everyone around you, and that included Rowan. Much more surprising was how much Arabella missed him.

"Good God, are you ill?" Her brother thundered from the foot of the stairs, a look of astonishment in his eyes.

Jemma trailed behind Nick, rubbing the small mound of her stomach, a chocolate pastry of some sort clutched in her hand.

Arabella's mood was so light she didn't even feel the need to point out to her sister-in-law that if she continued to stuff herself in such a way she'd be as big as a barn.

But I can think it. A smile crossed her lips.

Jemma was staring at her so hard she bumped into Nick's side before coming to a full stop alongside her husband, horror on her face.

"No, I'm not ill," she replied with her usual waspishness. "Why would you ask me such a thing? Do I look ill?" She waved a hand down the lovely new walking dress. "I'm going for a ride in Hyde Park, then a lemon ice at Gunter's."

"Gunter's? The park? Where is my snarling sister?" Nick questioned as she sailed past him. "Unchaperoned?"

Arabella suspected Nick knew where she was going and with who. After all, someone had told Rowan about her love of cherry tarts. "True. Would you and Jemma care to play chaperone?"

Jemma took a defiant bite of the pastry she held. "I can't think of anything more frightening."

Nick looked rather discomforted. "You should take your maid."

"Why? To guard my virtue? Edith is wonderful with hair but it's doubtful her talents extend in that direction. Besides, Aunt Maisy deems my outing to be perfectly acceptable. You forget, I have been to Gunter's numerous times with Miranda."

Nick looked at if he would say more but wisely did not.

Peabody came before her and made a slight bow. "Lord Malden awaits you in the drawing room, Lady Arabella."

❦

THE DAY WAS BEAUTIFUL AND SUNNY, WARM ENOUGH SO that the top of Rowan's curricle remained down. Besides the sun, keeping the top down was prudent and would help to remove any impropriety. The sun felt glorious on her face and she tilted her chin up, not caring if she ended up with freckles.

"I approve of the dress." Rowan glanced at her, the green glints in his eyes dancing with a beautiful light.

Arabella basked in his admiration. "I wasn't aware your approval of my clothing was necessary."

"It is if you want a lemon ice." A smile curled the full lips as the wind ruffled through his hair. Dressed in a coat of deep blue superfine, paired with dark brown breeches with his boots shined until they glowed, Rowan was almost too handsome to be real.

He's breathtaking. Her eyes glanced down to his hands, wishing he wasn't wearing gloves. Remembering the touch of his fingers, her face grew warm. "Thank you for the cherry tarts. They are my favorite."

"I was informed of your appreciation for Gunter's tarts. I'm told the cherries used are especially ripe and sweet." His eyes fell to her lips.

Arabella's skin tingled. "Malden..."

He leaned close to her and whispered. "We agreed, Bella, that I should not hear Malden again from your lips. Were we not so...*exposed* I would find it necessary to remind you again of your promise to me."

The warmth flowing down Arabella's body was not from the sun. Nor was it the least unpleasant.

"Rowan." She murmured as his foot slid beneath her skirts to touch hers.

⚜

THE PARK WAS HORRIBLY CONGESTED, EVERY PERSON IN London seeming to want to enjoy the bright sunny day. Ladies strolled in pairs or with gentlemen, sometimes with a maid following discreetly behind. A young boy chased his brother across the length of the green grass, laughing as he dodged a group of older women who twirled their parasols.

As a rule, Arabella didn't venture into the park on a regular basis, only doing so when Miranda wished, which was rare. Hyde Park was nothing but a parade of gentlemen and ladies who all wished to see and be seen. Each new Season brought a fresh crop of debutantes all seeking suitable matches while the eligible bachelors all did their best to avoid them. It was rather tiresome. In the past, Arabella found the park to be irritating and beneath her.

Before Malden.

She had relived their encounter after the opera at least a thousand times. Often, she fell asleep with a pillow clutched between her legs, ashamed and feeling like some innocent milksop who had no inkling where all that touching would lead. Arabella *did* know. She'd just not had any idea she would ever want such a thing. Nor had she anticipated wanting Rowan.

A wave of hair fell over his forehead, the golden highlights glowing amid the lush brown. A gentle breeze fluttered the strands and Arabella remembered the feel of his hair between her fingers. Like silk.

"What are you thinking Bella?" He gave her a half-smile.

Good God, she'd been staring at him. Rapidly she composed herself. "I was thinking of how much I will miss Miranda when she goes on her great adventure to Egypt. She's always adored mummies and such. Something she has in common with her brother, Lord Cambourne. If there is a dry, dusty lecture about, Miranda and Sutton will be there."

"I've never been particularly enamored of the ancients. I'm much more interested in the future. The way we have done things for centuries are changing. Our way of life will change."

She nodded in agreement. "People are leaving the safety of their hamlets and small villages to seek work at the factories. Eventually landowners, like your father and my brother, will face a shortage of labor to work their land. Girls who no longer wish to become wives or domestics are leaving the countryside to seek their fortunes in London's factories. Unfortunately, many of those young ladies find themselves living in St. Giles. A far cry from the glamorous urban life they envisioned."

Rowan shot her a look of surprise. "You are well-informed."

"I read the papers, my lord. And I am the patroness for an endless list of charities all of which attempt to provide for those who have fallen on hard times."

"The rapid growth of factories has indeed created a crisis. But factories are irrelevant unless they can bring their goods to market. There must be ample and efficient transportation." He slowed the horses to a sedate walk.

"I read a piece in one of Nick's journal's just the other day concerning the need to modernize ships for transatlantic voyages." Arabella found such topics fascinating. "Steam engines dramatically reduce the length of the crossing. My brother will have to modernize our fleet. If our ships make crossings faster, we can double in some cases, our import load." Arabella shot Rowan a look. "But you aren't necessarily speaking of my brother's ships, are you?"

Before he could answer Rowan was hailed by a passing carriage. As the vehicle pulled alongside them, a corpulent woman in mauve silk waved a gloved hand in greeting.

The lovely ash-blonde from the opera sat next to the woman. Lady Gwendolyn. Even the dislike twisting her lips as she saw Arabella didn't mar her golden beauty. The girl was really quite stunning, Arabella thought, with a sinking stomach. Jealously flared and simmered inside her.

"Lord Malden. How lovely to see you." The woman twittered and clasped a hand to her chest. "The park is lovely this time of day, is it not?"

Rowan tensed but he smiled pleasantly. "Lady White, Lady Gwendolyn. May I present Lady Arabella."

Lady White studiously ignored Arabella, barely sparing a glance in her direction.

Arabella's eyes narrowed. The cut was rather direct. And *foolish* of Lady White, considering who Arabella was.

"How is Lady Marsh, your dear mother, faring?" The feathers atop Lady's White's hat flapped about as she spoke. "I've called but she's not been receiving. Lady Marsh has not been herself lately, almost as if an *ill humor* or some other unwelcome *malaise* has descended upon her."

Lady Gwendolyn's face remained bland, but her eyes flicked over Arabella.

Arabella took a deep breath. Well that was something new, to be compared to a *malaise*. What was next? She was akin to the plague? Or perhaps someone would be brave enough to insist she reminded them of the pox.

Rowan's booted foot pressed atop the toe of her shoe, a silent request for her to hold her tongue.

"How odd, Lady White." He said in a perplexed tone. "My mother hosted Her Grace, the Duchess of Dunbar for tea just yesterday. Perhaps our butler misunderstood the nature of your visit when you called."

A flush stole up Lady White's overly powdered face.

"I'm sorry to have missed you at the opera, Lady White," Rowan continued. "However, I had the pleasure of seeing Lord White and Lady Gwendolyn in our box."

Lady Gwendolyn preened and batted her eyes at Rowan in a blatant attempt to gain his attention.

Rowan didn't so much as look in her direction.

Lady White gave a toothy smile recovering from his previous comment. "I was visiting my sister in Dorchester. I was devastated to miss such a lovely evening. Gwendolyn enjoyed herself immensely." She bestowed an indulgent smile on her daughter.

"A pity to be sure." Rowan was all smooth charm, but his eyes were hard as flint. "I was hoping to see you wear that beautiful brooch. The diamonds are *exquisite*. I happened upon Lord White as he purchased it. Such a masterpiece. A gift which declares completely the affections of the man purchasing it. I decided I *must* have one made exactly like it for Lady Arabella." He raised Arabella's hand and pressed a quick kiss to her knuckles. "I hope you don't mind."

Arabella blinked. Nick and Miranda had been correct. Rowan was *not* as nice as he pretended to be.

"Brooch?" Lady White stammered and blinked. Realization dawned in her eyes as she gave Rowan a brittle smile. "Why, of course."

Rowan continued to smile at Lady White, almost daring her to admit she'd received no brooch and the piece of jewelry had likely gone to Lord White's mistress. Arabella herself couldn't have given a better set down.

Lady Gwendolyn looked as if she wished to climb beneath the seat of their carriage. She stopped her mooning over Rowan and pretended to study a loose thread on her glove.

"Oh. Yes." She pretended to recall the brooch. "A beautiful piece, isn't it? Lord White does like to indulge in such tokens," Lady White bit out, clearly horrified. "We must be on our way, my lord. Please give my regards to Lady Marsh." She spared an ugly look at Arabella.

Rowan dipped his head. "Lady White, Lady Gwendolyn. He snapped the reins and the carriage moved forward.

After a moment, Arabella said, "Apparently I am not the only one who knows how to fling about an insult." Her heart ached in a pleasant way at his defense of her. "I don't think I deserve—"

"Probably not."

Arabella hissed under her breath and swatted him against the shoulder with one gloved hand. He immediately grabbed her wrist and pressed a kiss to her pulse.

"Lady White insulted you while her daughter watched. I find that she did so intolerable."

"Was there really a brooch?" Arabella questioned.

"Of course," he gave her a look of disbelief. "Quite beautiful. He was bragging about the gratefulness of his mistress for the gift. I believe she's an actress, a terrible one I understand. At any rate, Lady White will go home now and confront her husband. She will remind Lord White that while she does not have his affection, she would have his respect. She will rail at him and demand her own, more expensive, brooch. He will go off to his club and sulk." He winked at her. "No actual harm done, except to Lady White's ego. She will not insult you again."

Arabella laid her fingers on his sleeve, enjoying the feel of his muscles bunching beneath the coat. "You surprise me."

"Shouldn't you be telling me how I must allow you to flee to Italy? To become fat and learn to paint? Which," he laughed, "I sincerely doubt you have the patience for." He looked down at her and grew serious. "I find Bella, that you surprise me, as well."

𝕽 26 𝕽

He'd never thought watching a woman enjoy a lemon ice would be such an erotic experience.

Arabella made small sounds of satisfaction as she enjoyed her treat, and he wondered what other sounds she was capable of making. Even the way she licked her spoon gave Rowan improper thoughts. Her eyes were dark and mysterious as she watched him over her ice, one sable curl dangling over her shoulder as she ate. She'd surprised him by wearing a lovely frock of forest green and wearing her hair in a relaxed style. Her ensemble even included a matching reticule and earbobs. He imagined she'd chosen a scandalous chemise to compliment her dress as well, though he hadn't asked her. Arabella had a dark sensual quality to her making her more desirable than any other woman he'd known. And she was far more intelligent than he'd supposed.

Rowan found that particularly arousing.

She made another sound as she ate the remainder of the lemon ice and Rowan's blood surged between his legs. He'd heard that sound before as he stroked and caressed her after the opera and Arabella truly gave herself to him. Rowan

171

wanted more. *All of her*. Even the secrets he sensed she still kept from him.

"I don't suppose I could have another." A wistful smile pulled at her lips.

"You are beautiful when you smile." His eyes followed the movement of her tongue as she licked lemon ice off the corner of her mouth. "I long for you to do so more often."

Arabella shot him a sideways glance. "I know what Newsome is." She placed her empty spoon down, ignoring the compliment. But her cheeks pinked.

"Do you?" He hadn't really discussed his plans with anyone for the textile mills, only telling Nick they'd come into his possession. The properties needed modernization but more importantly, they required a way to get whatever they produced to market.

"Newsome is the name of a family in Surrey who owned several floundering textile mills. The river that powered the mills and was used to bring their goods to London has long been dammed, resulting in financial difficulties. A land dispute I believe." She leaned forward. "And I'm told the father gambles."

The father did indeed gamble and poorly. He'd been no match for Rowan's skills. "How would you know such a thing?" He had the urge to reach across the table and kiss her which would shock everyone at Gunter's.

"You may find this hard to believe, Rowan, but as I mentioned before, I *do* happen to read. Also, my brother was trained from an early age to run the duchy and our various family interests. Since I could not abide being separated from my brother, I was there for the tutelage as well. I speak French passably, adore mathematics, and know a reasonable amount of history. Particularly military history as the subject was a passion of my brother's."

"Why?" He knew part of the answer but wished to know all of it. All of her.

"I suppose because my grandfather knew my father could never run the estates, so he made sure Nick had the finest education from nearly the time he was born. I liked mathematics especially. I'm very good with sums."

"So am I." Rowan shook his head. "What I meant was, why could you not bear to be separated from your brother?"

Arabella looked down at the remains of her ice. She went very still. "I've told you," she said in a low voice, "he was all I had."

She *had* told him. At least some of it. The motivation for her deceit. There was more, but he resolved to leave the subject alone for now and not spoil the day.

"Why would you want the Newsome mills? You'll have to modernize them and there's no longer access to water. The river has been damned. You cannot run the mills without the river."

He raised a brow at her assumption.

"Steam also powers looms." Her dark eyes watched him. "As it does ships. And our ships as we discussed earlier, will soon be converting to steam. My brother cannot avoid it. Steam will shorten the journey back and forth to America and you will get your cotton sooner, won't you?"

"Clever girl." Rowan's heart thudded with desire for her. "What else?" His gaze flew to her lips, then lingered on the swell of her breasts. "I like the dress, by the way. Have I told you?"

"Yes." She tapped her fingers on the table. "If I guess correctly, will I receive another lemon ice?"

Rowan adored this playful, teasing, Arabella. "Absolutely."

"I think that the Newsome textile mills are only a hobby." She drew circles with her fingertips and all Rowan could think of was how badly he wanted her to touch him.

"A hobby?" He scoffed. "Why would you think that? Because I'm titled and should not be in trade? Your brother and his ships are not the only exception."

"No. You are much more ambitious than I realized. What you really want is a *reason* to build a *railroad*. The Newsome mills are only an excuse, aren't they?"

Rowan picked up her hand and toyed with her fingers, before bringing them to his lips. "I'll go get you another ice." It was incredibly improper, regardless of their betrothal and impending marriage, to behave in such a way, but Rowan didn't care.

Let them all look.

"I'll return in a moment."

Arabella nodded. "Of course, my lord." And she was smiling.

❧

ARABELLA WAS HAVING A MARVELOUS DAY. SHE EVEN FELT *lighthearted,* an emotion she hadn't experienced since she was a child. Peering through the crowded interior of Gunter's she could just make out Rowan's tall form as he disappeared to bring her another ice.

I must have guessed correctly.

And he appreciated her business sense. Nick did, of course. Truth be told, she and her brother operated more as partners in regard to the Tremaine fleet, then as the duke and his younger sister. She'd grown up learning the shipping business from Grandfather, among other things. Her family had long been known not just for their success at trading goods, but also trading in *secrets.* Taught from an early age to never discard information, Arabella hoarded facts and bits of gossip. She sensed the same hoarding of information in her future husband.

She could see Rowan's tall form through the window speaking to the clerk. As he waited, two men approached him. The younger man was speaking to Rowan urgently while his companion nodded every few seconds in agreement.

Arabella caught Rowan glancing out to the terrace to check on her before he began speaking to the two men.

She turned away from the window as the shadow of a man, directly behind her appeared.

"I didn't think he was ever going to give us a chance to talk."

THE LAST TWO MEN ROWAN EXPECTED TO SEE AT GUNTER'S were Sir Chatsworth and Mr. Hind. He suspected they'd been looking for him and had managed to track him here. Arabella had been correct he was planning a rail line. The Newsome mills were worthless with their only transportation route, the river, damned up. There was no rail at all in that part of Surrey despite there being several large villages in the area. The most direct route would need access through the edge of the estate of Squire Tidwell, a prominent landowner. Tidwell wanted nothing to do with the rail line and was proving rather obstinate.

"Mr. Hind, Sir Chatsworth, I didn't realize either of you gentlemen frequented Gunter's." He bestowed a smile on both men even though business was the last thing on his mind. Arabella was all he wished to consider at the moment.

"Malden, finally," Mr. Hind began. "I've unfortunate news, I'm afraid. All of my efforts concerning Tidwell have fallen on deaf ears. He refuses to even consider allowing access to his land. Nor will he sell the parcel."

Chatsworth nodded. "No amount of money it seems will sway him. The property is in trust for his daughter. The plot will come to her once she weds." He shrugged. "Unfortunately, the girl has not one suitor that we know of, my lord. Even so, there is no guarantee any husband would sell the land."

The smile on Rowan's face didn't falter. Everyone had their price he just hadn't found Tidwell's yet. The land *would* be his. Somehow. "Gentlemen, may we continue this conversation at another time? I am otherwise involved." He nodded to the terrace in Arabella's direction, surprised to find her gone from the table they'd been sitting at.

"Excuse me." Gripping Arabella's lemon ice, Rowan made his way back to the terrace, wondering where Arabella had gone.

ARABELLA FROZE AT THE SOUND OF BARKER'S VOICE. THE lemon ice curdled in her stomach.

"Perhaps you'd like to move to the edge of the terrace? There's some lovely blooms for you to admire."

"Get away from me," she hissed. "How dare you approach me again." Glancing inside, she could see Rowan was still engaged in conversation. Thankfully he hadn't looked in her direction.

"You stuck that knife in Corbett to keep him from talking. Get up. Walk to the terrace."

"I did no such thing. He was going to shoot—" She stood and slowly moved to the edge away from the window and bent her nose to a large purple flower. People moved past, but no one paid the least attention to her. Or Barker.

Barker laughed, an ugly guttural sound as he hovered a few feet to her left. "I saw you do it. I came up to help Corbett. He was my meal ticket. But you stabbed him.

Weren't your toff like he told the constable. See, that's what they call *intent*. That's what the constable would call it."

The flower caused Arabella's nose to itch. "It's not true," she whispered. Had she meant to kill Corbett? She panicked. Rowan could appear at any moment and must not see her with Barker. "How much? How much to make you go away?"

"Now see I knew we could come to an agreement."

Arabella didn't turn to look at him, instead she hurriedly searched through her reticle. "This is all I have." She took all the coins in her reticule in her palm and held her hand behind her as discreetly as she could.

"Not nearly enough," Barker snarled, taking the coins from her outstretched hand. "I'll be in touch. Perhaps I'll attend your wedding."

She grasped the flower before her, holding the fragile stem so firmly it snapped. Filled with loathing both for herself and Barker, Arabella could think of nothing else but the stabbing of Corbett.

A hand fell on her shoulder and she jumped, but it was only Rowan, holding out her lemon ice.

🐾

ARABELLA HAD BLAMED A HEADACHE, BROUGHT ON BY TWO lemon ices and the sun, for her somber mood on the drive home. She put a hand to her head, rather dramatically, and sighed.

Rowan wasn't impressed with her acting skills.

As he'd walked towards the terrace, Rowan could have sworn he saw a man hovering at Arabella's back as she looked at the flowers spilling from the railing. When he arrived at her side, there was no one there.

After leaving Arabella at the Dunbar residence, Rowan mused over his future wife as his carriage rolled through the streets. She was not only intelligent but highly educated. Her reasoning and ability to decipher what he was really doing with the Newsome properties was nothing less than brilliant.

Too bad I don't completely trust her.

He did not think he imagined the man on the terrace behind Arabella. Possibly it was nothing more than coincidence. Maybe it had simply been a gentleman who happened to only pass behind her. But her behavior afterward betrayed her. She was nervous. Unsettled.

He couldn't imagine what she could be hiding from him. Was she planning on fleeing to the Continent to avoid their marriage?

Doubtful. Her happiness at Gunter's had not been practiced. Her enjoyment of his company did not ring false. If anything, the heat in her eyes matched his own.

Rowan pictured her eating the lemon ice again and moved his thoughts from her odd behavior and toward a more pleasant direction. Their wedding night for instance.

❧ 27 ❧

Rowan's hand held hers firmly in the warmth of his. "You look beautiful. I am partial to you in blue. And red."

Heat pinked her cheeks at his reference to her red chemise. For the wedding ceremony today, Arabella had chosen another dark blue gown, this one shot with deep green thread. She knew the color would please him as would piling the heavy mass of her hair into an array of curls left to dangle over her shoulders. She wore her sapphire earrings. Arabella had never felt so beautiful.

If only her new mother-in-law would cease her weeping.

She strove to keep from frowning at Lady Marsh. While Arabella and certainly everyone else was aware of Lady Marsh's disapproval, the woman didn't need to wail as if she were attending a funeral. Lord Marsh sat with a stony look on his face, though he was careful to not show his displeasure as strongly as his wife. Not with the Duke and Duchess of Dunbar present.

Rowan said his vows in a deep, sure tone, squeezing her hand as he did so, in a sign of encouragement. Last night she'd had nightmares of him leaving her as the vicar requested his vows, while his family clapped their approval. She'd even dreamt he'd laughed as Corbett appeared, announcing to everyone Arabella had promised to marry him as he took her hand to become her rightful husband.

Arabella did not have a restful night.

Her voice only trembled slightly as she spoke the words that bound her forever to Rowan. The vicar said something else, but she was so focused on the ruby and diamond ring placed on her finger she barely heard him. The ring was heavy and only a little lose. Before she knew it, Rowan had brought her hand to his lips and pressed a kiss to her knuckles. The smile he bestowed upon her was full of wicked intent mixed with true affection and made Arabella's toes curl inside her slippers. She may have sighed.

Lady Marsh sniffed loudly.

Rowan tucked her hand securely in the crook of his arm as they were offered hugs of congratulations and well wishes. A dark-haired man approached, a smile on his swarthy face.

"Brendan," she cried happily, hugging her cousin. "I'd no idea you would venture to London for my wedding. You've not been to town in ages; I'd thought you'd forgotten the way. Rowan, may I introduce you to my cousin, Brendan, Lord Morwick."

The two men shook hands as Arabella's eyes took in her cousin. His hair, black as sin had grown overly long, nearly brushing his shoulders. His trousers didn't appear to match his coat and he looked a bit rumpled. Brendan cared little for clothing or the trappings of being an earl. He was happiest crawling through the caves that littered the moors outside his estate and studying rock formations. Overly large in height and build, like every other man who shared the bloodline of the Duke of Dunbar, Brendan, with his wild hair and olive complexion, resembled a pirate more than an earl.

"Congratulations on your wedding, love." Brendan whispered in her ear as she released him. "Let me know if he gives you any trouble."

Arabella nodded solemnly. "I shall."

The group proceeded to the dining room where an enormous wedding feast had been prepared in Rowan and Arabella's honor. One dish after another was brought out from a steady stream of servants, the aroma causing Arabella's mouth to water. She was starving. In addition to not sleeping, her nerves had not allowed her to eat anything.

As the conversation flowed around the table, Arabella sipped at her wine and waited for her nerves to calm. She looked at Rowan down the length of mahogany laden with food and found her new husband watching her. His mother was busy chattering away in one ear, but he seemed focused on Arabella and paid Lady Marsh no mind. When his gaze fell to her lips, heat flowed up Arabella's chest.

In the weeks leading up to their wedding, Rowan's slow seduction had inflamed Arabella to the point she thought of little else *but* her wedding night. No wonder he was considered a bit of a rake amongst the ladies of the *ton*. He did not flirt overtly with her, instead his hands would glide down the length of her spine as she walked. Or he'd casually tuck a strand of hair behind her ear, allowing his fingers to brush her cheek. He'd argue with her then kiss her savagely as if he would devour her whole.

Her desire for Rowan was rather terrifying.

After the meal was finished, the gentlemen retired to Lord Marsh's study for a short time to ply Rowan with whiskey or brandy before he and Arabella would leave. Rowan had purchased a handsome town home a short drive away as a wedding gift to her. Having no idea how to proceed with the decorating and furnishing of such a house, Arabella was at a bit of a loss. She would need to consult with her aunt, or possibly Miranda. The polite thing to do, however, would be to consult her new mother-in-law, Lady Marsh, the woman who was actively pretending Arabella didn't exist.

Miranda's grandmother, the Dowager Marchioness of Cambourne, came to Arabella's side to link arms. "Will you walk me in, my dear?" The green eyes were twinkling as she took in the tableau of the Marsh family versus Arabella. As they moved into the drawing room, the Dowager leaned in. "I shouldn't worry. Lady Marsh would never have approved of any woman Rowan chose without her assistance. She only disapproves of you *more*. I've never known her to be an unkind woman." The Dowager's brow wrinkled in thought. "She's been a bit overprotective since the death of her eldest son, some years ago. But that is not an excuse for her treatment. Should it continue I will have a word with her."

Arabella halted momentarily at the Dowager's words. Rowan had never mentioned an older brother but there was much they hadn't yet discussed or told each other. "Please don't worry yourself on my account. Lady Marsh has reason to dislike me and I'm not exactly the match she would have wished for her son." The Dowager doubtless knew the whole story, as she knew most things. "He did me a good turn and instead of being thanked, he is stuck with me."

"I do not think he minds." The Dowager intoned as Arabella led her to a large chair dominating the room. "Nor do I think you are distraught at having to marry that handsome scamp. Regardless of the circumstances, he is a good match for you." She squeezed Arabella's hand and nodded towards Arabella's hair. "I like this new Arabella. You no longer look as if you're sucking on a lemon."

Arabella felt the slight touch of the dowager's cane against her leg and the curl of her lips stopped.

"Don't start frowning, I shan't tolerate it on your wedding

day. Now bring me that girl." The Dowager pointed with her cane at Petra. "I wish to speak to her about her Season."

Arabella dipped and approached Petra and Lady Marsh. "Excuse me, Lady Marsh, but Lady Cambourne wishes to speak with Petra."

Lady Marsh clapped her hands, barely glancing at Arabella. "Oh Petra, this is a fortuitous occurrence. Perhaps the entire day won't be wasted." She hustled her daughter towards the Dowager without another word to Arabella.

My wedding is a waste of Lady Marsh's day. How lovely.

Arabella moved to stand at the window overlooking the gardens, pushing out thoughts of her mother-in-law's rudeness to mull over the words of the Dowager. Was Rowan pleased to have married her? She knew he desired her. Wanted to bed her. He'd never once told her he wished to end their betrothal, though she'd given him many opportunities. And she sensed he enjoyed her company.

Arabella laughed softly under her breath. If anyone had told her months ago she would marry Rowan, she would have snarled something insulting in their direction. *That* Arabella, the one whose bitterness seeped through every pore, still lingered just below the surface. She tried to keep her contained, although in the face of Lady Marsh's dislike, it was becoming increasingly difficult. She gave a pleasurable sigh as she looked out amongst the flowers and trees, realizing that she would tolerate all of Lady Marsh's ill-mannered sputtering for Rowan.

I am well and truly bound to him.

Guilt washed through her. The horrible lie she'd told about her kidnapping hovered around her as she repeated her vows. She'd been acutely aware she'd nearly spoken those same words to another man. A man whom she would have married for revenge. The lie threatened her current state of unexpected joy, the tiny seed of which was nurtured with every caress or teasing word from Rowan.

It was hard to believe she could be happy.

A bird fluttered about the rose bushes, soaring into the air and then dipping back down. She watched the bird for some time until it flew off, frightened off by something that even now shook the rose bush. Probably a cat. Arabella had seen a large tabby roaming the dining room while they ate.

Arabella clasped the sill of the window in a death grip, a sickening ball of fear forming in her stomach. It was not a cat but something far more predatory lurking in the Marsh garden.

Barker, looking less scruffy than he had at Gunter's, stood by the rose bush. It was clear by his stance he saw her at the window. With a flick of his wrist and a nod, he made his meaning clear. She was to meet him in the garden.

Arabella shook her head in refusal.

Barker shrugged and took a step towards the house, looking at her with a question on his coarse features.

Her mouth went dry, imagining Barker interrupting the wedding party. She snuck a look at the women chattering madly in the room. Miranda was still waving her hands about, clearly entertaining Jemma, Alex and Aunt Maisy with one of her stories. The Dowager held the rapt attention of Lady Marsh and Petra, both hanging on the older woman's every word. She supposed it should have bothered her, to see that everyone had forgotten her presence, but Arabella was grateful. She would handle Barker once and for all.

Moving towards the door, Arabella's hand fell to the knob. She turned and mumbled to the room that she wished to take some air.

Aunt Maisy looked up at her, smiling brightly. "Do you wish me to go with you?"

Her aunt was overly concerned Arabella needed her

council on what to expect from the marriage bed. She was probably hoping her advice was needed even though Arabella told her quite firmly, she was not in need of direction.

"No. I just need a bit of air." She gave her aunt a firm look.

Aunt Maisy gave a wistful sigh and returned to Miranda's conversation.

Arabella strode quickly out to the terrace and down the steps leading into the garden. Moving as far away from the large windows facing the garden as possible, she sought out a bench positioned at the furthest edge and behind a hedge of flowering myrtle and sat. She prayed no one would come looking for her, ears alert for any sound of footsteps on the gravel path. Afraid and incensed Barker would come here and invade her wedding, she became more determined to rid herself of the former groom.

"What a lovely bride you are, Lady Arabella. I stopped by in hopes I could congratulate you on your wedding day."

Barker stood directly behind her, his fetid breath causing her nose to wrinkle in distaste. She kept perfectly still, her voice low and quiet, her hands clasped on her lap as if she were contemplating the serenity of the garden. "What do you want? I've given you all the money I have."

He leaned closer and Arabella shrank away as he whispered in a guttural tone, "not true. Your brother's a duke. You've more money than I could spend in a lifetime." He looked down at her hand. "That's a lovely bauble."

Arabella immediately covered the ring Rowan had just placed on her finger with her hand. "Are you insane? What would I say to my new husband should I return from a turn about the garden without my wedding ring?"

"I don't give a shit what you'd tell him. Corbett promised me a large settlement. Seagraves too. Your bitch of an aunt hit poor Seagraves on the head. He's got headaches now.

Seagraves didn't deserve such treatment as he never would have hurt her."

Arabella snorted, her fear replaced with anger. "Seagraves *abducted* my aunt, you lunatic. What should she have done?"

"I'll tell you what you are going to do, Lady Arabella. I know all about you and your fancy toff. I've seen the house he bought you." A hand reached out and batted the sapphire earrings.

Arabella cringed and tried to slide away. "Don't touch me."

"Those gems hanging from your ears will fetch a nice price."

Arabella shook her head. "No. I'll bring you money tomorrow. I—"

"Did you know Corbett had a sister? Doesn't even know her brother's dead, I'll warrant. Poor girl." He gave a low chuckle. "Wouldn't she be surprised to know the *whole* truth. Her husband's a barrister."

The threat was quite clear. She could already imagine the story Barker would tell Corbett's sister. He would infer she'd changed her mind and then killed Corbett to marry Rowan. Given Arabella's past behavior, she thought it unlikely anyone would believe Corbett's death was an accident.

I should have confessed my stupidity well before now.

Slowly, she pulled the sapphires from her ears, knowing she had little choice. At least today. "I wish never to see you again, do you understand?" Her mind raced, wondering what she would say if anyone noticed the earrings gone from her ears.

I'll say the clasps were hurting my ears and I had to take them off and I must have dropped them in the garden.

"I knew you'd see reason, Lady Arabella." His hand opened at her side.

"That's enough to keep you for the rest of your life,

Barker. Do not bother me again." She dropped the jewels in his outstretched palm. "Are we finished?"

"I suppose we are. My congratulations again." The crackling of brush met her ears as he slithered off and left the garden.

Arabella sat staring at the rosebush for the longest time considering the options before her. She closed her eyes and focused on inhaling the sweet smell of the flowers and listening to the bird song, instructing her heart to stop beating so hard.

Rowan would never forgive her if he knew she'd omitted the truth. He would wonder if she *had* meant to kill Corbett. Her new husband would point at her willingness to pay Barker to keep such things from him. Not to mention her brother.

I was a different person then. I've changed.

She doubted that would matter. No one had ever assumed the best about Arabella; they were unlikely to start now.

28

Arabella was up to something.

Rowan wrapped the towel around his hips and stepped from the tub, ignoring the sputtering of his valet as water dripped all over the carpet. When he'd found her, sitting on the stone bench in his mother's garden, she'd been deathly pale. At first Rowan assumed it was nerves for the day had been a bit trying. His mother in particular had been difficult. It wasn't until they arrived at their new home that Rowan noticed the earrings she'd been wearing were gone. His new wife made a vague excuse about having dropped them in the garden as they pinched her ears.

"That will be all, Parker." He dismissed his valet.

"My lord—"

"Out. It's my wedding night. I doubt I need your assistance."

Parker gave an exasperated sigh, pointedly looking at the water on the carpet. After a moment he nodded and quietly left the room.

Mother had behaved dreadfully, but he didn't think that was the reason for Arabella's odd mood after leaving his parents. Nor did he think it was the loss of her earrings. With any other woman, Rowan may have assumed nerves due to the wedding night, but Arabella's behavior the night of the opera assured him of his wife's enthusiasm for her wifely duties. Whatever was bothering Arabella, she didn't trust Rowan enough to tell him.

The feeling was mutual.

He and Arabella were drawn to each other in a way Rowan didn't wholly understand. What would she say if she knew he'd wanted her for years? The pull towards Arabella was so strong, so primal, Rowan often had trouble keeping his physical distance from her. Today was particularly difficult. But for all that, Rowan found he still didn't trust her.

A soft knock sounded on the door and without turning he said, "Parker, I told you I had no more need—"

"It's me."

Arabella's voice was low and husky, the sound rasping over his skin as if she touched him. Few brides would grow so impatient on their wedding night as to seek out their groom. Rowan smiled to himself.

Clutching the towel to his hips, Rowan turned, knowing she would see how tented the towel had become. Perhaps he should drop the towel. It would be interesting to see what Arabella would do. She didn't frighten easily but seeing him naked with a raging erection might send her fleeing from the room.

The sight of her caused all amusement to flee.

The sable mass of her hair flowed wildly over her nearly bare shoulders. The nightgown she wore, a bit of white lace and silk, hid little from his gaze. He could just make out the dusky outline of her nipples beneath the almost sheer fabric. The entire concoction was full of ribbons and flounces, completely un-Arabella like.

Eyes the color of pitch looked down at the towel, and

back at his face. The plump lips of her mouth widened into a perfect "o", but she didn't look away. Nor did she stammer or blush. Instead her gaze on him became increasingly possessive, as if he belonged to her.

A shudder of longing ran through him, forceful and sharp.

Rowan held out his hand and Arabella threaded her fingers through his without hesitation.

The towel dropped to the floor.

⬥

BLOODY HELL.

Arabella didn't typically curse, though she certainly knew some choice words, after all, her brother *was* the Devil of Dunbar. And given her mother's predication for bringing her lovers home, she *had* seen a naked man before.

Just not Rowan. Dear God, not Rowan.

She'd often wondered what lie beneath the tailored coats and fine lawn of his shirts. She imagined the bunched muscles of his thighs that caused his breeches to be so indecently tight. A violent fluttering spiraled out from her stomach to settle between her thighs as her eyes roamed over him.

He's beautiful. No wonder every woman in the ton *is chasing him.*

Arabella had a rather possessive nature. She didn't share things well despite her generosity to orphans and widows. Jealously was also not an unfamiliar emotion. But the proprietary way she felt about Rowan was new to her. Different. *Powerful.*

Broad muscled shoulders topped an equally sculpted torso. Many men of the ton padded their coats to give the appearance of a fine figure but her new husband wasn't one of them. Not an ounce of fat shown on the rugged lines of his body.

Glorious. Magnificent.

His skin shone golden in candlelight. Small drops of water, missed when he'd dried himself, dripped down his chest from his still wet hair. As she watched, one droplet fell and slid down his chest, trailing down the flat toned stomach, to disappear in a thatch of dark hair.

Oh dear.

She tore her eyes back to his, determined to keep her gaze above his navel. Impossible with his arousal jutting out as if demanding her attention. Rowan seemed to have no inclination to cover himself. He curled his fingers around himself, stroking several times while she watched, gauging her reaction. "My sacrificial virgin has arrived. I'd no idea you'd be so impatient."

Arabella's pulse skipped, blood pumping furiously through her veins. The tips of her breasts chafed against the confines of the ridiculous nightgown Aunt Maisy insisted she have. She was fascinated by the length of him. What should she call...*it*? Her mother always referred to her lover's assets in a rather lusty way, as a *cock*.

She supposed she should look away. Possibly twitter and weep at the sight of a large, naked male who clearly desired her. But if Arabella had learned nothing else about the man before her, it was that Rowan appreciated that she was *not* shy and retiring. Her boldness aroused him, as evidenced by the size of his— *cock*. She looked up at him and narrowed her eyes. "Virgin sacrifice? I thought I had more the appearance of an overdone wedding cake. I have never worn so much lace in my life."

He reached out and wrapped an arm around her waist, pulling her against his still damp body.

"You will not be wearing that piece of lace long or likely ever again." He nuzzled the side of her neck.

"A shame." Though it wasn't. She detested frills and bows.

"Aunt Maisy assured me all bridegrooms desired their brides to be adorned in such silliness." She was trembling, both at the hardness pressed against her thigh and from the delicious anticipation radiating through her body.

He brushed his lips against hers. "Your aunt is incorrect. I prefer my bride to be clothed in as little as possible. Though I ache to seek you in your red chemise. Are you frightened, Bella? I don't wish you to be."

"No." She shook her head. "I mean...possibly a little."

The green in his eyes deepened. "Did I ever tell you I saw you once, long ago?" A finger slid down across her skin to the valley between her breasts. "You wore a ballgown the color of pink that reminded me of the early morning sky."

"You did? You never told me." It was difficult to think clearly when he touched her. Her breasts were swelling up towards him, eager for his hands, his mouth.

Rowan cupped one breast, the heat of his touch searing her through the thin silk and lace. "A ball, given by some member of the *ton* whose name I no longer recall. You were so very lovely. Haughty. No one dared approach you." A soft laugh escaped him. "After that, I never saw you in color again for years. For the longest time I thought you were in half-mourning." He gazed into her eyes intently. "No more browns or grays." His words held a tone of command. "Are we in agreement?"

When she didn't answer immediately, he gently squeezed her nipple between his thumb and forefinger until she whispered, "Yes. You seem to like me in blue."

"I have wanted you for a very long time, Arabella. I watched you at the few balls you attended, until you no longer went out. Difficult and dour woman that you are." Lips fell against hers, gentle and coaxing. "Do you wonder any longer why I came for you?"

"No." Arabella's body melted as she threaded her fingers

through the damp strands of his hair. The tips of her breasts rubbed deliciously against his chest, the sensitive peaks chafing against the lace and silk in an almost painful way. She moved her hands to cup both sides of his face, feeling the brush of his whiskers against the palms of her hands, and opened her mouth to his.

A low primitive sound rumbled from deep in his chest. Grabbing her hips, he edged closer to the bed. "Lie down."

A small feeling of trepidation mixed with the anticipation coursing through her. She backed up against the coverlet on her elbows, the nightgown inching up to bare her thighs as she did so.

Rowan appeared large and predatory as he pushed her knees apart to stand between her legs. "This," he tugged at the nightgown, "must come off, Arabella." Deft fingers tugged at the fragile ribbon holding the neck of the garment together.

A slight tearing sound met her ears as her breasts spilled out, her nipples hardening in the cool air of the room. His hands opened and circled the mounds, squeezing and rubbing the pads of his thumbs against the small peaks.

"Jesus, you're beautiful." Then he ripped the remainder of the fragile material with one sharp jerk of his hand.

She lay before him as if she were indeed a virgin about to be sacrificed to some pagan god. Rowan certainly looked the part as he loomed over her prone body. Half his large form lay in shadow while firelight gilded the other portion of his body with gold, his eyes dark with hunger as if he wished to devour her.

His hands stroked up the side of one breast, then down her side, tracing each rib. Fingers wove through the soft hair between her legs. "Finally, mine," he whispered. "Every bit of your darkness belongs to me."

An intoxicating haze of pleasure fell over her as she

watched him. Rowan understood her as no one else ever had. Accepted her. She *was* full of darkness and sometimes it threatened to overwhelm her.

"Yes." She sucked in her breath as the warmth of his mouth enveloped her nipple. His tongue tortured her breast, nipping and sucking until her entire body throbbed with the need for more.

His mouth left her breast and Arabella sighed in disappointment. He gave a quiet laugh as his lips pressed the underside of her breast before nibbling down her skin. Teeth grazed across her stomach making the muscles jump and twitch in pleasure.

This was the most exquisite form of torture. Her breathing became rough as every movement of his mouth sent another shock of moisture to her core. When he finally made his way to her navel, he paused.

"I think about tasting you, Bella." He murmured between nips of her flesh. "I want to savor you like fine wine."

"Rowan." His name left her lips almost like a plea. Her entire body ached and throbbed. Arabella knew what he wanted. Where he intended to put his mouth. She'd heard of such things, of course, but the thought of such being done to her? Arabella's legs squeezed shut.

"No, sweetheart. These are never to be shut to me." He nipped at her thigh. "You'll like this, Bella. I promise." A finger slid through her damp folds, gliding over the softness. Teasing her. "You are as beautiful here as everywhere else."

Arabella found she couldn't speak. Her hips twisted against him as the finger teased her already swollen flesh. He avoided the center of her pleasure and instead seemed content to stroke and caress her sensitive folds. It was maddening.

One finger slid inside her, thrusting gently.

"This is what you like." His breath was hot against her thigh.

"Yes." Arabella was panting like a wild animal, the need within her growing to a feverish pitch as it had the night he'd touched her in the coach.

Another finger followed the first, stretching and thrusting. Soft pressure fell against the small bit of flesh hidden within her folds as Rowan pressed his thumb to her in a rotating motion. "The things I wish to do to you, my lovely wife. So many things. We will spend whole days in bed." He pressed the underside of the small bundle of nerves and her hips lifted.

"Yes," she choked out, nearly mindless from the pleasure surging through her body.

"Think how much better this will feel when I use my mouth." One hand cupped her buttock and pressed her up towards his waiting mouth. He blew a soft puff of air through the hair of her mound. "You are lovely here. Do you ever touch yourself, Bella?"

"No—" Arabella fisted the coverlet in each hand as his tongue caressed her folds. Each stroke sent bolts of sensation across her body.

"I don't think you're being truthful." He paused, waiting.

"Yes, but—"

His mouth and tongue moved in unison, suckling her tender flesh until the lightest touch caused her to whimper. "Please." She arched trying to position herself more fully in his mouth. Bits of fire broke and flamed across her skin. The pressure intensified to a fever pitch. "Please, Rowan." She was begging. *Pleading*.

The fingers inside her curled.

Arabella threw back her head. He was killing her. Every nerve in her body coiled tight, ready to spring.

Rowan sucked her into his mouth, allowing the tip of his teeth to brush across the swollen piece of flesh.

White spots flashed before her eyes as her entire body arched and held before violently breaking apart. She cried out his name, her hands clutching at the coverlet atop the bed as the tremors surged through her body.

Rowan held her down, his mouth drawing out each contraction of her body, fingers moving inside her, drawing out her pleasure until Arabella lay limp and panting on the bed. Her eyes fluttered open to see Rowan's dark head between her thighs. She felt blissful. Positively wanton.

He kissed the inside of her thigh and looked up at her with a feral smile. Looming over her on all fours, possession flickered in the depths of his hazel eyes, as he leaned in to nuzzle the side of her neck. She felt the hard press of him as he positioned himself at her entrance.

"I'll try to be gentle, Arabella. But I'm—"

"Large." Heat fanned her cheeks. Ridiculous, considering what he'd just done to her. "Of course, I don't have anything to compare it to." She sputtered. "What if it doesn't fit?"

A trace of a smile crossed his lips before he kissed her gently.

She kissed him back, tasting herself. "I may be a little frightened."

His arms were tight, the cords of his muscles taut as he strove to keep himself in check. Slowly, he moved, pressing into her. She was slick and wet but still Arabella felt as if she were being stretched apart.

Arabella's body immediately clenched. She tried to close her legs.

"Relax, love." He whispered against her cheek. "I don't wish to hurt you more than is necessary."

Her hands clenched the hard lines of his buttocks, pulling him closer. "I know you won't hurt me." She kissed his neck, relishing the taste of his skin, then his mouth. Nipping his bottom lip, Arabella claimed his mouth with all the ferocity welling inside her, willing him to take her.

A low growl came from Rowan's chest. He thrust deep inside her with one stroke, seating himself more fully between her thighs.

A painful cry of surprise left her mouth. She bucked beneath him, her body wishing to throw off the intruder. *Dear God, it hurt.* He was too big. He would tear her apart. Rip her to shreds. She shut her eyes, blinking furiously, ashamed when a tear ran down her cheek.

Rowan didn't move. Kissing the tear running down her cheek he whispered, "I'm sorry. There was no help for it." He murmured soft, nonsensical words to her. His lips found her eyelids, the corner of her mouth, the curve of her jaw, each word and kiss soothing Arabella until she relaxed.

She could feel him, hard and pulsing deep inside her.

Rowan pulled out a halfway then thrust again.

Arabella clutched at his arms, knowing he was taking great care to not hurt her further. The pain abated with each sure stroke to be replaced with a mild burning sensation. Her insides felt battered and stretched to their limits. What had her mother liked about this act so much? No wonder they called it a duty. How in the world would she ever get used to this—"

Rowan took another deep, smooth stroke, and moved so that his body caught hers. The barest glimmer of the pleasure she'd experienced before resurfaced. "Oh."

"Oh, indeed. I see you are not impressed. I'll have to work harder, Lady Malden."

Each stroke teased to renew the pleasure she experienced before. Tentatively, she moved her hips, trying to find the pace he set.

"Better?" He didn't wait for her to answer, instead

Rowan's hand moved sinuously between their bodies, caressing her until she could feel the tightness coiling within her once more.

He lifted her hips up and took up a steady rhythm. His fingers would move between them, touching her just enough to drive her mad without offering the release she sought.

"Please, Rowan. Please." Arabella was a writhing ravenous thing. Begging for something only Rowan could give her. "Harder." Madness had come over her and she wished to break and shatter.

"Wait for me." Rowan nipped at the lobe of her ear. "Wait."

He pounded into her, stroking her flesh only once more before the orgasm slammed into Arabella. Her entire body arched against him as the pleasure radiated through her. She sobbed, her nails digging into the flesh of his back. Her body clamped down around his and she heard his breath catch.

"Jesus." He whispered. "I told you to wait." He thrust into her almost painfully, gripping her hips, all sign of the gentle lover gone. The cords of his neck tightened as he thrust one last time, and his breath left his lips in a soft moan as he collapsed against her.

Arabella lay panting with Rowan's weight atop her, her skin tingling as blood pumped through her limbs. She could hear his heart beating with hers, tasted the salt of his skin with her lips. Possessively, she clasped him tighter not willing for this feeling to end.

Somewhere along all her mistakes and bitterness, she'd done something she never thought would be possible. Especially for her.

She'd fallen in love.

🎕 29 🎕

*C*hrist.

Rowan's heart hammered in his chest. Rolling to his side, he was surprised to hear her slight protest as his body left hers. "Shhh." His mouth brushed hers. "I'm heavy."

A smile crossed her lips as her eyes fluttered closed. "Yes, but I like it." She looked peaceful. *Happy*.

His heart skipped a beat seeing that slight twist to her lips. The strength of her joy filled the air around them. When had her happiness become so important to him? He was giddy at the slightest hint of a smile from her lips. Pressing a kiss to her temple he smoothed back the dark mass of her hair, marveling at the softness of the strands. He threaded his fingers through the curls marveling at the way they slid through his fingers like silk to float gently over his chest.

"The things I will do to you, Bella," he whispered, already wanting her again. If he were to put into words what he felt at that moment, Rowan would have said, *completion*.

"I will allow it." She snuggled closer. "I feel the worst is over and thus can continue to tolerate your attentions."

"Don't be too sure." He nibbled on her ear.

Pushing herself up on an elbow, the dark pools of her eyes wandered over his face. She looked seductive and wild with her hair spilling over her naked shoulders, not a bit of virginal shyness apparent. Thank God she'd been dressing like a governess for most of her life or he'd be challenging half the men in the *ton* to duels despite her sour manner. She was rarely sour with him, however. Arabella could even be described as pleasant lately. Jemma jokingly asked at the wedding if Rowan was giving Arabella laudanum to make her more amenable.

He would like to think her change in manner was because of him.

Rowan was not a jealous man by nature. He bore affection for some of his bed partners and others had been purely for physical reasons. There had never been any commitment between he and his lovers. No promises made. Certainly, he'd not been possessive of any of those women. But none of those relationships compared to the way he felt about Arabella.

Challenging. Far more intelligent than was good for a woman. Dark. Prone to deceit. There were many ways to describe her.

Mine.

He'd known from the moment Lady Cupps-Foster asked him to retrieve her from Corbett. He went because she *was* his.

Her hand, slim and pale, trailed down his chest, the fingers threading through the dark hair. The hand paused at one of his nipples, rolling it gently between her fingers. She cast a sideways glance at him, wanting to see if her touch affected him. She moved her hand farther, splaying it across the center of his stomach. Her nails gently raked his skin.

This was interesting. His cock twitched at her approach.

Closing his eyes, Rowan was content to allow her to explore. Her touch, neither innocent nor experienced, was incredibly arousing. She paused at the line of hair which led below his waist.

"Go on." He whispered. "Unless you are afraid."

A snort of disbelief met his ears, followed by her fingers wrapping around the length of him. "I am many things, Malden, but not a coward."

"Indeed not, my love." His breath sucked in as her fingers circled his shaft. She gave him a light, exploratory stroke as if gauging his reaction. When he gave a grunt of pleasure she continued in her ministrations. "No more Malden." He choked out. "We agreed." A groan left his lips.

"Oh, yes. I forgot." She paused. "Did I not do that right? Are you sore as well?"

"I'm not sore." But his cock *was* swelling painfully beneath her touch. If she kept this up he would take her again and she *was* sore. His hand covered hers.

The dark eyes narrowed. "I am too bold."

He could feel her retreating from him, even though she hadn't moved. Arabella was so sensitive to the slightest rejection. He would need to be careful and pay close attention to his words and actions until she trusted him.

A frown started to form on her beautiful lips.

"Bella." He tucked a strand of hair behind her ear and kissed the end of her nose. "I happen to like your boldness. But even though I am not sore, you are. If you persist in your...*worship* of me—"

A small laugh escaped her. "Worship? Oh my, you are very full of yourself, Malden."

Her laughter aroused him more than any touch of her hand.

"Rowan. Next I know, you will be writing an ode to my eyes. Good Lord, or perhaps my," he wiggled his eyebrows.

"Cock." She said the word with absolutely no hesitation.

Christ. The way her lips moved as she said the word. She hadn't even blushed. Keeping his voice solemn he said, "Yes. Imagine the scandal. Even though I must admit, it is deserving of an ode or two."

Arabella giggled. It was the most beautiful sound Rowan had ever heard. Her laughter was the most potent of aphrodisiacs. His fingers ran across her ribs, gratified when she squirmed and twisted from his touch. Arabella, dour, austere woman, was ticklish.

"Stop, I beg you." Her lips parted in invitation as she spoke, the words turning seductive.

Rowan wrapped her hair around his wrist and pulled her mouth to his. "Bella," he said against her lips, "you will be *very* sore tomorrow."

❧ 30 ❦

The next several weeks passed in a cloud of absolute bliss.

Rowan, contrary to many gentlemen, enjoyed having an intelligent wife. She knew this because he told her so, asking her opinions on a variety of subjects. Rowan was fascinated with steam power, engines, railroads, anything connected to transportation. He was not interested in the way a scientist would be, but rather from a financial standpoint.

The renovations of the Newsome textile mills were a huge topic of conversation as he sought the best men to make the modernizations. He continued to advise several of his business acquaintances on investments and other financial matters. Arabella soon found herself hosting a small dinner party with several gentlemen and their wives. All of the men were in trade and enormously wealthy. She watched, fascinated, as Rowan picked their brains under the guise of his charm and affability. He made quiet deals in the days after the dinner party, becoming a silent partner so as not to stir up talk of his being in 'trade.' Her husband's thirst for business and creating wealth was insatiable.

As was his thirst for Arabella.

She'd been unprepared for the unbridled desire her husband had for her. The delights of Arabella's marriage often left her abed until mid-morning, her body still throbbing from her husband's attentions. Nor did he leave her after they made love. Rowan was adamant that they not sleep apart, even if, on those rare occasions, all they did was actually *sleep*.

While he spent his days away from the house, he made a point to dine with her in the evenings. One night he surprised her with a picnic in the garden. After nibbling on cold chicken and a bottle of wine, he lay down on the blanket and pulled her to him. For hours they did nothing but look up at the stars as he pointed out the various constellations. Neither of them was particularly enamored of mythology, so they spent the time piecing things together and arguing over who had the story of Cassiopeia correct. After being proven incorrect in her assumptions, Arabella was forced to pay a forfeit. Rowan stripped her naked beneath the large tree in the garden and made love to her in the cool grass. After, shivering from the cold, he wrapped her in the blanket and snuck her back into the house and carried her to bed.

She was certain the servants were scandalized.

Arabella found her previous bitterness was no match for her current happiness. As the weeks went by, she fell deeper in love with her husband. The fear of loving Rowan still lingered, but she learned to put her anxiety aside. It had no place in her marriage.

Late at night, as Rowan snored softly beside her, Arabella would wonder if she should tell him everything, starting with her lie about Corbett and ending with Barker's threats and blackmail. She would throw herself at her husband's feet and beg him to understand that she was no longer that bitter woman.

Rowan was wrong. She *was* a coward.

The fear of losing him kept Arabella's lips firmly shut. The thought of Rowan hating her, as he surely would, stopped her. She couldn't bear to have him look at her with revulsion. And so, she kept silent and waited for her guilt to abate. As the weeks wore on, she saw no more of Barker and determined the earrings had finally appeased him.

Still, Arabella felt strongly that the time had come for her to atone for at least *some* of her sins. When she and Rowan had been married a month, Arabella reached a decision.

31

"Her Grace is in the drawing room, Lady Malden." Peabody lifted his brows at her in surprise.

Well, why wouldn't he be a bit shocked? She'd never once sought Jemma's company. And she knew the old butler was incredibly protective of the duchess. "Thank you, Peabody." As Arabella passed the butler she paused, "for everything."

The older man's cheeks pinked. "My lady, it has been my greatest pleasure."

Arabella gave a snort of disbelief. "You suffered Grandfather, then Nick and especially *me*. I feel certain that if they gave battle commendations to house staff, your uniform would be decorated with medals."

Peabody's eyebrows raised into his hairline at her words before his lips turned up in what passed for a smile. "Congratulations again, my lady, on your marriage. May I say it seems to agree with you."

"You may." She strode forward and waited for Peabody to open the drawing room doors. "I shall not upset her in the least."

Peabody said nothing, only gave a short bow and opened the drawing room doors.

Her brother's wife sat on the large brocade sofa near the window with a view of the gardens. She was cleaning a beautiful set of pistols inlaid with ivory on the handles, the mound of her stomach glaringly apparent. It was a rather ridiculous scene, the pregnant duchess cleaning a pair of deadly pistols. Jemma was terribly eccentric. Arabella supposed that was one of the reasons Nick loved her.

She looked up at Arabella's entrance, with one raised brow. Her face remained carefully controlled and polite though her hand tightened on the hilt of the pistol.

I haven't the least doubt she'd like to shoot me. Nick says she's an excellent shot.

Peabody gave Jemma a pointed look and departed, leaving the drawing room doors open.

Arabella nodded towards the departing butler. "I suppose he's concerned that I might accost you, Your Grace. With the doors ajar he's certain to hear your screams for help."

Jemma resumed cleaning the pistol. "Peabody is overprotective. I rarely scream and my condition has not affected my shooting ability."

Arabella swallowed down the sharp retort that instantly came to mind. But she was not here to argue with her sister-in-law. "I shall refrain from causing Peabody any alarm. I should hate to have him wrestle me to the floor in an effort to protect you."

"Nick isn't here." Jemma turned to her. "I'm sure you can show yourself out." She raised the gun and pointed the weapon in Arabella's direction, pretending to check the sight.

She wasn't going to make this easy, but why should she? Perhaps her behavior was part of Arabella's penance. "It's just as well, I came to see you. If you would be so kind as to not shoot me with that thing, perhaps you'd like to know why."

Hazel eyes, so like Rowan's, looked up from the pistol. Her hand fell protectively over the rise of her stomach. She placed the pistol on the sofa but kept it within easy reach.

"How interesting. Are you here at your brother's behest?" She shook her head. "Bloody meddling duke that he is. Or perhaps Rowan?" She shrugged. "It doesn't matter. We'll tell them both we spoke. There is no need to continue what is bound to be an incredibly awkward conversation which will embarrass us both."

Arabella took a deep breath. It was rather difficult not to lose her temper with Jemma since everything her sister-in-law did irritated her beyond belief. But in this instance she deserved Jemma's disdain, considering Arabella's past actions.

"I am not here at my husband's request. Nor Nick's, though you are correct in that he is a meddling elderly matron trapped inside the body of a duke." Arabella gave a half-smile.

Her smile was not returned.

"I see." Jemma regarded her with barely concealed dislike.

Getting Jemma to hear her out was much more difficult than Arabella had anticipated. She'd had some bizarre assumption that being with child would cause her sister-in-law to soften towards her.

"Your Grace, I would only ask that you allow me to say what I've come to say before you voice your opinion. This will not take long, I promise. Please hear me out." Arabella paced back and forth across the thick rug of the drawing room, not daring to look her sister-in-law in the eye. Her hand twitched against her skirts though she tried to stop it.

"Whatever have you done to your hair?"

The words took Arabella by surprise. She halted. "Excuse me?" She reached up thinking something had gone awry when she took off her bonnet, but the smooth chignon still sat firmly at the base of her neck. A few lose strands of her hair were artfully left to fall against her shoulders. Her hair was *perfect*. "There is nothing wrong with my hair." Her eyes narrowed on Jemma. "I'm told pregnancy makes a woman do and say strange things." She couldn't stop the curl to her lip though she wasn't upset, just amused.

"Careful, Arabella. I'm the one with the pistol."

Arabella shut her eyes. When she'd considered apologizing, she'd envisioned Jemma smiling sweetly and accepting Arabella's request for forgiveness. How naïve of her. The very idea was preposterous. "I came here to make amends, if I can."

"You can't."

"I have wronged you—"

"The understatement of the century," Jemma snapped.

Arabella clenched her fists. "May I continue?"

"Yes, of course. How rude of me to interrupt. Though to be fair, I said I would listen, not make your act of contrition easy." Jemma's chin tilted up. "Do go on."

Arabella nodded. There was no excuse for her actions but at the time, she'd truly felt she was protecting her brother from a woman who would harm him. Jemma may never forgive her, but she did wish her sister-in-law to understand. Arabella had not acted purely out of malice.

"My entire childhood was spent with Grandfather railing against the man who framed my father, Phillip. Treason is always a terrible crime, but for my family, in particular, even the very mention of disloyalty is in direct opposition to a promise made long ago." How much had her brother shared with his wife? Did she guess at some of the things Nick had done for Crown and country?

"The Dunbars serve the Crown." Jemma held her gaze. "Always. You are telling me nothing I don't already know."

Arabella nodded in agreement. "Yes. You must understand that I was conditioned to hate this nameless man, whom we now know was your father, with my entire being. Nick as well. Not only for the act of treason, but..." Arabella swallowed as the memory of her parents bloodied bodies flashed before her eyes. She could still see her mother's hand clutching the wine goblet. "But for what came *after* the accusations of treason."

Jemma looked at Arabella with something akin to pity. "He's told me of what transpired that day. You and Nick saw them. A terrible thing."

"You've no idea." The coppery smell of her parent's blood still stung Arabella's nostrils.

"I don't suppose I do." Jemma was looking at her oddly, perhaps she was beginning to understand.

"Nick bore the brunt of Grandfather's need for vengeance and was reminded daily the responsibility of restoring our family's honor was *his*." Arabella rolled her eyes. "As if treason were the only thing standing between my parents and respectability. I'm sure he's told you. Phillip and Charlotte were the farthest thing from respectable. Nick and I were shunned, but feared. Respected and despised. I suppose we both became a little overprotective of the other."

Jemma slowly nodded. "Another understatement." But there was no judgement in her words.

"I have been very angry for a very long time, Jemma. For a variety of reasons, none of which I will further bore you with. But Nick was all I had in the world. My brother, who was my strength," she halted, "*my safe harbor*, became despondent at the news of your death. I could not protect him from the pain of your loss. I've never felt so powerless." Arabella turned away from her for a moment, remembering Nick locking himself in his study for days, the pile of empty whiskey bottles outside the door the only sign that he still lived. "I cannot express to you the terror I felt that my brother would do himself harm. I feared he would follow you to the grave. *Nick. The Devil of Dunbar*. And then to find the Jem he grieved was the traitor's daughter who miraculously returned from the dead." Arabella looked away. "I have never felt such betrayal in my life, nor such fear that you would destroy my brother. I was ripe for manipulation when I met the Corbetts."

She looked back to her sister-in-law. Jemma had paled and her eyes were wet with tears.

"I am not making any excuses for my behavior, for there are none to be had." Arabella continued. "But I truly thought I was acting in Nick's best interests, in my own selfish way. I was afraid I would lose him, that you would harm him in some way and—"

"Stop." Jemma brushed a tear from her cheek and turned away. "That is a time I can no longer speak of without weeping. You are not the only one that has made foolish choices fueled by pain and bitterness. If you know nothing else, know that I love Nick, with all of my heart. I will have no one hurt him again. Not me or you. *Anyone*." Her voice grew hard.

"I did not mean to upset you." Arabella's voice shook. Since her return from Wales she had observed her sister-in-law and knew how much Jemma loved Nick. "I was wrong about you and I am truly, deeply sorry. I was..." She hesitated slightly. "...someone else then."

Jemma sat still for the longest time, dabbing at her eyes with the same cloth she'd been cleaning the pistols with earlier. "I accept your apology, Arabella. I do not know if we can ever be friends, but at the very least, we have no need to be enemies."

A weight lifted from Arabella's shoulders.

"I believe, Arabella, that marriage to my cousin agrees with you."

"Indeed." She was not about to get into a discussion of

her marriage to Rowan with Jemma. "I bid you good day, Your Grace."

"Good day, Lady Malden." Her sister-in-law wiped another tear off her cheek, then began to polish the handle of her pistol in earnest.

ARABELLA SAT BACK AGAINST THE LEATHER SEAT OF HER carriage with a sigh of relief. The conversation with her sister-in-law had stirred up her emotions, and God knows her thoughts were in a constant state of upheaval. Life had been much simpler when it had been just she and Nick with occasional visits from Aunt Maisy or Miranda.

She rapped on the roof of the coach. "Bond Street."

Arabella was quite wealthy, something she'd never given much thought to. She had gobs of money and rarely spent any of it, finding such a pursuit to be frivolous. But not today. Aunt Maisy declared shopping to be a wonderful way to pass the time particularly when a problem picked at one's mind. Arabella had to agree.

The carriage rolled to a stop at the far corner of the street and Arabella stepped out, giving a nod to the young groom to follow at a discreet distance. Rowan would be furious to know she'd gone out and about with no escort, only a boy barely able to shave, to tote her packages. But just now, Arabella was in a rebellious mood. If she must be in love with her husband, so be it, but being a completely obedient wife held no appeal for Arabella. Besides, she'd had enough of Rowan's family for one day.

Strolling along, she purchased new gloves for both herself and Rowan, as well as a lovely coin purse for Aunt Maisy, to replace the one taken by Corbett. Next, she stopped at Thrumbadge's, the booksellers. Speaking directly to the clerk, she purchased a copy of *Experimental Researches in Electricity* by the scientist Michael Faraday. Rowan loved technology although his current passion was steam and railroads. Arabella was willing to bet he would find Faraday's work to be of interest. She had read several of Faraday's articles and found his research fascinating.

Humming to herself, she paid the clerk and handed her wrapped package to the waiting groom. A warm feeling centered over her heart. She enjoyed buying Rowan gifts and her husband was very effusive in his gratitude. After purchasing him some stationary he'd locked the parlor door and they'd spent an enjoyable afternoon. The divan would never be the same. Her cheeks flamed at the memory.

My God I've turned into one of those women who moons over her husband.

As Arabella rounded the corner towards her carriage, she was preoccupied with thoughts of Rowan. Primarily his naked backside which she'd admired that morning as he'd walked to his dressing room. Smiling to herself, she nearly ran into a pair of women coming from the opposite direction.

Lady Gwendolyn and another young lady.

Turned out in a froth of pink and lace, Lady Gwendolyn batted her round blue eyes at Arabella with dismay. The perfect rosebud of a mouth pursed in dislike as she put as much distance between herself and Arabella as possible. As if Arabella were a leper.

Arabella nodded politely to Lady Gwendolyn and her friend, moving past the pair as quickly as possible. Whispers and malicious giggles met her ears, but Arabella did not turn around. Instead, she hummed louder to drown out the sound. As she and the groom approached the coach, she directed the young man to secure the packages.

"Oh, dear." Rowan's gloves were missing from the stack. She was still carrying them when she'd entered Thrumbadge's and must have set the package down as she spoke to the clerk.

"I've left something at Thrumbadge's" She said over her shoulder as she headed back down the street. I'll return in a moment."

"Lady Malden." The groom reddened as he tried to balance the load of books. "Please wait and I'll escort you." He looked up at the driver for assistance.

"Don't be ridiculous. You'll be able to watch me from where you stand. Please stay with the carriage and secure my purchases." Her words held a note of command as she hurried down the street to the booksellers. Unfortunately, she hadn't left the package at Thrumbadge's for the clerk claimed he'd not seen it. After muttering a few choice words under her breath, Arabella decided perhaps the footman had dropped the gloves. As she made her way back the way she'd come Arabella kept her eyes down, hoping she'd spot the dropped package.

"Lady Malden, how lovely to see you out and about."

The words startled her momentarily and she halted, dread seeping over her chest. A shadow moved out of a narrow alley between Thrumbadge's and the tobacco shop. As the shadow moved closer, she could see the malicious sneer on his lips as he looked at her.

"Don't you want to stop and say hello to an old friend?" He held up a small package wrapped in brown paper. Rowan's gloves. "Are you looking for this?"

Barker.

She reached out and he stepped nimbly back into the alley holding the package out in a teasing manner.

"Give it to me." Arabella shot a nervous glance to her waiting carriage. Her footman was busy loading the packages and trading gossip with the driver.

Barker's lips drew back in approval as she stepped into the

narrow alley, probably enjoying her discomfort. He was nicely turned out. A new coat. Shiny, black expensive boots. Had his features not been so course, he would have blended in very well on Bond Street. Possibly even been mistaken as a gentleman.

"That's more like it." He allowed her to take the package from his hands.

She turned to go but his next sentence stopped her.

"I could shock everyone on Bond Street, all these fancy ladies out for a stroll, with the most interesting story. The tale of how Lady Arabella ended up at that inn. With Corbett."

Anger swelled within her. She'd given him her earrings. She was finally happy. How she longed for some sort of a weapon to dispatch Barker from her life. He would never stop demanding money from her she realized. Never stop threatening her new life. Must she pay for her sins forever? "I'll not give you another cent. I've confessed everything to my brother and husband," she lied. "If you approach me again, I'll make sure you spend the rest of your miserable days rotting in Newgate with nothing but the rats gnawing on your toes."

Barker's nostril's flared at her words. "You bitch."

"So I've been told." She turned swiftly on her heel and strode away, hoping Barker would take her threat to heart and bother her no more. If she heard from him again, she may have to take her cousin, Brendan, into her confidence and ask his assistance.

I should tell Rowan.

Arabella discarded the thought immediately not willing to risk her newfound happiness.

"My lady?" The groom, his Adams apple bobbing nervously, looked over her shoulder to where Barker had been standing. She suspected the lad was rather terrified of her. Rightly so.

"He found this," she held up the package. "And returned it to me. This is a gift for Lord Malden; have a care in the future with my purchases." Rather unkind of her but between seeing Jemma and Barker's unexpected appearance, Arabella wasn't feeling especially charitable. "I'd like to be taken home now. I'm rather tired."

The poor groom had paled considerably. "Yes, my lady."

Once in the carriage, Arabella clasped her hands together firmly and told herself all would be well despite the rising sense of dread she felt.

❧ 32 ❧

Rowan handed his coat to the waiting footman and took his wife's arm as they entered Lord and Lady Galspred's home. As they made their way towards the ballroom, Rowan snuck another appreciative look at Arabella. She was stunning tonight in a gown of deep ever-green trimmed with gold braid. The globes of her breasts rose and fell against the fabric, threatening to flee the tight confines of her bodice. He doubted she had ever worn anything quite so daring. Lust shot through him as he caught a whiff of bergamot in her hair. Even though he'd taken her against the wall of their dressing room just a short time ago, he wanted her again. There was bound to be a deserted alcove or small parlor in this house somewhere where they could disappear for a discreet moment.

He felt the movement of Arabella's hand against her skirts a sure sign of her agitation. He released her elbow to lace his fingers through hers. "Buck up Lady Malden, it's only a ball, and a rather small one at that." While Arabella had become comfortable acting as hostess in their own home for his business associates, Rowan still felt her hesitation at attending larger events, especially without her formerly severe persona at her disposal.

A low hiss came from her lips. An annoyed Arabella was much preferable to one who was nervous.

Rowan chuckled softly. "Be charming." He said sternly. "And pray try to smile. Just a bit. Not like a crocodile about to devour a child." Pulling her close, he pressed a light kiss to her earlobe to take the sting from his words.

He and Arabella had not been hiding from the *ton*, but neither had they sought out the company of society. With Miranda gone to Egypt and Lady Cupps-Foster visiting Bath, Arabella's lack of callers was noticeable. The only invitations she received were for charity teas or luncheons, most of which requested a donation from her. Rowan's own mother should have called on her new daughter-in-law, but in a breach of etiquette, she had failed to do so. The rest of the *ton*, sensing Lady Marsh's displeasure, followed suit.

Rowan would deal with his mother later. His tolerance of her behavior was at an end.

Arabella immediately lifted her chin as they approached their hosts, her armor of bored disdain already evident on her face. No one would *dare* cut a Dunbar of course, but Arabella still expected the dislike of society. He'd told her several times Lord Galspred and he were old friends. Lady Galspred, a lovely woman whom society adored, would take Arabella under her wing.

"Malden." Galspred clapped his shoulder.

Rowan smiled. "May I present my wife, Lady Malden."

Galspred's eyes roved discreetly over Arabella, paying a bit more attention than Rowan liked to the gentle swell of her breasts. "Lady Malden, a great pleasure to finally meet. No wonder we've seen little of Malden. I should not wish to leave you waiting at home either."

Arabella's lips tilted. "You are too kind, Lord Galspred."

"My wife, Lady Galspred." Galspred turned to a woman next to him wearing powdered blue and a great spray of peacock feathers in her hair. Winnie, as Galspred referred to his wife, was small and delicate, with light brown hair and enormous blue eyes.

Lady Galspred took Arabella's hand. "Welcome, and congratulations on your wedding, Lady Malden."

Winnie hadn't a mean or malicious bone in her body, but neither did she possess an ounce of intelligence. Arabella would swallow poor Lady Galspred in one bite if she became annoyed.

Arabella murmured a low greeting followed by a pleasant smile.

"Come, Lady Malden." Lady Galspred took her arm. "Let me introduce you to some of my other guests."

Arabella allowed herself to be led away, dark eyes narrowed as she spared Rowan a backward glance, promising retribution.

Behave. Rowan mouthed to her. He would sleep with one eye open tonight, though seeing Arabella in that dress, he doubted he would sleep much.

"You've allied yourself with a very powerful family, though I wouldn't have thought it necessary as your cousin is already wed to the Duke. Tell me, are the rumors true?" Galspred's eyebrows wiggled. "Witchcraft and black magic?"

"Not in the least." Rowan took a glass of wine from a passing servant, frowning slightly at his friend's remark. This was the type of stupid innuendo Arabella had been tolerating her whole life. The remark annoyed Rowan.

"I'd heard rumors of Lady Arabella, of course. I was given to understand she was unpleasant and generally dressed like an elderly matron. I'm glad to find my information to be untrue, at least on one part." He stroked his beard. "I'm sure the enormity of her dowry would more than make up for a shrewish nature."

"She isn't a shrew." Rowan's gaze followed Arabella as she floated along behind Lady Galspred. The sable mass of her hair was caught up in a loose knot at the back to allow several curls to tumble seductively about her shoulders. She was easily the most beautiful woman in the room and the most intelligent. Even though she was across the room from him, Rowan still felt tethered to her, her every movement drawing him along in her wake.

And she's mine.

Male eyes turned in appreciation as Arabella moved across the ballroom. If she was aware of the looks she garnered, she showed no sign. Several ladies, eyes widening at Arabella's appearance, snapped open their fans to confer behind them.

He caught the mulish tilt of Arabella's chin and knew she *had* noticed the women likely gossiping about her. Looking over his glass, Rowan caught a flash of ash blonde hair.

Lady Gwendolyn.

Seeing Rowan across the room she fluttered her fan and eyelashes to gain his attention.

He nodded politely but did not approach her. He assumed her parents to be somewhere in the ballroom and instantly regretted coming this evening. Lord White's badgering to forgive his debts had grown more insistent, especially now that Rowan had married Arabella.

Lady Galspred was making introductions to a small group clustered in one corner. A young man, tall and lean with red gold hair leaned over Lady Galspred's hand, looking in appreciation at Arabella, awaiting an introduction.

"Mr. Longstreet." Galspred caught Rowan's glance. "He's related to someone with a title but for the life of me, I can't remember just now. Winnie will know."

Longstreet was buzzing around Arabella like a very determined bee. He was smiling over her hand and must have said something amusing for his wife laughed.

Jealously slammed into Rowan. *He* was the only one to make his wife laugh. He had the sudden urge to tear young Longstreet limb from limb.

"Malden? Are you well?"

"Why do you ask?" Rowan bit out, his eyes never leaving the lecherous Longstreet. He grabbed another glass of wine from a passing servant.

"You appear a bit hostile just now towards young Longstreet. Don't worry; he's harmless. His heart belongs to some squire's daughter, I believe. Can't marry her as he's poor as a church mouse. Fancies himself an artist."

"Then why is he hovering about my wife?" Rowan spat out before he could think.

"Probably wishes to paint her, Malden." Galspred gave him an odd look and lowered his voice. "The story you and she were secretly courting and rode to Scotland on a wave of passion, changed your minds and decided to wed properly is ridiculous. You're meticulous in your plans. Once you've set on something you see it through, rarely altering your path. I doubt you would have done something so impetuous."

Rowan stayed silent, too busy watching Longstreet hovering about Arabella to be concerned with Galspred's assumptions.

"We were all shocked of course, that you didn't offer for Lady Gwendolyn. Lord White—"

"Was incorrect. I never had any intention of wedding his daughter."

Galspred nodded. "So it would seem. Most of London believes you wanted the alliance with Dunbar and your wife's enormous dowry. The betting book at White's is ten to one

Dunbar tripled her settlement to ensure your agreement. A veritable king's ransom."

"*Careful*, Galspred." Rowan sipped his wine as the anger slowly spooled inside of him. "Besides, you shouldn't be betting on anything." Galspred's lavish lifestyle had nearly driven him to bankruptcy. Rowan had lent his friend a substantial amount of money to keep the debt collectors from the door so Winnie could continue to throw frivolous events such as these.

A surprised look crossed Galspred's face at Rowan's anger. "I meant no disrespect." His eyes widened. "*Good Lord*. You *wanted* to marry her. You *were* courting her."

"Shut up, Galspred." Rowan walked away from whatever else his friend was unwise enough to say. What he'd just admitted to Galspred was something Rowan hadn't even admitted to himself.

He'd gone after Arabella. *Saved* her from Corbett. If anyone had a right to Arabella, *all* of Arabella, it was Rowan. Not that silly red-haired pup Longstreet who was currently fawning all over her.

Bloody Hell.

He *was* behaving like a jealous husband. Rowan clenched his fists and moved towards the gaming tables, determined to enjoy himself and not spend the evening dancing attendance on his wife.

Halfway across the ballroom, fingers lingered against his arm.

"Lord Malden. How lovely to see you."

Lady Gwendolyn stood before him, her blue eyes wide and fathomless. She was a pretty girl with her blonde hair and petite figure. But there was none of the overt sensuality his wife possessed. Nor intelligence. Nor darkness. She would make some gentleman a wonderful wife for she would be pleasing and demure and unlike Arabella in every way possible. He would never have married her no matter his mother's machinations.

Bowing he took her hand and greeted her. "Lady Gwendolyn, how nice to see you. I am glad to see you looking well." She had probably been told to expect an offer from him at any time and was likely embarrassed nothing had come to pass. He felt a rush of sympathy for the lovely Gwendolyn and pasted a polite smile on his face.

"Lady Malden looks lovely this evening." Her voice wavered slightly. "The dark green suits her. No wonder she's collected so many admirers."

Rowan raised a brow. "Has she?"

"Well, yes, Lord Malden. Your wife is quite sought after. I saw a man just the other day follow her down Bond Street just to speak to her."

Rowan's gaze flew to Arabella. Dear God, she was clapping her hands at something Longstreet said, which only made him angrier. He'd known she'd gone to Bond Street. Maybe she'd run into one of the acquaintances from one of the dinner parties they'd hosted. But if that were the case, why hadn't she mentioned it?

She's up to something.

He must have scowled because Lady Gwendolyn twittered. "Oh my, I've said something untoward." Her eyes welled with tears. "I do hope I didn't upset you."

"Not at all." Over the last month, Rowan thought he'd grown to know his wife well. He did not mistake what was between them, even though he wasn't sure what to call the emotion. But the truth was, he still didn't trust her.

"Excuse me." He bowed to Gwendolyn. "I've a seat waiting at the tables."

❦ 33 ❧

"Another." He waved his empty glass at a servant. It had been several hours since Rowan left the ball-room and he'd been playing cards for the better part of the evening. *Losing* at cards would be a better term. He was drinking too much and playing poorly, his mind more focused on Arabella than the game. Nursing his boiling jealousy and doubt with scotch now instead of wine, Rowan thought it was high time he claimed his wife.

He stood and strode swiftly into the ballroom, searching the thinning crowd for a sign of Arabella. Had she been looking for him? Or had Longstreet or some other gentlemen kept her too busy to miss him?

Longstreet, his copper hair shining under the lights, was spinning around the dance floor with a dark-haired woman. A woman who belonged to Rowan.

Arabella.

He moved towards the side of the room to observe his wife. Not surprisingly, Arabella didn't dance well at all. Lack of practice, he supposed, for she'd spent years either as a wall-

224

flower or not attending events where dancing took place at all.

Longstreet didn't seem to mind.

Arabella was no longer smiling up at the young man; she was too busy concentrating on the movement of her feet.

Longstreet winced as she stepped on his toe.

She leaned in to whisper to Longstreet, probably an apology, as the dance ended. The pair strolled towards the group of ladies she'd been introduced to earlier.

Lady Galspred welcomed her with a smile and took her arm.

Longstreet lingered for a few more minutes, speaking to Arabella and completely ignoring the pretty young girl who was making calf eyes at him. Rowan found nothing to recommend the young man. Gritting his teeth, Rowan made his way to his wife's side.

Rowan made a deep bow to the group. "I'm afraid Lady Malden and I must take our leave."

Arabella narrowed her eyes at him but said nothing. She began to introduce him to Longstreet, but Rowan only nodded at the man and took her elbow to lead her away. Arabella tugged at his grip on her arm and he tightened his fingers.

"Malden, cease your death grip on my elbow if you please."

"What did I tell you about calling me that?" His grip grew tighter, his anger hotter.

"I am glad for your arrival. I was about to pretend to have a fit of the vapors just to escape the inane banter but didn't know where to find you. If you sought to torture me this evening you have succeeded beyond your wildest imaginings." Arabella frowned. "Mr. Longstreet was the only bright spot and even my attention in him was beginning to wane."

Rowan looked up and down the line of coaches and spying

his own, led her over. "Home," he instructed his driver as her lifted Arabella inside. "It did not appear so."

She sat across from him and arranged her skirts, regarding him with a question in her dark eyes. "You're in an ill humor. And you smell of scotch." She leaned forward. "Are you foxed?"

ARABELLA SNIFFED THE AIR AGAIN. ROWAN *WAS* FOXED. AND angry. His large body fairly vibrated with ice cold rage as if she'd done something horrible. She hadn't. She'd allowed the twittering Lady Galspred, a woman with the personality of a boiled turnip, to introduce her to a larger group of uninteresting ladies. She'd laughed at the inane banter. Danced with Longstreet and engaged him in conversation gleaning bits of information from him.

All because she'd promised Rowan she would behave.

It was *exhausting* to be social and she wasn't at all sure she cared for it. Before her banishment to Wales, Arabella hadn't really attended many social functions. If she did, it was usually to benefit a charity or some other worthy cause she supported. Sometimes she'd attend a ball or some other event if Miranda begged her, but even so the two of them only stood against the wall and whispered about everyone in the room. The *ton* had deemed Miranda scandalous and Arabella...*sour*.

Rowan was looking out the window, his hands curled into fists. He deliberately ignored her, barely glancing in her direction as the carriage rolled towards their home.

The first trickles of anxiety ran down her spine.

"Rowan?"

His eyes were glacial upon her. "Stop talking."

Arabella fell back at the quiet growl, inching her body

out of his reach. She'd never been afraid of Rowan; in truth, he had never given her cause. Despite the amount of sarcasm and insults she had often thrown his way he'd never once hurt her. Had Barker found Rowan and told him the truth?

"I can explain," she whispered, prepared to beg his understanding.

He smiled at her. Not his usual charming twist of the lips which lit his handsome face, but a frosty grimace which filled her with apprehension. "We're home."

The carriage barely stopped before Rowan leapt down, grabbing her wrist to lead her into the house. He only stopped to fling his coat at the butler before grabbing her wrist again and pulling her up the stairs.

"Rowan stop. The servants—"

"Will assume nothing if they wish to remain employed."

He thundered up the steps, stopping just outside her bedroom door. He flung it open with a bang, dragging her behind him.

"Begone." He commanded her maid. "I'll see to my wife this evening."

Arabella struggled against his hold on her wrist.

Her maid, Edith, look askance at them both. She shot a worried look at Arabella then back to Rowan. "My lord—"

"Get. Out." Rowan's voice was little more than an icy whisper.

Edith scurried out, bobbing once and then shut the door behind her.

"Have you taken to terrifying the servants?" Arabella shook him off. "I am in no mood for your foul temper. Nor your drunken bumbling. I witnessed enough of such behavior with my father." Fear of discovery had made her waspish and she truly did not care for this hard, angry man who watched her as if he would pounce at any time.

"Take off your dress." The words snarled out. "Now." His eyes, cold and predatory, had darkened to a murky green.

"I am in no mood—"

"You should be more concerned about *my* mood," he murmured in a silky tone. "Much more concerned."

Arabella swallowed. "You've dismissed my maid." Her fear only served to heighten the ache beginning between her legs. She was aroused and if the tightness of Rowan's breeches were any indication, he was as well.

"How careless of me. I shall act as your maid." He shoved his knuckles down between her breasts, ripping her gown to the waist. Several buttons fell and rolled about her ankles as the fragile silk hung shredded, gaping open to her chemise.

"How dare you." Arabella was breathing hard, the ache between her legs becoming more insistent. She had never seen Rowan lose control.

"Take off the dress, Arabella, least I rip the remainder of it from your body." He stalked forward.

Arabella took a step back, grabbing the ends of her dress together.

"No corset tonight? Well you certainly don't need one." His gaze lingered on her slender waist. "I approve of the chemise, at least. Did you choose that for me or someone else?" He reached out to tease her nipple through the sheer black and gold silk covering her breasts.

Someone else? "I have no idea what you're talking about." Relief flooded her, but also confusion. This was not about Barker, although she couldn't for the life of her figure out exactly *what* this was about.

"Stop talking. Take. It. Off."

Not an ounce of warmth came from him. She'd only seen him look like this one other time, when he'd confronted Corbett. Hands shaking, she pulled the dress from her shoulders and it fell to the floor in a pool of green.

"Turn around." He pushed her so she lay over the small couch at the foot of her bed. "Put your hands on the bedpost"

Moisture seeped between her thighs, her body excited in spite of the situation she found herself in. She obeyed him, placing her hands on the cool mahogany of the bedpost. The position raised her buttocks, the chemise riding up her thighs. Within minutes his neckcloth wrapped around her hands, binding her to the bedpost. She tugged on her hands and found them secure.

Rough hands jerked and tugged at her underclothes until the fragile cotton was ripped from her, exposing the lower half of her body. He loomed behind her, the heat of his body searing the flesh of her buttocks. A palm grasped one cheek, squeezing the mound in his hands.

"I rather like you in this position." The flat of his hand slapped her.

She jerked at the sting of his palm. "Malden —"

Another swat greeted her words. "What did I tell you about calling me by that name?"

Before she could reply, his fingers pushed inside her, thrusting slowly in and out.

"Rowan." She moaned, pushing her hips back against his fingers, wanting more. Needing more.

He pulled back his hand. "Are you wet for *me,* Arabella? Or is it all your new admirers?"

"No...I..." She couldn't speak. His fingers thrust back inside her, flicking against her folds in a harsh caress. She was helpless. Exposed. She bit her lip to keep from begging.

He nipped at the skin of her buttocks. "Longstreet, perhaps?"

Rowan is jealous. Jealous of Longstreet. Her heart fluttered even as her body pleaded for release.

His other hand wrapped around her waist and stroked her from the front, gliding through her wet folds. Caressing and teasing Arabella until she nearly fainted from the pleasure of his touch. Aching with need, her hips writhed. A light stroke touched the swollen flesh and she whimpered. "How dare you accuse me of flirting with Longstreet."

His response was another light caress. Over and over he brought her to the edge, only to retreat until Arabella became mindless, her arousal painful.

"Turn your head. See what I see."

The full-length mirror next to her vanity reflected a woman, her hair falling around her shoulders in disarray, her only clothing a torn decadent chemise pushed up from her hips. Her buttocks rose high positioned on the arm of the couch. A beautifully handsome man stood behind the woman, fully clothed, his manner predatory. The man's hands roamed over the lower half of her body, his fingers disappearing from view as he caressed her. She had never seen anything so erotic.

Rowan's eyes held hers in the mirror. Possessiveness stamped every line of his face. He was bloody furious. *And jealous*.

"Rowan." Her voice hitched as he continued to torment her, and she pulled back against the silk binding her wrists. She was panting now, ready to beg and plead with him if only he would give her what her body so desperately needed. As her muscles began to clamp down, Rowan pulled back his fingers, refusing to allow her the release only he could give her.

"No." She whispered, ashamed to find her hips pushing back. "Damn you."

A warm hand traced the outline of her spine, then settled, splaying across the column of her neck. His fingers threaded through her hair, pulling her head back gently.

"To whom do you belong?" His breath, warm and scented

of scotch whispered in her ear, before his teeth grazed her neck.

"Myself," she murmured, still defiant though barely able of coherent thought. Anger rose in her that he, of all people, would assume her to have become a shameless flirt. It pained Arabella that he would think her like her mother. "You are not my master, you—"

Her words were cut off as his fingers continued to torment her. A small moan left her lips.

"I can do this all night, Bella. Who do you belong to?" His lips nipped at the curve of her neck again. "I will hear you say it."

Her eyes filled with frustrated tears. She was wild with need and tugged back on the cloth around her wrists.

"Tell me, Bella. I want to make sure you understand."

"You," she whispered. "I belong only to you, Rowan. You came for me."

Her reward was immediate. Fingers slid against her, lightly stroking before taking the nub between his fingers. He pinched slowly and deliberately, his head resting on her back.

Arabella cried out, as the orgasm crested through her body. She bucked, twisting as he held her in place. Spots appeared before her eyes and she became mindless as the pleasure coursed through her. She panted, trying to catch her breath as the tremors slowed and abated.

"Again," Rowan whispered.

Already oversensitive, the merest touch of his fingers against her sex brought another wave of release. Over and over, Rowan coaxed her body to peak and shatter until she sobbed his name into the cushions of the couch.

A low growl sounded behind her as he wrapped one hand around her neck and finally entered her with one hard thrust. He took her ferociously, without mercy, pounding into her trembling body with a need no less fierce than her own. He was claiming her, possessing her as no other man ever would.

"Mine. No one else, Arabella. If you seek to take a lover, think again." Another hard thrust. "Ours is not a marriage of convenience. Do I make myself clear?"

Her already tortured body could only accept and pull him in, inner muscles tightening like a vise around his length.

"Witch." He breathed against her neck. The base of his palm pushed against the top of her oversensitive sex.

Another blinding climax shook her, and Arabella could barely summon a whimper.

Rowan slammed into her once more and stopped.

His breath fanned against her neck, then he abruptly stepped back and pulled up his trousers. He reached over to untie her but left the length of his neck-cloth dangling from one of her wrists. The hard length of his arousal tented his formal trousers.

"Rowan," she whispered.

He said nothing, just picked her up by the waist, holding her against his side as if she were a bag of grain, and strode towards his room. She imagined this was how Vikings took their captive women.

He wasn't done with her.

Arabella smiled to herself. She didn't struggle.

❧ 34 ☙

As Rowan tossed Arabella on the bed taking in the scandalous chemise and tumble of dark hair, he realized two things simultaneously. One, he was behaving like a jealous barbarian. Two, he was in love with his wife.

At the moment, neither realization made him happy.

For years he'd watched Arabella at the few social events she'd attended. He would attempt to engage her in conversation only to receive a scathing remark or some other sarcastic observation for his efforts. It didn't matter. He'd been drawn to her like a moth to a flame, wanting her no matter how much disdain she showed him. He would see her across a room and imagine her hair released from the tight braids she wore, the dark mass whirling about the pale mounds of her breasts like a seductive hurricane.

Much as she looked now.

No matter how Lady Cupps-Foster pleaded with him, had Rowan not wished to rescue Arabella from Corbett, he would have sent for a Bow Street runner. His desire for her had never been simple lust.

I have always wanted her. I welcomed our forced betrothal.

As he looked down at the beautiful woman laying like some pagan feast on his bed, he wondered if he should ever admit such a thing to her, fearing to give Arabella the upper hand, especially since he wasn't certain of her feelings. Did she love him?

Lady Gwendolyn's carefully dropped comments about Arabella had aroused his already heightened suspicions. Intentionally. Perhaps he'd misjudged Gwendolyn; after all, hell hath no fury like a woman scorned. But Gwendolyn was right about one thing. Arabella *had* managed to garner male attention. Every man at Galspred's had watched her, probably shocked at the changed appearance of the formerly sour, austere Lady Arabella. He'd reacted badly, allowing too much scotch to mix with Gwendolyn's words until jealousy had clouded his vision.

She rolled over on the bed and crawled on all fours to the edge, sitting back on her heels. One delicate ripened berry of a nipple peeked out through a tear in her chemise winking with impudence. Arabella wasn't the least put out with his behavior. Her features were soft and full of longing.

For him.

Without a word, her fingers worked the buttons of his shirt, the palms moving across the planes of his chest. Her nails raked against his torso as the fabric fell away. Bergamot filled his nose, along with the smell of her arousal. A potent combination.

His breathing grew ragged, his cock hardening to the point of pain. He'd delayed his own release, not ready to end his possession of her so soon. Now he groaned as she leaned taller and pressed the heat of her mouth to the hollow of his throat. She bent, kissing down his chest until she reached the curve of his navel. Her hands took either side of his trousers, tugging at the material until Rowan pushed her hands away and shucked his pants.

A dark question lingered in her eyes as she grasped the length of him in her hand.

"God, yes," he choked out, sucking in his breath.

Arabella stroked back and forth, watching him. "Like this?" She stroked firmly as her other hand pushed the chemise down to bare her breasts. Boldly, she ran her finger over one taut nipple while she stroked him.

Rowan groaned. "Christ." His tongue flicked across the hardened peak.

She kissed the line of his jaw until she reached the edge of his ear. "Malden."

"Rowan—" His voice faltered against her breast as her thumb slid over the top of his cock and he straightened. "I rode all over fucking England for you."

"Not all over England." She bent and kissed his stomach. "You didn't even have to go all the way to Scotland. You found me in Lancashire." Her head bent lower.

Rowan groaned as her tongue ran the length of his arousal. This particular act was something he had not yet broached, but as usual, Arabella surprised him with her enthusiasm.

"Fair enough," he whispered.

Arabella had him fully in her mouth, her tongue twirling around his shaft. She sucked and licked, driving him slightly mad with her ministrations. When her hand lowered to further grasp him, he took ahold of her shoulders and gently pushed her away. He wouldn't last one more minute if she continued. "Lay down."

A small pout formed on her lips, but she complied.

His hand ran down over her breasts to the hollow between her legs. "I will *always* come for you, Bella. No matter where you would go, I would find you. You belong to me."

"Yes." A satisfied smile tilted one side of her mouth.

His mouth moved down the luscious curves of her body. He *loved* her. Adored her. Every dour inch. She was less unpleasant, and smiled more often than not, but Arabella still had her moments.

Placing a hand beneath one plump buttock he entered her slowly, savoring the soft warmth that encased him. She was saying his name, her hands trailing down his back to clasp his hips and pull him closer. He took with great care, his love for her marking every movement, worshiping every inch of her glorious body, as the truth of his heart was laid bare before her.

Cupping her face in his hands he watched Arabella as her release took her, the sound of his name on her lips propelling him over the edge. The force of his release left him bared before her and his heart nearly stopped. Overcome with emotion, he buried his face in the sweet-smelling mass of her hair, clutching her to him as if he would never let her go.

Arabella snuggled closer to the large male body, sinking deep into the warmth that was Rowan. Joy flooded through her, a foreign emotion and one fraught with pitfalls and worry. She had never thought to feel such love for another human being. She, Arabella Tremaine, the sour, unpleasant sister of the Duke of Dunbar who'd conspired to have her sister-in-law abducted was in love.

Truthfully, I'm still somewhat unpleasant, even when I try not to be, though Rowan doesn't seem put off. And I'm not at all sure I won't do something rotten in the future.

"Bella." Rowan's warm body moved, pinning her to the

mattress. He pressed his forehead to hers. "What are you thinking?"

The thought of telling Rowan she loved him was terrifying. She could barely admit the truth to herself let alone the object of her affection. Certainly, his jealousy towards Longstreet would indicate he cared somewhat. "I'm thinking that my conversation with Longstreet was quite innocent."

"I do not wish to discuss Longstreet." A dangerous note entered his words. "Did I hurt you? Before?"

She shook her head. "No, of course not. Will you take a mistress?"

Rowan looked down at her, his dark hair falling about the high cheekbones and the slashes of gold and green in his eyes. "Why in God's name would I take a mistress?"

Because I'm afraid you'll tire of me. You may feel I'm not worth the effort. Especially when you find out about Corbett.

"Most married gentlemen take a mistress at some point, do they not?" She bit her lip.

"You would be accepting? If I were to take a mistress?" he said quietly, staring at her intently.

She tried to pull away. "If that is what you wished, I would have very little choice in the matter, would I?" No, she wanted to scream at him. She *wouldn't* be fine with such an arrangement. Given her rather possessive nature, she was fairly certain any mistress of Rowan's would meet with an unfortunate carriage accident.

"I will not be taking a mistress." His voice lowered to a violent purr. "And rest assured, *you* will have no other man in your bed but *me*. I am not most husbands and you are not most wives. If you wanted a typical marriage within the *ton* you should have married someone else." He bit her shoulder and she gasped at the sudden flash of pain. "I thought I'd made myself clear, Lady Malden."

Arabella's body curved, molding against his. His words filled her with happiness. And hope.

"I see you require further instruction." He moved to hover over her. "You are very stubborn, Bella. I may need to reinforce this lesson repeatedly until you understand."

"I am a slow learner, Malden," she whispered.

❦ 35 ❦

"Come."

Rowan looked up to find Arabella in the doorway of his study looking fresh and seductive in a rather wispy morning gown of pale rose. Only the shadows under her eyes reminded him she'd not been allowed much sleep last night. Even now after leaving her snoring softly in his bed a few hours ago, he wanted her again.

A new level of intimacy had been forged between them last night and Rowan's feelings towards his wife had only been reinforced. What she thought, he wasn't certain. Arabella, unlike most women, did not wear her emotions on her sleeve. She was cagey, controlled and often difficult to decipher, though he read her better than most.

His fingers itched to rake through the heavy mass of her hair, which Edith, her maid, had artfully pulled back from her face and wound into a lose chignon at her neck. He preferred her hair down, especially as they were at home, but the messy bun she had taken to wearing was vastly preferable to the tight braids and austere hairstyle she'd worn before.

"Am I interrupting?" Without waiting for him to answer,

239

Arabella strode forward, obviously determined and not about to be deterred should he tell her she *was* bothering him.

Rowan set down the report from his solicitor on renovations to the Newsome textile mills, although he supposed a name change was in order.

Arabella's eyes narrowed as she glanced at the report. Her breasts swelled against the demure neckline of the dress and Rowan found himself thinking of her delicious nipples. It was very distracting.

As if sensing the direction of his thoughts, she gave him a sideways lusty glance, before seating herself on the couch. The fingers of one hand trailed against the leather, in a caress, watching him.

Bloody tease.

The length of him tightened painfully beneath the desk, remembering the feel of those long, delicate fingers touching him last night. He'd been fortunate to marry a deeply sensual woman whose sexual needs matched his own. After their current conversation, which he was certain had something to do with the renovations of the mills, Rowan had every intention of throwing up those wispy skirts and taking her atop his desk.

She lifted a brow and looked at him with more than a hint of her typical mulishness. "There was a reason I was speaking to Longstreet though you didn't give me an opportunity to tell you so." A slight pout graced her plump lips.

His mood souring at the mention of Longstreet, Rowan sat back in his chair. "Must we continue to bring him up?" A sigh escaped him. "Go on." He had several fantasies about Arabella that centered around her mouth. Her bottom lip especially was plump and full. The mouth of a courtesan.

"Rowan." She admonished him in a harsh tone though her eyes twinkled. "Pay attention."

"I am. I'm paying particular attention to your mouth."

A deep flush stained her cheeks, which surprised him, *especially* after last night. "Mr. Longstreet was completely harmless. He was flirting with me but not for the reasons you assume. More importantly, he is in love with the daughter of a country squire."

Rowan ceased his study of her mouth. "Why is Longstreet's love life of any importance to me? And I didn't care for his flirting."

"Yes. I surmised such from your behavior last night." Arabella gave him a pointed look. "You wish to build a rail line through Surrey, without such, the Newsome mills have no value to the textile empire you are building."

"Who said I was building a textile empire?" Arabella paid attention to every comment or dropped hint. He suspected she'd 'accidently' glanced at his papers when he was at his club. Honestly, Rowan would have given them to her to read had she asked.

Her lips twisted further. "I've seen your ledger."

Ah. He'd forgotten seducing her while working on his ledgers late last week. She'd run her finger over the columns while he fumbled under her skirts and found several mistakes.

Clever, brilliant girl.

"The most direct route," she continued, "will take you through the property of a local farmer. You could go around, of course, but the expense will be much higher and several miles of track wasted."

Rowan sat back, eyeing his wife with renewed respect. "How do you know that?"

"I can read a map. And I've traveled through the area on the way to visit my cousin, Spence. Longstreet is in love with Squire Tidwell's daughter, Marianne."

"Again, why is Longstreet's love life my concern?" His eyes fell to her breasts as he considered her words. "What color chemise are you wearing?"

"Red. The land is part of Marianne's dowry, which her husband will control once she is wed."

Rowan's mind examined the information, sliding the pieces around in his mind, marveling at the absolute brilliance of his wife.

"Come here," he growled.

Arabella stood and walked to him, her luscious plump mouth pursing in annoyance. "You aren't listening. I'm about to get to the best part."

"Don't let me stop you." He bent and lifted her skirts, finding the slit in her drawers. God she was wet. Slick. He couldn't wait to sink himself into her. "Why hasn't Tidwell accepted Longstreet's suit for his daughter?"

Arabella gasped and clutched the lapels of his coat while his fingers slid into her warmth. "He has no means." A small whimper left her mouth. "Tidwell wishes Longstreet to distinguish himself and prove he can provide for Marianne. Which I find rather petty, considering Tidwell is quite wealthy and could easily support them."

"Longstreet must prove himself. But," he pulled her close and brushed her lips with his, "how does this information help me? Do you wish me to purchase the man a commission in the army?" The young man didn't look the type who would enjoy the military.

"Yes," she panted, pushing against his hand. "But not the type of commission you are thinking of. He's a painter. An artist. He needs a large commission and a wealthy patron to prove to Tidwell he can support Marianne. If he can do so, Tidwell has promised his blessing." Her fingers slid through his hair. "Longstreet will be here within the hour to introduce himself and begin your portrait."

Rowan spun Arabella around and pressed her down atop his desk, not caring that his papers spilled to the floor. He tugged at his trousers until his cock sprang free and thrust into her, watching the way her eyelashes fluttered against the rise of her cheeks. She arched against him whispering, "Longstreet is dull as dishwater, but he will give you access to the property or sell it outright once he is wed."

"How long will such a thing take?" Rowan took Arabella's hands and held them over her head lacing their fingers together. She was far more intelligent than even he had given her credit for. Were she a man, Arabella would be a master of business and industry.

"Not long. Marianne grows impatient and I suspect Longstreet has already ruined her." The sentence ended on a whimper as his hips rocked against hers. She cried out, her body clasping his and Rowan groaned at the intensity.

Arabella gasped as the inkwell rolled off the desk to stain the expensive rug covering the floor. "The rug."

"It doesn't matter." As Rowan struggled to bring his breathing back to normal he bent his lips to hers, all the while thinking that of all the assets he possessed, Arabella was the most valuable.

❦ 36 ❦

An invitation had finally arrived. Actually, two. The first was to attend the nuptials of Mr. Longstreet and Miss Marianne Tidwell. Rowan had embraced his patronage of Mr. Longstreet but instead of having his own portrait painted, he had asked the young man to paint Arabella. She sent their regrets along with a lovely gift.

The second invitation was not nearly as welcome. She and Rowan had been invited to dine at the home of Rowan's parents, Lord and Lady Marsh. Arabella wished to send her regrets to Lady Marsh as well. She considered taking to her bed and pretending illness but decided against such subterfuge.

As the carriage rolled towards the Marsh home, Arabella hoped Lady Marsh wouldn't resort to poisoning her soup.

Arabella had not seen her new in-laws since the wedding, nor did Lady Marsh call on her. The last fact, in particular, caused much gossip within the *ton*. At a luncheon for Soldiers' Widows, of which Arabella was a large contributor, several ladies bantered about the words '*annulment*' and '*divorce*' when whispering of Arabella's marriage. Lady Gwendolyn had apparently made her opinion on the situation clear at a musicale the night before saying she would not 'look askance' at a man for his past mistakes.

Arabella, careful to keep a polite smile on her face while overhearing the attendees of the luncheon wager on the demise of her marriage, longed to point out an annulment would require a public declaration that Rowan could not perform his husbandly duties. She doubted Lord Marsh would wish his son's ability to father an heir questioned. The option of divorce was patently ridiculous. Such a thing required an act of Parliament, a tedious and lengthy process. And she would have to agree.

"You're frowning, my love." Rowan's lips curved into an amused smile. "No, wait, I feel certain it's actually a sneer." He leaned over to kiss her, stopping the sharp retort forming on her lips. The green and gold of his eyes glinted as he tucked a piece of hair behind her ear. "Thank you, Bella, for not coming down with a mysterious illness at the last moment."

"Would you have accepted such an excuse? If so, there is still time for me to leap from the carriage." The entire evening had her feeling rather cowardly. Especially after tolerating the speculation of her marriage at the charity luncheon earlier today.

He picked up her hand and pressed a kiss against her pulse. "I will reward your sacrifice most handsomely."

Arabella shivered in pleasure as his teeth grazed her skin. "The carriage ride is not long enough for such nonsense, my lord."

"Nonsense? I see I will have to change your mind once we return home." He pulled her close. "You are a stubborn woman and I find I must continue to explain the nature of our marriage to you."

She giggled at his teasing, wishing they were already home.

"Your laughter is a lovely sound. My favorite in all of the world." His finger traced the line of her jaw before he kissed her soundly again.

The words sent her heart fluttering. How did he do that? With the merest touch or casual word, Arabella's entire being glowed from the inside out.

Rowan exited the carriage and held out his hand, large and warm. His fingers wrapped around hers. "Courage, Bella."

ROWAN'S FIRST INCLINATION WAS TO DECLINE HIS MOTHER'S invitation to dine, but he didn't want to be estranged from his family no matter their poor behavior. He hoped the invitation meant a loosening of his parent's disapproval of Arabella.

As he entered the drawing room, Rowan's hopes were dashed.

Surprise showed on his mother's face as she caught sight of Arabella. They weren't expecting his wife to accompany him tonight, that much was obvious.

Lord Marsh discreetly murmured something to a waiting footman. Probably requesting an additional place be set.

"Darling." His mother greeted him with warmth, before turning. "Arabella." Her mouth tightened into a pucker. "How lovely to see you."

When the invitation to dinner had arrived, addressed only to him, Rowan assumed his mother was merely being peevish. She had a tendency to be a bit spiteful if she hadn't gotten her way. He looked down at her plump form, artfully encased in violet. Most people would find such a statement difficult to believe, but Rowan had been on the receiving end of his mother's manipulation for most of his life.

He squeezed Arabella's hand. His wife was far too intelligent to not comprehend his mother's surprise and he didn't wish her hurt by it.

Arabella dipped gracefully in greeting. "Thank you for the invitation." She emphasized the word as she gave his mother a look that would curdle cream.

Mother's cheeks pinked. "Of course."

Rowan gave his mother a pointed look. Arabella didn't need his protection but if necessary, she would have it.

His father came forward, clapping Rowan on the shoulder in greeting. He smiled politely at Arabella. "We are so happy to see you both." He gestured to the large, brocade sofa. "Sit."

"I expected Petra to join us," Rowan said as he settled himself on the couch and pulled Arabella down next to him.

Her hand gripped his tightly, though outwardly not a bit of discomfort showed. Her features remained serene.

"She'll be down in a moment. A ride in the park earlier wore her out, poor thing. She's so many suitors I fear she'll become exhausted before the Season ends." Mother fluttered her hands.

"Has she a favorite?" If Petra didn't, he was certain Mother did.

"Lord Percival Dunning," she snapped back without preamble. A sound at the door stopped her from saying more. "Ah, there she is."

Rowan doubted seriously his sister's choice of husband was Lord Dunning. Petra would never choose a man who was half a head shorter and a good twenty years older than herself.

Petra, dressed in some diaphanous gown covered in ribbons, fairly skipped into the drawing room. She was humming but stopped immediately upon seeing Arabella on the couch. Not known for her discretion, she gave both their parents an odd look before pasting a small, polite smile on her lips.

Rowan was beginning to wish both he and Arabella had begged off with a headache.

৩৯৫

NONE OF ROWAN'S FAMILY WOULD MAKE DECENT CARD players. Their dislike of Arabella was on full view and difficult to overlook.

Arabella took a deep breath and tried to maintain the calm, serene manner she was striving to project. Under no circumstances would she allow Lady Marsh or the insipid Petra to intimidate her. She'd assumed, wrongly it appeared, the dinner invitation was Lady Marsh's version of extending an olive branch to her. Arabella reminded herself Rowan's family had *every* reason to dislike her and very few to embrace her. She didn't give a fig for any of them, but she *did* care for Rowan. He loved his family, but she didn't need to. Arabella need only tolerate their presence in her life.

Resolved to tolerance, Arabella decided to engage Petra in conversation over dinner. Arabella knew the girl was enjoying the Season, likely her last if the hints Lady Marsh dropped were any indication.

At the announcement that dinner awaited them in the dining room, Lady Marsh stood and immediately attached herself to Rowan in a blatant display of motherly possession.

Arabella stood and walked slowly towards the drawing room, certain Lord Marsh would walk with Petra and leave her alone. Surprisingly, he did not. Instead he offered an arm to each of them.

"I hope you like duck, Arabella." His tone was polite, almost cordial. She was not fooled for an instant.

"Yes, my lord. It is one of my favorites." A small lie.

248

Honestly, she had no opinion on the duck nor anything Lord Marsh's cook might have prepared. Her discomfort of the evening had ruined her appetite.

He nodded, as if approving her choice and brought her to her seat, but before she could sit her husband appeared at her side. He settled her in the chair allowing his fingers to linger over her shoulder before brushing her collarbone. The simple action spoke volumes.

Lady Marsh's nostrils flared in irritation reminding Arabella of a bull about to charge. Were her mother-in-law to have a pistol Arabella doubted she'd survive the first course.

The conversation flowed around Arabella as a line of liveried footmen brought an array of silver platters to the table. What little food she ate was delicious. The dinner had been specially prepared for Rowan. Roasted duck served with potatoes in a wine cream sauce was one of his favorite dishes. He made a show of thanking his mother for remembering and Lady Marsh beamed from her end of the table.

She tried and failed to engage her mother-in-law in conversation but received only curt one-word answers, snorts of disbelief or careless waves of the lady's beringed hands. Her mother-in-law's behavior towards her was noticed by everyone at the table. Lord Marsh shot his wife several warning looks, which she did not heed.

Rowan's parents questioned him on a variety of subjects in which he gave pat answers. He laughed and entertained them with bits of gossip, as if he spent his days flitting about the *ton* enjoying all the delights society offered. He never mentioned the textile mills nor the rail line he would soon build. There was no discussion of steam, a topic Rowan debated with her endlessly. Her husband worked either with his solicitor or in his study, brow wrinkled in concentration. He employed two secretaries. Sometimes if he were completely immersed Rowan would lose all track of time and Arabella had to remind him to eat.

He caught her eye as he twirled the stem of his glass, a silent plea for understanding.

Rowan was rather skilled at projecting an amused, devil may care attitude which for some reason his parents admired. The only mention of anything serious was a brief conversation on the repairs needed to a roof at one of Lord Marsh's holdings which Rowan promised to see to.

The Dowager had mentioned Rowan once had an elder brother who perished many years ago. Arabella had broached the subject once, but her husband put her off. After seeing tonight's display, she figured out quickly that Rowan's elder brother had not only been the heir, but Lady Marsh's favorite. Arabella understood Rowan's behavior as she was well-versed in pretending to be someone she wasn't.

But I'm not any longer.

Turning her attention to Petra, Arabella was mildly successful in getting Rowan's sister to speak about the Season. While Petra mentioned several young gentlemen's names, Lord Percival Dunning was not one of them. Arabella almost felt sorry for Petra. Clearly Lady Marsh had already mapped out her daughter's future.

Gratefully she pushed back from the table as the meal ended. Rowan had spoken little to her as his parents managed to monopolize most of the conversation. Lady Marsh chattered throughout the meal deliberately excluding Arabella. She'd even brought up Lady Gwendolyn several times.

"Rowan, let us retire for a drink before joining the ladies." Lord Marsh clasped Rowan's arm and nodded.

Arabella watched with dismay as they retreated to enjoy a brandy and a cheroot. Determined to continue to project a serene manner, she followed Lady Marsh and Petra to the drawing room, comparing the situation to a felon being forced to the gallows. Or perhaps Marie Antoinette on her way to the guillotine. Nothing positive could come of her spending time with Rowan's mother and sister. The separation of the sexes after dinner was a ridiculous tradition and just now, Arabella wished fervently it didn't exist. The urge to stay with Rowan was so strong, she nearly turned on her heel to follow him.

Lady Marsh immediately perched on the divan, reaching out to grab her daughter's hand, forcing Petra to sit next to her, leaving Arabella to choose one of the uncomfortable looking chairs across from them.

"I believe I'll have a sherry." Lady Marsh intoned to a waiting servant, not bothering to offer a sherry to Arabella.

She wouldn't wish one anyway. Sherry was not something Arabella cared for. In the time she'd been married she had enjoyed wine with her husband and tried spirits, but nothing so missish as sherry. She wondered what Lady Marsh would do if she asked politely for a glass of scotch. While she didn't care for the aftereffects, Arabella thought becoming numb to the veiled insults of her mother-in-law held vast appeal.

As she settled herself in the chair, Arabella decided she'd had quite enough of Lady Marsh's behavior. Clasping her hands in her lap she surveyed both women with a bold stare.

Petra returned her gaze instead of looking away as she used to. It appeared Rowan's sister had gained additional backbone. Likely Jemma's influence.

"How did you enjoy Lady Galsped's fete the other night?"

It took Arabella a moment to realize Lady Marsh addressed her. She would not meet Arabella's eyes but glanced instead at a painting on the wall.

Perhaps she thinks I have the power to turn her to stone should she look directly at me.

"I found Lord and Lady Galsped to be excellent hosts," Arabella answered, "and the music to be delightful." She flushed slightly thinking of what had come *after* the evening at the Galspeds. The things Rowan had done to her. "I danced."

Lady Marsh pursed her lips and turned to her daughter. "Did you know, Petra, Lady Gwendolyn attended?" Her eyes slid to Arabella. "Are you acquainted with Lady Gwendolyn, Arabella?"

Arabella's hand twitched against her skirts. "We've been introduced." She kept her tone mild.

"Such a *dear* girl. Quite a catch." Lady Marsh sipped at her sherry and shrugged. "I appreciate the fact she is forgiving of mistakes and exhibits patience. One never knows when the wheels of fate will turn in another direction."

"Mother." Petra hissed under her breath in admonishment. "*Stop.*"

Good Lord, was Petra trying to protect Arabella? The very idea was absurd, but possibly she'd underestimated Perfectly Perfect Petra.

"Lord White is highly regarded in Parliament. He's told me there are ways to correct mistakes, especially those made under duress. Not common, of course, but possible."

This time Petra frowned in horror at her mother.

Lady Marsh insinuated, and none too subtly, Rowan could seek a divorce under the condition that he'd been forced to marry Arabella and, in the process, made clear her preference for the saintly Lady Gwendolyn.

At least now I know the source of the gossip I heard earlier today.

The idea Rowan could no longer be hers nearly caused a hitch in her breathing. Divorce or annulment were ludicrous, but as she looked at the determination stamped across Lady Marsh's face, Arabella decided the notion *wasn't* so ridiculous. Nor impossible. And the thought was quite painful. The hurt rapidly crystalized into something much more useful.

Anger.

"Lady Marsh." Arabella stood and walked over to her mother-in-law. She tilted her chin at just the right angle of arrogance and laced her words with ice. It was time to remind Lady Marsh exactly who she insulted. Arabella might be a baron's wife by marriage, but she *was* the daughter and sister of a duke, neatly outranking Lady Marsh.

"Please feel free to speak plainly. I am not considered unintelligent, and I grow tired of your innuendo." Arabella allowed a sneer to cross her lips. She would not be cowed by the likes of Lady Marsh.

LADY MARSH'S COMPLEXION TURNED TO BEET. "RUDE AND impolite." Her cheeks puffed. "*We* did not approve of this marriage, no matter how dear Nick is to us."

"You are *afraid* of my brother," Arabella snapped, ignoring Lady Marsh's sharp intake of breath. "That is not at all the same as affection. I assure you my brother knows the difference."

Lady Marsh sat down her sherry with force, spilling the dark liquid across the table. "*My* son is an honorable man," she sputtered. "And far more than *you* deserve. You'll *ruin* him. Keep him from his duty. *Destroy* every ounce of decency in him." The curls around her temples shook with rage. "I can only hope the *poison* that lies within you does not find its way into Rowan and destroy him." With a flurry of violet skirts, Lady Marsh stood, facing Arabella as if she was considering tackling her to the floor. "I will do everything in my power to release my son from your clutches." She turned her back on both Arabella and Petra, her angry footsteps echoing on the hardwood floors as she departed the room.

"Well," Arabella snapped, "I was going to ask her opinion on the redecoration of our new home, but I suppose I'll have to do without your mother's advice."

"I am sorry for her behavior." "Petra looked down at her hands for a moment, then continued in a controlled tone. "My mother is less than clear-headed at times and especially where Rowan is concerned. It's because..." Petra waved her hand as if pushing the words aside. "She behaves badly when thwarted, as you have just witnessed." Her gaze pierced Arabella. "Rowan never wished to marry Gwendolyn. But he *did* wish to marry you." She raised a golden brow. "Though I'm not at all sure *why*."

Arabella resisted the urge to swat Petra, not appreciating the back handed compliment given all she'd had to endure this evening. "Will you let Rowan know I've taken the carriage?"

"I do not think —"

"Then don't. *Think* that is. I feel certain your mother does enough thinking for you."

Petra's eyes grew hostile. "Not all of it. You are not the only one pretending to be demure, though I'm far better at it."

Arabella started towards the door. "I find myself feeling rather ill and must return home. Perhaps the duck was too rich. I bid you good evening, Lady Petra."

Petra nodded. "He will not be pleased."

Arabella didn't know if Petra meant Rowan would not be pleased with Lady Marsh's behavior or her own and decided it didn't matter.

"ANNULMENT IS A POSSIBILITY IF YOU CAN PROVE SHE married you under false pretenses or you were to admit you were unable to consummate the marriage." His father gave him a hopeful look.

Rowan tossed back the scotch, allowing the amber liquid

to sear down his throat. The conversation had taken an ugly turn. He was so incredibly furious, Rowan dared not speak.

"Divorce is more difficult," Lord Marsh continued. "White would use his influence but such a thing could take years. Parliament would approve the action much quicker were you to prove Arabella adulterous. Given her mother's reputation, inferring the apple doesn't fall far from the tree is an excellent strategy."

"She is not," Rowan flung the words at his father, "adulterous." Had he known his father's offer of an after-dinner drink was actually an attempt to browbeat him into discarding his wife, Rowan would have grabbed Arabella and fled the Marsh residence.

His father shot him a speculative look. "How can you possibly be certain? She's incredibly devious. White—"

"Has no idea what he's talking about. You assume I *wish* to rid myself of Arabella. I thought I made my decision perfectly clear to you when I told you I would wed her." His voice grew hard. "Imagine how His Grace would feel were you to ask me to discard his sister and in doing so destroy her reputation beyond repair. I thought you bore him some affection."

Lord Marsh had the grace to look embarrassed. The leather chair squeaked as he sat back, holding the glass of brandy he sipped to his chest.

"I do bear Nick a great deal of affection. He has been an excellent husband to your cousin and he treats your mother and I well." His entire form deflated. "The very idea is *rather* preposterous when said out loud. Your mother has done nothing but harangue me day and night about your marriage. She is convinced you did not marry Arabella of your own free will, that your honor led you to make a decision and in doing so, ruined your life."

"Honor had absolutely nothing to do with my decision.

Do you really think I could be forced to marry against my will?"

"No. I don't suppose you could be. Forgive me for suggesting such. I promised your mother I would...offer you *options*."

Rowan's parents knew the story of Corbett and Arabella's subsequent rescue, but he'd insisted they not contradict the story that Rowan and Arabella had been secretly courting. It hadn't mattered, the entire *ton* still assumed he'd been forced, coerced or threatened to marry Arabella, his only consolation her enormous dowry. He knew now he should never have told his family the truth, especially his mother. She honestly believed he would have married Gwendolyn if not for Arabella.

"Do you wish to know why Lord White pushes his daughter at Mother so forcefully?" Rowan watched his father over the top of his glass before taking a sip.

His father grew still, and his eyes slid away. "I'm not certain I do."

"Allow me to enlighten you. What little time your *dear* friend doesn't spend sowing dissention in our family he spends avoiding the duns beating at his door. White is rapidly bankrupting his estate. I have his markers, Father. All of them. Well over *ten thousand pounds* worth. White's taste in mistresses is rather expensive. Lady White's extravagance runs unfettered. He wishes me to marry his daughter so I will forgive his debts."

"Dear God." The color leeched from his father's face. "I'd no idea."

"Are you more surprised by the amount of your friend's debt or the fact I have so much capital at my disposal?"

"Neither, actually." Lord Marsh shut his eyes and pinched the bridge of his nose. "You have always been good with numbers and financial dealings. Clever. You do not tell me, and I do not ask, but I hear things. I know you are involved in trade. I suspect your ambitions stretch much farther than being a mere earl." A faint smile crossed his lips and his eyes opened. "Unlike me in every way possible. I should have known there was another issue at hand for I couldn't understand White's determination. He's all but convinced your mother the benefit of your marrying Gwendolyn far outweighs any scandal from the dissolution of your marriage."

Rowan opened his mouth to reply when the door to the study burst open to reveal his mother, the violet silk swirling about her body in her distress.

"Dear Lord, she is a *trial*. Rude. Snobbish. Lacking in any manners," Lady Marsh uttered, her hand placed dramatically against her forehead. "Please tell me, my lord," she addressed his father, "that you have talked some sense into our son. Thankfully Lady Gwendolyn is the most patient of creatures."

"I hope so Mother, for she will be waiting a lifetime." Rowan set his glass down thinking how ridiculous a creature his mother was, though he loved her dearly. "I hate to disappoint you but I've no intention of annulling my marriage. It has been consummated." He looked his mother dead in the eye. "Repeatedly."

His mother's hand flew to her throat as if to stifle a scream, whether from his vulgarity or the idea that even now, Arabella could be carrying her grandchild. Then she gave him a brilliant smile. "Lord White assures me that while a divorce would be difficult, neither is it impossible, especially if His Grace does not impede the process. We will wait a few more months and I will speak to Jemma—"

Rowan slammed his palm down on the table with such force both his parents jerked in alarm. "Let me be clear, Mother, lest you misunderstand. Never did I *ever*, consider marrying Lady Gwendolyn. I would not have agreed to a match under any circumstances. I find her unappealing in every sense and dislike her parents."

"You don't mean that." Her lower lip quivered.

"I do." If he didn't leave this instant, he would say something regrettable. "Now if you'll excuse me, I'll collect Arabella and take my leave."

"She's already left." His mother looked towards his father. "After threatening me."

"Threatening you?" He gave a snort of disbelief. "What did you say to her?" Rowan demanded. He had underestimated his mother and would not do so again. She'd deliberately provoked Arabella, he was certain.

"Nothing. She is simply ill-mannered and hostile." His mother swallowed. "Not right for you in any way."

Rowan moved until he loomed over his mother's diminutive form. "Mother, I *love* you. Truly. And because I do, I have tolerated for years your persistence to meddle in my life. I have tried to be a dutiful son." He raked a hand through his hair. "I now see that has been a mistake for it has allowed you to believe I am someone I am not." He took his mother's hand. "I am *not* James. I will *never* be James. You adored him. He was the heir and I the spare. I blame myself nearly every day for his death though there is little I could have done to stop such from happening. I have tried to please you."

His mother's eyes welled with tears. "Do not—" She took a breath.

"I tire of this game, Mother. *I* was the son who came home dirty. Whom you caught cursing at a village boy after I blackened his eye. I was disobedient. Stole the pies from Cook. I used to dice in the kitchens with the grooms. I have been ruthless in business sometimes ruining a gentleman to gain what I wish. I've kept mistresses. I am good at cards though I pretend I am poor at it because it's an advantage. I spend my days in *trade*."

She was shaking her head. "No. You are an honorable man. A gentleman. Perfect. Dutiful."

"No, Mother," he said as gently as he could. "That was James."

A great sob came from his mother and she pushed him away. "Why are you saying such things to me? Her influence over you has led you to lie to me in such a way." His father rose from his seat and wrapped his arms around her to mutter soothing words in her ear. "James would never speak to me of such unsavory things."

Rowan looked to his father and said more forcefully, "But I am *not* James. And I was not forced to marry Arabella, I *wanted* to marry her no matter the original circumstances. I will not discard her because you aren't pleased. Truthfully, I worry for your sanity that you continue to undermine my marriage. I do not wish us to be estranged, Mother. But if you continue down this path, I will not visit you again nor welcome you in *our* home."

"You don't mean that." His mother was sobbing now, clutching at his father.

"I do." Rowan bowed to both his parents. "The duck was excellent. I bid you good night."

37

Arabella paced across the floor of her room, her hand twitching against the dressing robe. She had come upstairs immediately upon her arrival and ordered a bath wishing to wash the sting of rejection from her skin. The scorching water did nothing to wash away Lady Marsh's dislike. It was almost as if the woman could see the stain of the Great Lie, as she had taken to calling her acceptance of Corbett's proposal. It was as if Rowan's mother could sniff the air around Arabella discerning she was a bad seed, capable of ruining his life just by association.

I need to tell Rowan. Admit to all of it.

A fierce pounding echoed in her chest, the first tremors of fear at the thought of admitting how truly awful she was. Or had been. Rowan would discard her. Force her to live elsewhere. Possibly even send her back to Wales. In every instance, the end result was the same. He would hate her for proving his mother had been right all along about Arabella.

The wet strands of her hair whipped around her body at the sound of footsteps moving in the bed chamber next door.

She heard Rowan dismiss his valet before the door between their rooms swung open. Would he be angry she had left?

"Contrary, mulish woman." He padded on bare feet to her, ripping off his neckcloth as he did so. He had already shed his coat and waistcoat.

"The duck did not agree with me. I was ill."

The fine lawn of his shirt joined the neckcloth on the floor. He kicked both away.

Arabella found she couldn't speak when faced with the utter masculine beauty of Rowan. She couldn't look away from his torso, watching in fascination the way his muscles rippled as he moved towards her. A low hum of desire vibrated across her body. Her fingers fluttered against her robe wanting to touch the golden kissed skin.

I love you, her heart whispered.

"I feel certain something else made you ill." A hand reached out and loosened the tie holding her robe together. The garment fell apart exposing a sheer white chemise trimmed in red ribbon. After the disastrous dinner and her abrupt departure from the Marsh home, she wished to placate him.

Hunger flared in his face at the sight of the chemise.

"I could not stay a moment longer, Rowan." Lifting her chin, she dared him to chastise her. "I tried."

His eyes were focused somewhere below her chin. "Jesus. Where did you get this one? I can see your nipples." A large hand cupped her breast. "I do not blame you, Bella." Lips brushed hers. "Petra stopped me in the foyer and told me what happened. I'm actually amazed at your self-control. My mother deserved far worse from you."

"But you deserve better. I'm ill-mannered and waspish in addition to being contrary. I am also quick to anger." Arabella gasped as his fingers caressed her through the sheer fabric.

Rowan's hand dropped from her breast to gently cup her cheek. His breath wafted across her skin. "I married you because I wanted you. I still do." He whispered against her lips. "Every minute of every hour. Your scathing tongue does nothing to dissuade me unless you aren't using it properly." An impish grin tilted his lips as he placed a tender kiss to her mouth. He pressed his forehead to hers.

A tear slid down Arabella's cheek. *I've become a milksop. Rowan has turned me into a sniveling woman.*

Still she held his words tight to her heart deciding she didn't care if she became a watering pot. Her fingers slid around his waist to pull him closer to her. With a deep sigh she relaxed against the hard planes of his chest.

They didn't speak for the longest time. Rowan's fingers traced tiny circles between her shoulder blades and every so often he would press his lips to her hair. She could hear the fire Edith stoked earlier crackling and the beat of Rowan's heart beneath her cheek. Arabella had never felt so safe. Secure.

Finally, a rumble came from his chest and he picked her up. "Time for bed, Lady Malden." He walked towards the door separating their rooms. "My beautiful Bella," he whispered in her ear before laying her atop the coverlet.

Rowan lay next to her, his hands exploring every line and curve of her body, stripping the chemise from her body in slow intervals. He worshipped her with his mouth and hands, wringing such intense pleasure from her, Arabella thought she would die from his ministrations. When finally she lay boneless and sated, only then did he finally join his body with hers to seek his own release.

Arabella moaned his name, as she wrapped her body around his. Here was her safe harbor. The place she would always long to be. A member of the very family she'd sworn to hate and punish had now become the very center of her existence.

I will tell him everything. Corbett. The Great Lie. Barker.

The words that terrified her finally spilled from her lips as he thrust inside her.

"I love you."

❧ 38 ❧

"**M**y lady, come see what has arrived for you."

Arabella looked up from the letter she was writing. Aunt Maisy had left nearly a fortnight ago, returning to the moors with Brendan at his insistence. Putting the letter aside, she looked at her maid in amusement.

Edith was leaping from foot to foot in excitement. "Packages have arrived for you, my lady. From Madame Moliere's. The famous modiste." The maid's face shone with rapture.

"I'm well aware of who Madame Moliere is." The modiste had created Arabella's wedding trousseau under the direction of Aunt Maisy. "I'm sure she's sent the riding habit I ordered some time ago. There's no need to become so ridiculously giddy."

"Begging your pardon, my lady, but I don't think it's your riding habit. There's too many packages and red ribbon."

Arabella put the pen into the inkwell and stretched her neck before turning. She hadn't much sleep last night as Rowan had been insatiable. An image of Rowan the previous evening, sitting naked in a chair before the fire, sipping at his scotch while he watched her bathe slipped into her mind and heat flew up Arabella's cheeks. That she could still blush at what transpired after her bath was rather surprising.

When sleep finally did come last night, it was not peaceful. Barker's repulsive form invaded her dreams of late, probably owing to her resolution to confess everything to Rowan. It had been several weeks since the evening they'd dined at the home of his parents, but still, Arabella couldn't bring herself to tell him. The time had not seemed right and her bubble of happiness felt too fragile.

She must stop delaying the inevitable.

While Barker appeared in her dreams, he did not do so while she was awake. The more time that went by without seeing him, the more assurance Arabella felt he was gone from her life forever.

"My lady?" Edith was still hopping about like a deranged rabbit. "Shall I have them bring the boxes in?"

At the nod from Arabella, Edith flew from the room, only to return with two burly footmen each carrying a stack of boxes wrapped in red ribbon. When the footmen had shut the door, she turned to Edith.

I haven't ordered anything else." Mystified at the sheer amount of boxes now littering her private parlor, Arabella shook her head. "There must be a mistake."

"I don't think so, my lady." The maid took the largest box and placed it on Arabella's lap. It was wound with bright red satin ribbon and smelled of bergamot, her favorite scent. "This fell from the ribbon." Her maid held out a small embossed card.

Opening the envelope, Arabella immediately recognized Rowan's bold scrawl.

'You should always wear red, my love.'

Warmth burst over her chest inciting her heart to beat with joy at her husband's regard.

"It's from your husband, my lady?" Edith was peeking over her shoulder and Arabella hastily tucked the card up her sleeve.

"Yes." Carefully she unfurled the ribbon, wishing to draw out the pleasure as long as possible. No one had ever gifted her in such a lavish way. She supposed her dour manner hadn't allowed anyone the opportunity. Another shaft of sunlight spilled through her entire being at the thought of Rowan invading Madame Moliere's on her behalf.

Lifting the lid of the box she was greeted by a swath of tissue paper. Pushing the paper aside, Arabella sat back in wonderment.

How beautiful.

Inside the mound of tissue sat a stunning gown of crimson velvet.

"Oh, my lady," Edith whispered in awe. "'Tis the most beautiful gown I've ever seen."

Tiny bits of gold dripped from the bodice to the folds of the skirt where the delicate strands formed an intricate pattern. The hidden pattern would shimmer and flash as the wearer walked, and fairly sparkle when she danced. Gold braid decorated the hem and sleeves. The neckline was rather scandalous and would hug her breasts and push the tops into view. The color of the gown was the perfect foil for Arabella's sable hair and dark eyes. Rubbing her hands across the velvet, Arabella mused the gown must have cost Rowan a small fortune.

"Oh, Rowan," she whispered under her breath. "Maybe you love me just a little."

"My lady, did you say something?" Edith held out another box to her.

Arabella shook her head. "I fear my husband is rather extravagant."

The box she opened next contained gloves to match the

dress. But the third box caused Arabella to wave the girl away. "Take the dress upstairs immediately so that it doesn't wrinkle."

Edith took up the box containing the dress. "I'll be right back, my lady."

Once the maid retreated, shutting the door behind her, Arabella pushed aside the tissue. A crimson chemise of pure silk lay in the box. Gold thread shot through the silk, mimicking the design of the gown. The very sight of the chemise conjured up a host of erotic thoughts in Arabella. She pressed her thighs together to staunch the delicious ache. Rowan would not be home for several hours.

What a wicked man I've married.

The remainder of the undergarments were equally scandalous. Another box held sheer black stockings and a matching garter. Just as the door opened to Edith, Arabella picked up the final box. Smaller than the rest, Madame Moliere's initials did not grace the top.

Tugging at the ribbon, she opened the box to find a small jewelry case and another note.

'*I will always come for you.*'

Reaching inside, her fingers curled around a thin gold chain from which a blood red ruby dangled. The teardrop shaped stone was surrounded by gold filigree and fairly glowed as it caught the sunlight streaming through the parlor window.

"Shall I have the rest of the boxes brought to your rooms, my lady?" Edith was smiling at her, nearly as thrilled as Arabella with the array of gifts littering the room.

"Yes." She felt tears pricking the backs of her eyes.

He has turned me into a watering pot.

"I'll carry this up myself." She closed the small box and held it to her heart, fairly skipping up the stairs to her room.

❧ 39 ❧

rabella's earlier joy slowly turned to dread as the day wore on and Rowan failed to appear, nor did he send a note. As the hour grew later, she declined the offer of a tray in her room, certain Rowan would arrive at any moment.

He did not.

She ate alone in the large dining room, ignoring the curious looks of the servants. Barely tasting her food, she nibbled at the roasted duck which she'd asked Cook to prepare especially for her husband. When she could not drag out the meal any longer, Arabella made her way upstairs, the taste of the duck lingering bitterly in her mouth. Her stomach knotted and rolled as if she were aboard a ship during a storm. As the hour grew later, her anxiety increased.

Unable to sleep, she finally decided to go down to Rowan's study and work on a stack of ledgers sitting on his desk. Reviewing the columns of numbers had a calming effect and she hoped after an hour or so she would be able to sleep. Or that her husband would return home.

Settling herself in Rowan's chair, she breathed in the scent of tobacco and leather, two things she always associated with him. His delay in returning home, she told herself, was probably due to a late meeting. He'd merely forgotten to send a note to her. Opening the top ledger which had to do with cotton shipments, Arabella went to work, making careful notes along the margin for Rowan to review later.

ARABELLA JERKED AWAKE AS A THUD SOUNDED OUTSIDE THE study door. She blinked the sleep from her eyes, wincing at the stiffness of her neck. She'd spent the night asleep at Rowan's desk, the ledger still on her lap. Gray light filtered through the curtains heralding the dawn. Birds began to chirp in the gardens as morning slowly stole over London. Her candle was barely more than a stub and the fire had gone out.

Another thud sounded and the study door was flung open.

"I should have known I'd find you here. Fixing my books, are you?" Rowan strode into the study, followed by the smell of stale cigar smoke and alcohol. His clothes were rumpled and there was a tear in the shoulder of his coat. The ends of his hair stuck up at odd angles and his eyes were shadowed and bloodshot. He shut the doors to the study behind him with an exaggerated flourish.

He smells as if he's spent the night in a brothel.

Arabella clenched her fists. She was angry and worried and now jealously seeped into her thoughts. "Good morning, my lord." The words came out in a hiss even though she tried to contain her temper.

"Good Morning, my dear, *deceitful* wife." Loathing and disgust dripped from every word, his features frozen into an icy mask.

Arabella stayed wisely behind the desk as the thing which she'd most feared finally took shape. She grabbed the bits of her earlier anger around her using it as a shield against her rising panic. "Where have you been? You smell as if you've spent the night—"

"At a brothel? Would that I had but you've ruined such a thing for me. Have I been drinking? Most assuredly. Unfortunately, no amount of alcohol can wash away the truth. But then, you probably wouldn't understand. Truth being a *foreign* concept to you." An ugly sound erupted from him. "You are *unbelievable*."

A terrible swirling black mass threatened to drown her. "How dare you speak to me in such a way." She tried to stand, and her legs failed her. She was going to be violently ill.

He knows. He knows. Somehow, he knows.

Rowan approached the desk, his legs unsteady. The smell of alcohol grew stronger. Gazing coldly at her, he settled onto the couch. "Lying bitch."

The words slapped at her, shattering her into a million small pieces. Her palms flattened across the desk. "Rowan—"

"You were *never* kidnapped." His voice grew low and dark. *Never taken.*" He laughed, a horrible choked sound. "*Never* in danger. I merely interrupted a lover's quarrel, didn't I? How convenient I showed up at just the right time. I wonder if you would have stabbed him anyway?"

Arabella shook her head. "No. Please let me explain."

"Don't you want to know how I found out?" Reaching into his pocket he threw something small across the space that separated them, hitting her smack in the chest. A sapphire earring. *Her* sapphire earring.

"I suppose I should be glad you didn't give him your wedding ring, though I believe sapphires may be worth slightly more than a ruby. I didn't believe him at first until I visited the pawn shop. You actually *agreed* to marry Corbett." He stood and slunk to the sidebar and poured himself a full glass of scotch.

"How did you find out?" she whispered. But she knew of course. Barker.

"Apparently you missed a payment, *my love*."

The sarcasm and hatred in his tone sliced into her like a blade. She was trembling and quickly she pulled her hands into her lap, clasping them firmly. "I was so very angry and Corbett...*manipulated* me. I know that is not an excuse but—"

"Barker came to me requesting money or he'd turn over his suspicions about you to Constable McLauren. I heard the entire sordid tale. Apparently, Corbett confided in Barker. A marriage of *revenge*. Punish all of us in one fell swoop. No matter it would have destroyed your brother. Jemma. Your aunt. Good God, you *are* horrible."

"I am not that girl anymore." Her voice cracked with emotion. "You know I'm not." Arabella felt as if she were drowning in her own darkness and regret.

"Well, Barker," he poured himself another glass, "is convinced you meant to kill Corbett. I'm inclined to believe him. I find murder to be completely within your character. You also enjoy deceit, kidnapping, and blackmail. It's a wonder you haven't ended up in Newgate. No wonder Nick sent you to Wales."

Arabella shook her head. "Corbett fell out the window."

Rowan snorted. "Yes, conveniently for you. I'm sure you would have pushed him if he hadn't slipped. What a bloody relief his death must have been. And there I was, riding in like some fucking hero to save you from yourself. You must have cheered your good luck imagining all the ways you could use me. I'm sure you didn't think your brother would force us to marry. No wonder you kept trying to run off to the Continent."

"No." She shook her head violently. "I lied about Corbett but nothing else. *Nothing* else." Despite her best efforts, Rowan had found out. And he *hated* her, just as she knew he would. The pain and betrayal etched on his face was like a knife to her heart.

"I am no longer willing to play your fool." His lip curled in revulsion. "*Christ*, I defended you to my family."

"I did a horrible, *terrible* thing in accepting his proposal. But I could not have gone through with marrying him. Things were different then. *I* was different then. Please, listen to me." She was cold all over, her mistakes of the past taking away from her the one thing she wanted.

"You'll never change." He snorted. "Always scheming. Lying. *Betraying.* I wish to God I'd never touched you."

Her heart cracked open as her very soul bled out. A tear ran down her cheek and she wiped it away. "I love you."

"Love?" he snarled at her. "*This* isn't love, Arabella. I just like fucking you."

She fell back against the chair. The vulgarity of his words shading every intimacy they'd shared, tearing the happiness from her. Had it meant nothing to him? Shutting her eyes against the blatant disgust in his face, she forced herself to stand.

"Fine," she hissed, summoning all of the bitterness that rapidly filled the hollowness left by his impending loss. "Then divorce me as your mother wishes. Get your act of parliament and marry your precious Lady Gwendolyn. I'll not fight you. Better yet, why not sue for an annulment? I'll be glad to testify that you are *unable* to satisfy me."

His knuckles turned white as his grasp tightened on the glass in his hand. For a moment she feared he would throw the crystal at her head. His face grew hard and unrelenting, lips curling into a grimace as if speaking to her caused him physical pain.

"If that's what it takes to be *rid* of you, so be it. And now," he grabbed the entire decanter off the sideboard and waved her toward the door, "get the fuck out of my study."

Arabella raised her chin, refusing to allow him to see the devastation of his words. She stood and moved towards the study door. She had become unmoored, set adrift like a rat-infested ship, cast out to sea by the one person she wasn't sure she could live without.

"Don't forget to shut the door."

Spots swam before her eyes as she focused on keeping her breathing even, afraid she might faint as she made her way upstairs. Reaching the safety of her chamber she marched directly to the door separating her rooms from Rowan's and locked it. With a small cry, Arabella fell to her knees, pushing her forehead to the rug, welcoming the chafing of the fibers against her skin. Nothing would ever wash away the stain of the person she used to be. She would never escape that Arabella.

Rowan's disgust was deserved. She *had* lied. But his affection had so quickly turned to hatred, she wondered if he'd ever cared for her at all.

Annulment or divorce, what did it matter? Whichever he chose, her reputation would be in shreds, her future assured. London would offer her no refuge. The proceedings may well take years, but once free, she could travel to the Continent and never return. Alone. Adrift for the remainder of her life. Curling into a ball on the floor, Arabella wondered if it were truly possible to die from a broken heart.

I will not die from a broken heart. My punishment is far worse. I must live with one.

❧ 40 ❧

"**L**ord Malden?"

Rowan looked up from his dinner, a bowl of something rather mushy and unappetizing he assumed to be stew. He wasn't sure. The Fox Hole, a tiny tavern on the outskirts of Dorking in Surrey was not known for fine cuisine. He did not choose the tavern for the quality of the food but rather the proximity to the patch of land formerly belonging to Squire Tidwell.

"Hello Hind. I'd wondered where you'd gotten off to." Reginald Hind was truly the architect of the rail line project and Rowan's business partner. Son of an Oxford professor, Hind possessed a rather unique education. He was an architect by trade but had vast knowledge of engineering. Not wealthy in the least, he'd found Rowan quite by accident, drawn together by their mutual love of the advances in industry and transportation.

"I've found our surveyor, Johnson. He got lost coming through the woods," Mr. Hind said as he lowered himself into the seat across the table. Raising his hand, he summoned the barmaid over and ordered an ale.

"Our surveyor lost his way? Doesn't bode well for our project, does it?" Mr. Johnson, the surveyor, was two days late in joining Hind in Dorking. Rowan had wondered if the man would indeed arrive. Hind never had any doubts.

"Well, my lord," Hind stroked the ends of the bushy mustache hanging from the top of his lip, "the woods are especially thick this time of year. Easy to get turned around when you don't know your way. I've put him up in a boarding house run by a widow." Hind wiggled his eyebrows. "A very merry widow."

Rowan sat back and took a draught of his ale. He couldn't care less about the sexual escapades of Hind, of which there were many. Rowan found he didn't care for many things as of late. Food held no taste. Drinking himself to oblivion had only worked for a short time. He even visited his former mistress hoping to stir some sort of feeling within him but experienced not a hint of arousal.

I miss Arabella.

Longing for her pierced him as Hind drawled on about the widow who ran the boarding house. Rowan worked from early in the morning until late in the evenings, sometimes falling asleep in the small parlor of the house in Dorking he rented. He'd fled here after his confrontation with Arabella. Ironically the sale of Longstreet's land to him came only minutes before Barker approached Rowan at his solicitor's office. Barker, smug and full of dislike for Arabella, made a mistake. Hopefully he was contemplating the error of his ways while sitting in prison.

"Malden? Are you listening to me?" Hind clapped his hands as a bowl of the stew was placed before him.

"You are bound for disappointment." Rowan nodded to the bowl. "I've yet to determine whether it's lamb or beef."

Hind shrugged and put a spoonful in his mouth. "I have things well in hand here, should you wish to return to

London. There's no need for you to stay. We've had every-thing in place for months only waiting on the land. I'm still not sure how you managed such a thing." He frowned as he chewed. "Good God, you're right."

Rowan had been avoiding London. At first, he'd been so angry with Arabella his only thought had been to get as far away from her as possible. He'd left her a terse note only saying he'd gone away on business. He hadn't trusted himself to speak to her. As the weeks slid by and he attempted to bury himself in the rail project and renovating the mills, Rowan was able to view things with more objectivity. He thought back to her reasons for involving herself with Corbett in the first place, the anger towards her brother and Jemma. It was easy to see how in a fit of pique she would agree to such a thing as marriage. Arabella wished to lash out, hurting those around her as she'd been hurt.

Knowing her as he did, Rowan could see all of it so clearly. Arabella nearly paid for her bitterness with a marriage to Corbett. Even knowing her motivation, the sense of betrayal he felt would not dissipate. She'd lied to him and he had yet to forgive her.

"Perhaps after the survey is completed," Rowan said.

Petra had implored Rowan to return more than once. His mother, in particular, wished him home, her joy blatant at the estrangement between he and Arabella, though she didn't know the cause. Mother was hosting a ball in Petra's honor to celebrate his sister's birthday and what she hoped would be an offer from Lord Dunning.

After finishing their stew, he and Hind walked back to the small cottage Rowan rented to share a drink and further discuss the clearing of Tidwell's land. He lit a cheroot, blowing smoke into the late afternoon air and debated his return to London.

"Looks like London has found you, Malden." Hind

nodded towards the large, expensive coach and matched horses sitting outside the cottage. Four large footmen in livery and the driver stood around the vehicle.

Damn. Rowan didn't need to see the coat of arms on the door to know who was probably sitting in the small parlor sipping his scotch.

Hind's eyes widened as the crest came into view. "I believe I'll pass on your offer of the drink my lord, as it appears you've a visitor."

"I'll see you tomorrow as we start the survey." Rowan shook his hand and watched Hind walk off in the direction of the boarding house. Nodding to the footmen and driver he entered the cottage, irritated at the invasion of Surrey by the Duke of Dunbar.

His Grace sat in the parlor, his overlarge form massive in the tiny space. A chair groaned beneath his big frame. A glass of scotch dangled from one hand as if he'd nothing better to do than come to Surrey to interrogate Rowan.

"Your Grace." Rowan greeted his brother-in-law. He had no desire to discuss Arabella with Nick.

His Grace raised a brow at his tone. "I helped myself. I didn't think you'd mind. The chair, however, is not happy with my presence. It's quite ancient. I'm sure the legs are about to give at any time."

"I didn't realize you were coming to visit, Your Grace. I can give you a tour of the land if you wish, but the survey has not been completed."

"Nick." He frowned. "You are a member of my family and I've given you leave to use my Christian name several times. I may be a duke but I'm feeling rather 'your graced' to death as of late." His mismatched eyes held a speculative look. "And I'm not here to view our investment, as well you know."

"Here to meddle then?" The Duke of Dunbar was known

to arrange people and events to his satisfaction. The habit was incredibly annoying.

"I do not meddle." He sounded offended.

A small bark of laughter left Rowan. "Jemma compares you to an elderly matron of the *ton* with your machinations."

A pained look crossed the duke's face. "She has confessed everything to me, Malden. I wish she had done so at the first. I underestimated the extent of my sister's anger which was more directed at me than anyone. Bella is very complicated, which of course, doesn't excuse her behavior."

"No, it does not," Rowan said in a quiet voice. "She should have told *me*."

"Given your dislike of her at the time, she felt certain you would leave her to Corbett." A growl came from Nick.

"I never disliked her." Rowan wasn't afraid of the man before him, even though nearly everyone else in London was. "I've always wanted her." He gave the duke a hard look. "Does that surprise you? But she should have told me instead of allowing herself to be blackmailed and leaving me to feel the fool."

"Is that why you left? Because you feel foolish?"

"I needed a moment to think. I cannot be objective in London."

"What will you do?" The chair creaked loudly as Nick tried to get more comfortable.

Rowan walked to the sideboard and poured a large scotch. He took a sip before replying. "I plan to renovate the mills while the rail is being laid." He'd been pondering that very thing. What *would* he do about Arabella?

"Am I sending her back to Wales or to the Continent? If she is to go to the Continent the preference is Italy, though I'm not sure why. She's never particularly cared for the Italians, but she has expressed a desire to paint."

"Neither." Rowan's heart thudded dully. "And she lacks the

patience to study painting." He didn't care for the thought of Arabella being so far from him. Hell, Surrey was too far.

"Will you seek a divorce? Or an annulment? You can claim she married you under false pretenses." The larger man shifted again, and his lips grew tight. "I will not stand in your way nor claim displeasure. I suppose I could send her to Scotland. A convent stands on my holdings there."

Rowan snorted. "She'd be terrorizing the nuns within a week. Even I would not punish innocents in such a way. I appreciate your counsel however unnecessary it is." He'd never truly considered a more permanent solution to his estrangement from Arabella. The thought of divorcing or annulling his marriage in spite of the ugly words he'd hurled at her, was inconceivable. He'd come to that conclusion a week after he left London.

"My sister is an awful person."

"She isn't," Rowan murmured. "Or at the very least, she isn't anymore. And she's *my* wife. If anyone knows what Arabella is, it is me. I will decide her fate, not you, Your Grace."

If Nick was shocked by his words, he gave no indication. He nodded and stood, an oddly sympathetic look on his face. "I'll see myself out, Rowan."

"Safe journey back to London, Nick. Give my love to Jemma." He said the last over his shoulder at he moved back to the sideboard to refill his glass. He watched through the parlor window, as the Duke of Dunbar's coach pulled away. The argument between his head and his heart battled inside him.

He would leave for London the day after tomorrow.

❧ 41 ❧

"**D**ear God, I never pictured you moping about looking as if you would perish from despair."

Arabella turned from her contemplation of the rain-soaked gardens to face her sister-in-law, Her Grace, the Duchess of Dunbar. Unfortunately, she was in no mood for sparring although it held a certain appeal. Now that she felt certain Rowan meant to discard her, Arabella wasn't disposed to being polite to any member of his family.

"Hello *Jem*." She used her brother's nickname for his wife knowing how it angered her sister-in-law. "Come to gloat?"

Jemma cocked a brow and looked for a spot in which to seat her ever-increasing form. Her eyes alit on the couch. "Partially."

"How did you get in without being announced?" Arabella wished to be left alone to contemplate her fate. No word from Rowan in weeks, though she had a vague idea he was in Surrey somewhere. It wasn't unusual for married couples to lead separate lives, but their estrangement so soon after the wedding and before an heir was produced caused a significant amount of gossip. Lady Marsh must be skipping around making calls on every acquaintance she had in London to cheerfully spread the news.

"I'm a duchess. No one denies me entry." Jemma patted her stomach in the most annoying way. "I've come to speak to you about the celebration of Petra's birthday."

"Pregnancy has addled you." Arabella gave a short laugh. "I've no intention of attending anything in honor of Petra. Why would I? Aren't you afraid Precious Perfect Petra will be scandalized by my presence? Certainly, your aunt will not wish me there."

"Can you ring for tea? I'm starving." Jemma gave the small mound another pat. "Hopefully your cook has made something with chocolate." She gave Arabella a hard look. "Stop your pacing and sit *down*. And regardless of the circumstances, you are still Rowan's wife and to avoid such an event would only make things worse."

Arabella shot her a look of dislike deliberately ignoring her request.

"There have been several references in the society pages," Jemma said carefully. "You are taking the papers are you not?"

Arabella looked away. "Yes." The papers had been full of thinly veiled references that an annulment was in the works over the rather unfortunate marriage of Lady Arabella to Lord Malden. "They say my brother coerced Rowan and he, being terrified of Nick. and being an honorable gentleman, agreed to the marriage under duress."

Jemma snorted. "That's rich. Rowan is not nearly as honorable as he appears. Nor is he particularly terrified of Nick." She put a finger to her lip. "I've always found it odd he isn't. At any rate, I surmised at first Rowan allowed the betrothal to you merely to annoy my aunt and avoid Lady Gwendolyn." Dislike flashed across her face. "I don't particularly care for Gwendolyn. Shallow. Insipid. Made several rude comments about my husband." Jemma gave her a pointed look. "Please ring for tea before I waste away."

"We finally agree on something, *Jem*. I don't care for her either." Arabella rang for tea wishing Jemma would get to the point of her visit. "Although I think Lady Gwendolyn is exactly who Rowan *should* be with. She's rather perfect for him." Arabella bit her lip. "I assume he will request an annulment and claim I deceived him. Which I did."

"Had you wed Corbett you would not have been married very long," her sister-in-law said with certainty. "I would have shot him myself if no one else did."

"A duchess should have better decorum than to go around brandishing pistols." Arabella rebuked her. "Rowan deserves better than to be saddled to me. He should be married to a woman not riddled with the dislike of society. One who is flawless and possessed of a pleasing disposition. I am bitter and damaged with few redeeming qualities. You above everyone know that to be true. *Jem*."

"My God, Arabella, do you hear yourself? You are wallowing in self-pity." Jemma tried to resettle her form. "If you don't gather some backbone then it would be best for you to be sent away. Possibly Australia."

Arabella's hands clenched. She had the worst desire to box Jemma's ears no matter she was with child.

"True, my aunt doesn't care for you. But you are making a mistake in assuming she is in control of this situation." She sighed in relief as the tea cart was rolled in. "Oh, Thank God. Finally."

"You'll grow to be enormous if you keep eating. Like a giant ball of butter."

Jemma shot her an ugly look. "If you've been paying the *least* bit of attention you would know my cousin values imperfection. He seems to like a dour personality. Unpleasantness. The ability to empty a room with only a sneer. In short, *you*."

Jemma placed several small sandwiches on a plate and proceeded to eat them with relish.

Arabella's hand twitched into her skirts. Jemma's words had stirred the briefest flicker of hope. "Why are you saying these things to me?"

Jemma eyed the teacakes. "Where is the dress?"

Arabella felt the blood drain from her face. "Excuse me?"

"The crimson dress. The color chosen especially for you. He loves you in red. Who do you think went with him? *Me*."

Arabella's mouth popped open at the words. "Surely not."

"I was shocked as well. I reminded him of our mutual dislike. But, as it turns out, it was fortuitous I accompanied him to Madame Moliere's. He would have forgotten the matching gloves had I not reminded him. Though Rowan needed little prodding to remember the...*underthings* that went with the gown. Oh, Arabella, I'd *no* idea."

Arabella reddened. "There was also a necklace. Did you assist with that purchase as well?"

"No. My cousin knows his baubles." Another sandwich found its way into her hands. "May I be blunt, Arabella?"

"Dear God, please. I grow exhausted watching you eat the entire contents of the tea tray. I expect you to burst at any moment." Arabella's nerves already on edge from Jemma's visit were stretched taut.

"I'm trying to help you. Though you don't deserve my kindness. Rest assured I still dislike you. I'm doing this for Rowan, whom I love dearly."

"Thank you for clearing that up," Arabella sputtered back. An ache was beginning behind her temples.

Jemma stood and brushed a few stray crumbs from her skirts. "All of life is a gamble, Arabella. If you want Rowan, you must fight for him. Petra's party is in two days and she's already written to her brother he must be there. Gwendolyn will be in attendance and telling anyone who will listen you are to be discarded in her favor. Do you really wish to relin-quish Rowan to that pea-wit?"

"No." The words cut to the quick. She wasn't about to let go of her husband so easily.

"Wear the dress and demand his attention." Jemma snatched the remaining sandwich off the tray. "Arabella, he was caught off guard when Barker approached him. Yes, he was incredibly angry and disgusted with what you almost did. As we all were. But," Jemma gave a great sigh, "even I concede that you are not the same person who made such a poor decision."

Arabella looked down at her hands as her sister-in-law raised herself off the couch and waddled to the door. She looked over her shoulder at Arabella.

"Do not let love go so easily."

42

Arabella paced towards her dressing room and halted at the sight of the crimson ballgown left where Edith had hung it. She shook her head, walking back into her bedroom.

"I can't do such a thing," she muttered out loud. "What if he rejects me outright? Gives me the cut direct in front of everyone?"

What if he doesn't?

She spun about and headed back to the dressing room. Since Jemma's visit, Arabella had done nothing but consider her sister-in-law's suggestion. Wear the red dress. Attend Petra's ball. Seduce Rowan.

But what if he no longer wants me?

Chewing on her fingernail, Arabella considered her options. She was a woman of action and rather rash decisions on occasion. Not always with the best outcome.

She shot another look at the ballgown. Could a man who didn't want her have chosen such a dress for her? Or the undergarments that went with it?

She looked again to the door separating her rooms from Rowan's and walked slowly towards it. Lowering her hand, she threw the lock with a soft click and swung open the door.

The faint smell of leather and tobacco invaded her nostrils along with a clean masculine scent that was all Rowan's. She inhaled deeply almost feeling his arms around her. Walking to the enormous bed, she ran her fingers over the dark blue coverlet, remembering the nights spent on this bed naked, her body wrapped around his. A book lay on the side table, a piece of leather sticking out to mark the reader's last page. The tome was Mr. Faraday's, the gift she'd brought him from Thrumbadge's. He'd been reading excerpts out loud and debating the finer points with her wearing his dressing robe and nothing else before their estrangement.

Arabella clutched a hand to her stomach, feeling his loss keenly. For the first few days after their argument she'd thought he would return to the house, but instead he fled to Surrey, so repulsed by her he couldn't bear the sight of her. She'd survived for twenty-six years without him and could certainly continue with her life, she'd finally convinced herself. She could start afresh and move to the Continent. Maybe America, although the accent grated on her ears.

But none of those things would stop her from missing Rowan.

The thought of approaching her husband at Petra's ball in what was essentially hostile territory was rather daunting. While she was assured he would attend the celebration for his sister, he'd not sent word to the servants to ready his chambers, nor sent her a note that he would return. He did not mean to come home to her. He had not forgiven her.

"He cannot just discard me." Her hands clenched. "I will not allow him to do so. Not without a fight." Jemma, though Arabella was loath to admit it, was correct. If Arabella wanted her husband, she would need to convince him of her sincerity. The alternative was to relinquish Rowan and make plans to leave London; Arabella was far too possessive to give in so easily.

Full of resolve she stalked back to her room and closed the door behind her. She purposefully did not lock it. Grabbing the bell pull she rang for Edith and a bath.

It was time for Arabella to claim her husband.

"What do you *mean* she's not here?"

Rowan was tired, dusty and needed to see his wife. The journey from Surrey had taken far too long, or perhaps it was only his own impatience which made it seem so. After the Duke of Dunbar left Surrey, Rowan had done nothing but try to reconcile his disappointment in what he viewed as her betrayal with his feelings for her. It was unfair for Rowan to punish the woman she was now for the mistakes made as the unpleasant girl she'd been. And he didn't wish to spend the rest of his life missing her. The last few weeks felt as if he'd lost part of his soul.

"Forgive me, my lord. Lady Malden is not at home. She has gone out for the evening."

Their butler, a rather portly man with the whimsical name of Oberon, looked up at Rowan with apology. "Would you like your rooms prepared my lord? We were unaware of your return."

"Yes. Immediately. And find someone who knows where Lady Malden has gone." Rowan regarded the butler, frustration making his voice caustic. "*Now.*"

Oberon bowed, his mustache quivering at Rowan's displeasure. "Immediately, my lord." The butler clapped his hands and a footman appeared. "See to his lordship's things."

Rowan raked a hand through his hair and took the stairs

up to his chambers. Good God, he'd ridden as if the devil was after him and Arabella wasn't here? She didn't attend parties. Nor musicales. God knows she detested the opera. Where would she go? Especially alone? A flash of jealousy caused his step to falter. Had she sought a lover after he deserted her and even now was with him?

Storming into his rooms Rowan called for his valet, Parker. He'd left Parker in London when he left for Surrey, much to the valet's displeasure.

"My lord." Parker appeared out of nowhere.

"How do you do that, Parker?" Rowan greeted his valet over his shoulder. "Popping up whenever your name is whispered. Where do you hide when I am not in residence?"

A slight frown crossed Parker's lips. "A good valet anticipates his employer's needs, my lord. I'll have a bath prepared."

"Ssh." Rowan snapped as a sound came from Arabella's room. "And my evening clothes. I've a wife to find and a ball to attend." Could Oberon have been wrong? Was Arabella hiding in her room?

Leaving Parker sputtering at being shushed, Rowan placing his hand on the knob, throwing open the door with a bang.

Edith, Arabella's lady's maid gave a cry of alarm. Wet towels dropped from her outstretched arms. "Lord Malden." She hastily dipped into a curtsy. "Begging your pardon, my lord. We didn't expect you home."

"I neglected to send word in my haste to return." He looked down at the wet towels. "Where is Lady Malden?"

"I—" the maid stuttered.

Rowan's heart caught at Edith's hesitation. Dear Lord, Arabella *had* taken a lover. A growl came from him and the maid stepped back. "*Where* is she?"

"Lady Marsh is hosting a ball tonight, my lord." The maid reddened.

"Yes, I'm aware, for my sister."

"Begging your pardon, my lord, but Lady Malden's gone looking for you. At your sister's celebration."

43

Rowan strode through his mother's ballroom ignoring the curious glances and quiet whispers his appearance garnered. He imagined his mother had gleefully spread the news around London of her son's separation from Arabella so soon after the wedding and a potential annulment which would result. Not even the damage to his manhood would deter her.

Mother would be disappointed.

Lord and Lady White hovered about in the ballroom, Lord White watching him with avarice. Gwendolyn, possibly tired of Rowan's constant rejection, looked away as he passed by.

But there was no sign of Arabella. Perhaps Edith had misunderstood her plans?

"There you are." Petra breezed towards him, pale blue skirts fluttering behind her. "I hope I didn't interrupt your fun, playing with trains and such." Petra smiled up at him looking beautiful with her glossy blonde hair pulled up into a series of ringlets to frame her face.

Rowan smiled down at his sister. "It's your birthday. I

dared not disregard such a momentous event. I'm sure Mother has the entire evening choreographed to her satisfaction. Mother wrote me she's certain Dunning will offer for you tonight."

Petra shrugged in a careless manner. "Dunning is not my preference. He's nice enough and certainly wealthy, but there's no spark." She snapped her gloved hands.

"Spark? Most marriages are based on property, security and status. Rarely are they based on a *spark*."

"*Yours* is," Petra replied tartly. "You look at Arabella as if she were an enormous tea cake you wish to devour."

He regarded his sister in shock. When had Petra become so direct? And so well-versed in such things? "I see Jemma has been influencing you. You'd best not allow Mother to know." His eyes roamed the room beyond his sister's shoulder. Where was she?

"I know more than you think. Are you looking for someone?" Petra gave him an innocent look. "You need to direct your gaze just there." She tilted her head to a darkened corner by the punch bowl.

Bella.

Arabella stood alone and aloof, as she had the first time Rowan saw her. Only tonight her dress was not a pale rose but crimson. She moved slightly and the gold threads sewn into the velvet winked in the candlelight. The ruby he'd bought for her dangled provocatively between the valley of her breasts. The cut of the gown left little to the imagination and he instantly regretted that Arabella no longer favored necklines starting at her chin. With her dark hair piled high atop her head and just a touch of red to her lips, Arabella looked *decadent*. A sensual feast in slippers.

Jesus. His trousers tightened. *She's never wearing that damn dress again in public.*

"What will you do?" Petra repeated the question the Duke of Dunbar had asked him not two days ago.

Rowan didn't answer. "You helped her." His eyes never left Arabella who had yet to look in his direction. "Why?"

"Possibly." Petra waved her fan. "I prefer to think of it as helping *you*." She lay a hand on his arm. "Arabella loves you madly, Rowan. So much so, she is braving Mother, the Whites and half of London to prove it to you. If Jemma can forgive her, *you* can. She may always be slightly terrible." Petra's lips twisted. "But I suppose that makes her interesting." Then she added, "I believe she is truly sorry and not unredeemable."

"She is not unredeemable," he whispered. "Thank you, Petra."

His sister swatted him with her fan. "Do not forget the service I've done you. I may yet need your assistance. I've no intention of marrying Dunning no matter Mother's scheming." She sailed off towards a group of young ladies, all waving in her direction.

Rowan turned, his gaze tracing every curve of the beautiful woman in red. It was time to claim his wife.

As he started towards Arabella, she caught sight of him.

Eyes, dark like pitch watched his approach. She lifted her chin in challenge, perhaps daring him to cut her in front of the room, which of course he had no intention of doing. A twitching hand against her skirts proved her bravado false. Arabella was nervous. Frightened. *Brave.*

Heat rose up his skin thinking of her and how badly he wished to touch her. Taste all the delicious hollows and curves of her body, so delightfully displayed in the crimson gown.

The dark lashes brushed against her cheek as she lowered her eyes and her lips parted before her head raised.

What Rowan saw in her eyes took his breath away, the

dark pools full of longing as if her soul were speaking to him. Had he not been sure of Arabella or feared she would play him false again, her eyes told him different. Possession glinted briefly, a small hint of her reluctance to share him with anyone else. He knew that about her and accepted such, for he didn't wish to share her either.

Bergamot, such an odd scent for a woman, filled his nostrils, rippling across his skin, tempting him with her nearness. Rowan wished to be far from this ballroom, alone with her where he could inhale her scent as his body covered hers. The matching chemise he purchased likely lay beneath the crimson velvet, caressing her skin as he wished to do.

He had wondered until this moment if he would be able to forgive her.

I need not have worried.

The strands of a waltz sounded from the orchestra and she held out her hand.

"Will you dance with me, Malden?" Her voice was husky.

"Rowan." He swung her onto the dance floor and into the steps of the waltz.

۞

AT THE TOUCH OF HIS HAND, WARMTH RADIATED THROUGH her as if she suddenly stepped into the sun after standing in the rain for hours. Arabella leaned into Rowan, her body molding against his. The gold braid lining her bodice teased his chest, catching against the buttons of his shirt. Each brush across her breasts was agonizing, making her long to be alone with him.

The ballroom buzzed with speculation as dozens of eyes watched them dance.

His hand splayed against the small of her back. "Hello,

Bella." The deep growl echoed and bounced through her to finally settle between her thighs. Green and gold lights flashed in his eyes as he stared down at her. Still, she could not completely read his mood and worried over it. Was he glad to see her?

"Do you like the dress?" she murmured.

His gaze heated, dropping to the valley between her breasts where the ruby hung, then raised to focus on her lips. He swung her around gracefully, moving his legs further into her skirts, the hard length of him pressed briefly against her thigh. "I would like the gown better were it on the floor of my bedroom and you naked against the coverlet."

Arabella tripped and narrowly avoided stepping on his toes. At least that question was answered. He still desired her at least physically. "Poor of you to say such an outrageous thing when I am trying not to embarrass us both," she snapped.

"There's my girl. Not the shy wallflower standing alone. I miss her, you know." He nuzzled briefly against her neck

"Do you? Your lack of communication would tell me otherwise." Her head turned away from his, not wishing him to see the moisture gathering behind her eyes. What had she expected? That he would completely put aside his distrust upon seeing her?

"We have both behaved badly," he agreed.

"Me more so than you," she murmured into his shoulder, clasping the muscles beneath his fine evening coat. He smelled heavenly, that particular mixture of leather, tobacco and something that was only Rowan.

He pressed his lips lightly against her temple and the fingers at her waist tightened their grip. "Shh, Bella."

"I was afraid you wouldn't come," she whispered, her voice breaking just a bit knowing she could not fall apart in a ballroom full of the *ton*. "Or see me and flee the premises."

A frown crossed his beautiful mouth and Arabella longed to press her fingers to his lips.

"We cannot have this conversation here, where half of London watches." He danced her over to the terrace doors leading to the garden. Grabbing her hand, he led her out onto the terrace and down a small set of marble steps, stopping beneath a large tree.

The cool evening air chilled her shoulders and arms, helping to chase away her melancholy. She told herself it was far better she know his feelings rather than guess at them. Still her heart beat furiously. He was watching her, his face thoughtful, waiting for her to speak.

She pulled back on his arm and he let her go. Too quickly, she thought.

"Please, Malden," she started unsteadily, "if you cannot forgive me, I...I will sign whatever you wish." The words wrung from her painfully. "I will understand your choice."

Rowan gave a snort of disbelief. "No, you won't."

"I can. It would be unfair to trap either of us in a marriage based only on our baser desires, a lack of trust and a mutual appreciation for correcting ledgers."

"Baser desires?"

A slow burn of anger crawled up the length of her chest at his attitude. Anger was useful and gave her the illusion of power though her heart shattered with every word she spoke. "Or we can continue to live apart. I will find a house of my own to let. I have my own money," she hastened to add. "You will not be required to support me."

"I'm afraid I am not in agreement with your strategy." He crossed his arms.

Arabella swallowed. He would not make this easy, but what did she expect? She'd shown up dressed in this extrava-gant gown to try to seduce her husband into forgetting what a terrible person she *was*. It was incredibly unfair. She was changed. Could Rowan not see it?

"The Continent then. Or America. My cousin Spence is in India. I've always wished to visit." A brittle laugh bubbled out of her. "See tigers and such."

"Are you insane?" He stepped away from the tree and took hold of her arms as if he would shake her.

"Then what do you want me to do?" A sob left her.

"I am not here for my sister's birthday, Arabella. I went to our home first and you, bloody contrary woman that you are, decided to attend a ball. Something you don't particularly care for. The only thing more surprising would be if you'd attended the opera." He pulled her close, encasing her in the warmth and security of his embrace.

A deep ragged breath came from her. "You came here to find me?"

"Bella," he said softly. "I will *always* come for you. No matter where you go. I'm only sorry it took me so long. And I have missed you desperately."

She brushed at a tear. "I've done some rather unkind things motivated by my own anger at the world around me. I thought while in Wales I had come to terms with my jealousy and bitterness. But then Corbett..." She swallowed, remembering the fear of being trapped with him. "I should have told you. Trusted you with the very worst of myself, but I was so ashamed. "

"I know." He kissed her gently. "You are not perfect, but neither am I. If we are to move forward, there must be no more secrets between us. No scheming or deceit." His mouth hinted at a smile. "No dressing like a distressed swallow about to attend a funeral. And I will leave the country should I see even one braid gracing your head." He pressed his forehead to hers. "Can you live with my terms?"

Arabella nodded. "I am still unsure concerning the braids, but I can agree to everything else."

"Good." He kissed the tip of her nose, his eyes growing serious. "I was very lonely without you, Bella." Placing her hand against his heart, Rowan whispered. "This only beats when you are near."

She pressed a kiss to his lips. "Take me home, Malden."

EPILOGUE

S *ix months later*

"Is there something you wish to tell me, Lady Malden?"

Arabella looked up from her ledger and stretched her neck. "Yes. This chair is terribly uncomfortable. I'm certain we can afford one whose springs are not about to push through the leather at any moment. How you sit here each day is beyond me."

Rowan ignored her waspish tone. She wasn't feeling well and refused to admit it.

She opened her mouth to say something else when her face turned a disturbing shade of green. The pen hovered over the ledger and as he watched, Arabella swallowed several times.

Rowan stood and went to the door to request tea.

"I do not believe I care for duck even though it is a favorite of yours."

He moved to the sideboard and removed the chamber pot he'd discreetly hidden earlier. "I do not think it was the duck,

Bella. You've been ill more than once in the last several weeks and can barely tolerate a carriage ride."

Arabella narrowed her eyes at him. "It *is* the duck. You were driving too fast through the park which is why I became discomfited.

Discomfited. Rowan wanted to laugh out loud. He'd had to stop discreetly behind a tree while her breakfast came back up. He was concerned that Arabella didn't wish to admit what was truly wrong with her. Was she not happy?

Why do you have a chamber pot in here? What—"

Rowan sprinted to the desk replacing the ledger before her with the chamber pot. He was not a moment too soon. Poor Bella. He rubbed her back while the spasms shook her. For weeks she hadn't been sleeping well and became sick nearly every afternoon at the same time. Worried his wife was truly ill, Rowan confided in his mother. Lady Marsh smiled knowingly and sent Bella a box of cherry tarts.

Bella assumed his mother was trying to poison her, suspicious of any overture Lady Marsh would make. While the relationship between Bella and his mother had improved, it was still rather...*contentious* at times. Thankfully, Mother was too busy hovering over Petra, determined to marry her off, to pay much attention to Arabella. That would likely change though in light of recent developments.

"I think I need to lie down."

Carefully, Rowan wiped her mouth with his handkerchief before picking her up and carrying her to the couch.

"I am capable of making my way to the couch, Malden."

"Lay down." He sat and placed her head in his lap, his fingers sliding through the mass of her hair to loosen the pins. "Better?"

She nodded, purring like a kitten as he gently massaged her scalp while they waited on the tea tray.

Rowan looked down at her with a smile. The woman in

his arms meant everything to him and now Arabella would give him the most precious of gifts. Unlike many of his friends, Rowan did not view his marriage as a necessary evil. He and Arabella were partners in all things. She was fiercely loyal, brilliant in trade and a skilled negotiator. She terrified Hind as well as the manager he'd hired at the textile mills. But neither man could argue with her business acumen. Arabella was usually correct. Rowan adored her.

"Stop smiling like an idiot. I'm quite afraid." The dark eyes shone with a hint of tears. "What if I'm not any good at it? I did not have the best example, after all. What if I make a mess of things?"

His finger slid down her jawline. "You won't, my love." She would be a wonderful mother although he expected her to be slightly overprotective.

"How can you be so sure?"

He smoothed the worry line from her forehead. "I love you."

She smiled and closed her eyes. "I still think it might be the duck."

If you enjoyed WICKEDLY YOURS I would greatly appreciate you leaving a review. Reviews keep me writing!

CLICK HERE TO DOWNLOAD THE NEXT BOOK NOW...

Tall, Dark & Wicked.

And if you just started getting Wicked...start with Alex and Sutton's story in Wicked's Scandal.

ABOUT THE AUTHOR

Kathleen Ayers has been a hopeful romantic since the tender age of fourteen when she first purchased a copy of Sweet Savage Love at a garage sale while her mother was looking at antique animal planters. Since then she's read hundreds of historical romances and fallen in love dozens of times. Kathleen lives in Houston with her husband, a college-aged son who pops in to have his laundry done and two very spoiled dogs.

Sign up for Kathleen's newsletter:
www.kathleenayers.com

Like Kathleen on Facebook
www.facebook.com/kayersauthor

Join Kathleen's Facebook Group
Historically Hot with Kathleen Ayers

Follow Kathleen on Bookbub
bookbub.com/authors/kathleen-ayers

Made in the USA
Columbia, SC
20 July 2020

14230703R00183